COMPLIMENTS OF

WAPPINGERS CONGRESS OF TEACHERS

WCT

THIS BOOK BELONGS TO:

FIONA

FIONA

MEREDITH MOORE

An Imprint of Penguin Random House

razOr
bill

An Imprint of Penguin Random House
Penguin.com

ISBN: 978-1-59514-784-4

Printed in the United States of America

3 5 7 9 10 8 6 4 2

To Greg and Jenn

For being part of my family
and making me part of yours

CHAPTER 1

I step out of the tiny outdoor train station to find a village that consists of only three other buildings: a general store with a floral dress and piles of toothpaste in the window, a crumbling post office, and a pub, the one place open at this hour. The grass-covered mountains of the Scottish Highlands rise above it all, appearing as massive shadows in the dim light from the overcast moon. A few old men sit drinking pints outside the pub across the street, but otherwise the town is deserted, the only sound the rustling of leaves tumbling along the cobblestones.

I'm the only one who got off the train in Almsley, this tiny little place, and the only other person at the station is a clerk reading a glossy tabloid in the information booth. No one's here to pick me up. I check the clock hanging above the platform: 8:00. Right on time.

I try to calm my quickening breath and settle onto the bench outside the station. That woman, Mabel, is just running a little bit late. I don't have any British pounds left for a cab to Fintair Castle, but I'm sure I can manage to find it on my own if I need to.

The wind bites into me and whistles past my ear. I hug my ragged coat even closer. It's only late September, but the wind here grows vicious as the night wears on. I sit on that bench until I can't feel my fingers and then grab my patched-up duffel bag and lug it over to the pub. No use freezing outside if no one's coming to get me.

The pub is a cozy, worn-down, jovial sort of place. People of all ages crowd around the bar and lounge in the tattered green plaid armchairs by the fire. Two girls, one with dyed black hair and an impressive amount of cleavage and the other with wavy blond hair and a very short skirt, hold court in the middle of the room, surrounded by nervous male admirers. I skirt around them and head for the seat closest to the bright orange fire, drawn by the warmth.

A guy sits opposite me, staring into the flames, his curly brown hair shining with glints of red in the firelight. He doesn't look up to acknowledge me, though I'm only a yard away from him. I roll my eyes as I unwrap my scarf and stretch my hands toward the fire. The thin gloves I found in the Mulespur

Salvation Army have done nothing to keep my hands warm, and I stifle a sigh as the feeling begins to return to them. West Texas had no pervasive cold like this, even in the dead of winter. For a moment, I almost miss the sunbaked red dirt I just left behind.

I look up and see that the guy is staring at me. I blink, but he doesn't turn away.

"Can I help you?" I ask in the voice that my friend, Hex, taught me to use on creepers. It's a menacing, pointed thing, meant to pierce, but he doesn't even flinch.

He quirks an eyebrow in surprise, then shakes his head and looks back at the fire.

The dyed-black-hair-and-cleavage girl circles behind his chair. I watch her from the corner of my eye. She looks like she's stalking a particularly tasty kind of prey. "You up for a pint, then, love?" she asks, placing herself between him and the fire, one hand expertly resting on her cocked hip.

"Not tonight," he says, looking through the girl like he can still see the flames behind her. His accent is something like the Scottish brogue I kept hearing on the train, but it's crisper somehow. Cleaner. It reminds me so much of my mother's, and I realize suddenly that I'm blinking back tears.

"Come on," she says, bending down lower, no doubt to position her cleavage right in his face. "You've had a rough time of it. Let me make it better."

He finally looks up at her. "I'm fine," he says firmly, staring her down until she walks away.

She makes a clucking noise to save face and then escapes back to her circle of admirers. I don't blame her. There's something icy and unforgiving in those green eyes of his.

I realize that I'm staring openly at him when those cold green eyes shift to mine. And then they soften, and I realize that he must see the tears conjured up by his familiar accent.

And that's my cue to leave. I grab my scarf and my duffel bag and fling myself out of that little pub before he can say anything. Before he can see anything else.

There's a man with a thick overcoat standing across the street at the train station, and when he sees me looking at him, he heads toward me. He has shockingly white hair, deep wrinkles, and a broad smile. "You must be Fiona Smith, then?" he asks, taking my duffel bag before I can tell him that no one's called me Fiona in years. I'm Fee now. "Sorry I'm late," he continues. "We've had a bit of a situation at the house, but everything's sorted now. Poppy's very excited to meet you."

Poppy, the eleven-year-old girl I've come here to nanny.

Her mother, Lady Lillian Moffat—Lily, as my mom called her—grew up with my mother here in Scotland and recently invited me here for this job. But then two weeks ago, I got the Google Alert on my phone. I'd just bought this scarf and gloves and too-flimsy coat, preparing for my new life back in my mother's home country. I was on my phone, waiting for my aunt to come pick me up, and when the alert pinged, I thought it would be just a puff piece about Lord and Lady Moffat, the glamorous owners of the *Scottish Telegraph* newspaper, at yet another social gathering. Their smiling faces were often slathered across the *Daily Mail* site, though as hard as I looked, I could never find photos of Poppy or her older brother, Charlie.

It wasn't a photo of Lily and Harold this time, though. It was a picture of their mangled car.

I had never met them. I'd only spoken to Lily a few times on the phone, her voice crackling and quiet across what sounded like a bad connection. She had been my mother's best friend once. And even though it was hard for them to keep in contact after my mother ran away from the life Lily eventually took over, Mom always said she was witty and fun, someone worth knowing. And now I'd never know her.

Reading the news story, I sat down hard on the curb, my eyes filling with tears for this woman I didn't know who had died much too young, just like my own mother. For the son and daughter she left behind. I almost turned around and returned all the cold-weather clothing I'd just bought, but my aunt swerved into the parking lot and honked her horn in a long, angry screech, and I couldn't keep her waiting.

The call from the head housekeeper came a couple of days later. I'd already told my manager at the Buffalo Head Café that I would be staying, resigning myself to the fact that I wouldn't ever get out of Mulespur. That I would be surrounded by drugged-out cowboys and sunburned oilfield workers for the rest of my life. That I would never escape the stifling resentment of my aunt's home.

But Mabel, the housekeeper, told me that I was still wanted. "You may be asked to take on more responsibilities than originally planned," she told me, her brogue thick but her warning clear. "Master Charlie is legally in charge of Poppy, but he has to run the family business now. She needs someone to look after her." Her voice broke a little at that, and I could hear the undercurrent of grief in her tone. "You'll receive the same salary as previously negotiated." I'd never "negotiated" a salary—Lily could have offered me nothing but room and board and I would have still jumped at the chance.

So I kept the winter clothes and flew over the Atlantic Ocean on my first plane.

"I'm Albert, by the way," the old man says, extending his hand and breaking me out of my thoughts. "Forgot to introduce myself. That's the way of it when you get to be my age. I'm the driver. The chauffeur, Lady Lillian liked to call it. She always liked things to be fancier than they were."

That explains why she hired me as an *au pair*, not a nanny. *You'll be the perfect companion for Poppy,* she'd written in the email that came out of the blue. She wrote that even though she'd never met me.

I shake Albert's weathered hand and follow him to a large black car. He opens the rear passenger door for me, and I consider protesting, insisting I sit up front with him, but he raises his eyebrows at me, and I slide in without a word.

I buckle myself in, and now I know there's no turning back.

I don't know why I agreed to this. Why I thought I could do this. As the car travels out of the little crossroads town and up the winding mountain roads, I clench my hands together.

In my ear, I can hear my mother whisper: *You can do this, Fiona. And you will.*

I pick at the cuticle of my left index finger, my bad habit, and stare out the window, trying not to react. My mother's voice hasn't popped into my head much over the past few years, but I heard her in the airport back in Lubbock, too, as I stood in front of a bathroom mirror and tried not to have a panic attack over getting on a plane for the first time. *You'll be fine, hen,* she said, using her Scottish pet name for me.

It's just a grief reaction, I tell myself. It's not actually her, and I'm fully aware of this. It's my way of coping with a stressful situation. It's normal. I'm just freaking out because I am now somehow responsible for taking care of a girl who just lost her mother, too.

I've never known my father—he abandoned my mother before I was born. My mother had given up her life of privilege in Scotland to marry a wannabe rock star from America who was passing through the UK. Lily had warned her that he would ruin her life, that she would become someone so different that she wouldn't recognize herself. But my mother ignored her, left the fiancé her parents had picked out for her, and followed my father to a little apartment in Austin. Love, obsessive love, had put her in danger, leading her down a path she could never recover from. Her parents disowned her promptly, and after about seven years, my father ran off without a word while she was pregnant with me.

Despite everything, she made my life nothing short of charming. We lived in a garage apartment in a neighborhood with addicts and gang members and the kindest, most caring neighbors we could have wished for. Mom made sure I never knew how poor we were. She filled my life with brightly painted yellow walls and stories of princesses who slew dragons and, above all else, music and literature. Sir Walter Scott and Robert Burns always reminded her of home, and she'd read their work aloud for me, so that I could have a taste of that homeland, too. She told me tales of Celtic myths, the *bean nighe*, and fairies who led travelers off the roads. Strong princesses who fought their own battles. Ghosts and goblins and ghouls were my favorites, and she made up stories about all of them.

All that happiness, all those stories, died when she did, when I was twelve.

After that, I moved from the lively bustle of Austin to the hot, dead-end town of Mulespur to live with my father's older sister, the only family I had left. My mother's parents, the Cavendishes, died after she left Scotland. No one could get in touch with my father—he'd thoroughly vanished long before. "Probably dead in a ditch somewhere," my aunt said once before spitting on the ground. "Good riddance." My aunt put me in the back room of her little shotgun stone house, but not without warning me that she could get rid of me anytime she wanted. I grew up and went to high school and counted down the days until I could be free.

I was studying for my last final when Lily's email came. I'd known that she'd married the man my mother was supposed to, Lord Harold Moffat. They had a young daughter who needed an au pair for the school year. She wrote that she had kept an eye on me ever since my mother died, spurred by the memory of her friend, for whom she still felt obligation and affection. If I didn't have any plans for the next year, there was a position available for me in her home.

When Mom left Scotland, Lily took my mother's fiancé and carefully planned future, and Mom didn't begrudge her any of it. "I have you," she told me. "I have freedom."

Albert turns into a dusty dirt drive, revealing a view so magnificent that I can't help but gasp. Trees from the surrounding patch of forest line the road, their branches curving over to reach the other side, creating a space like the nave of a great cathedral. Spotlights shine down from the trees, fighting against the darkness of the night, creating shadows all around us.

"The avenue's been here since the mid-eighteen hundreds. The mistress was very proud of it." His voice is low and hushed, that particular tone of grief. He must have been very close to Lily to feel her loss like that.

We drive for what seems like miles through the cathedral of trees, until they suddenly fade away and reveal a long lawn with a reflecting pool, and a building that is definitely a castle. There is a central rectangular stone tower with several wings branching out from it. Dozens of windows line the walls, and the gray turrets and multiple chimneys reach up into the sky, lit by bright floodlights and the dim moon. We enter through an arched gateway into a stone courtyard, and the size of the castle stretching up around us overwhelms me.

I did a bit of research on the family before I came, eager to learn more about the people I was going to live with. The

Moffats have owned this castle for centuries, though Lord Harold bucked the family tradition of living off the land when he bought a national newspaper as well. The paper, the *Scottish Telegraph*, did not have a website I could access without a paid subscription, but as far as I could tell, it was established, respected, and serious.

No wonder his castle is so well maintained.

Albert stops the car in front of the door. "Here you are, then," he says, hopping out so that he can open my door.

I take a deep breath before I unbuckle my seat belt and get out of the car. This can't be real life. I must have stepped into one of my mother's fairy tales. All that's missing is the dragon I'm supposed to slay.

Albert knocks on the massive front door, then looks back at me with a kind smile, though there's still that observant glint in his eyes. "It'll be good to have some new young blood in the house, lass. You might bring some happiness to the poor little girl."

I straighten my shoulders and nod.

An old woman opens the door, her dark gray hair pinned under a white cap that seems to belong to another era. She looks me over, her eyes flicking to my feet and back to my face, and I shift my weight from one foot to the other. I should have worn my nice black pants and the onc presentable sweater I have. Instead, I'm in my secondhand coat and only pair of jeans, the ones I have to wear with a belt to keep them on my hips and a safety pin holding the sides of the back pocket together so my underwear won't show through. I withdraw all expression from my face and counter this woman's enduring stare. She can't cow me.

"Come on, Mabel, you going to let the poor girl in or not?" Albert says.

Mabel. The head housekeeper, the one who spoke to me on the phone and told me they still wanted me. She doesn't look like she wants me now, though. She purses her lips and nods. "Follow me."

I say nothing as I walk across the threshold into the most stunning entrance I've ever seen. A stairway curves up and up, its dark wood gleaming in the light from the large crystal chandelier dripping delicately from the ceiling. The walls are the same rough gray stone blocks as the outside and are covered with faded tapestries and paintings of men and women from another time. There are tables and bureaus covered with gold and silver knickknacks, and an actual suit of arms stands stiffly in one corner of the room. I try not to let the awe show on my face.

"It's Fiona, is it?" Mabel says, her eyes now examining my long, red, curly hair. It's the best feature I inherited from my beautiful mother and the one thing that tends to catch people's eyes. The rest of me is plain: straight nose, dark brown eyes, pale skin with a few freckles.

"Fee," I correct, and her eyes grow even narrower.

"Hmm. Well, come on, then." Her accent is fairly thick, and her voice is low. I have to lean in closer to hear her. She leads me past the staircase, through a suite of rooms with overstuffed crimson couches, fresh flowers, and fluffy crimson armchairs, until we reach a room that is markedly drabber. A large stove dominates the middle of it, and the walls are lined with cabinets and shining copper pots. "These are the servants' areas," Mabel explains. "The kitchen, the servants' staircase leading up to the rooms in the attic. When you're with Miss Poppy, you may use the grand staircase and the main house. But at all other times, it's best you stick to these quarters."

I try not to raise my eyebrows, but she isn't looking at me anyway. She starts ascending the dark, winding servants' staircase. We travel up five flights, until my knees are weak and I'm wheezing.

The door on the sixth floor opens up to a hallway of white-washed walls, solid wood doors, and a ceiling so low I can reach up and touch it. "The servants' living quarters," Mabel explains. She stops in front of a room several doors down and opens it with a key from the heavy chain at her waist. "Your room," she says, handing me the key. I step inside to see a narrow twin bed, a nightstand, a small fireplace, a desk, a dresser, and a sliver of a window.

"Acceptable?" Mabel asks.

I nod, unable to speak. My room at my aunt's didn't have a window. It was stuffy and always hot, and the light from the bare bulb in the ceiling made it irrevocably dreary. This room is clean and cheery.

She must think I'm disappointed, because she says, "You'll get used to it."

I nod again.

"You've missed dinner. I could have the cook prepare something for you and send it up," she offers, but the twist in her lips makes it clear that it's an offer I should refuse.

"I'm too tired to eat," I lie. My stomach has been growling the past few hours.

She nods. "I'll leave you to sleep, then. Miss Poppy is already sound asleep, poor thing. Master Charlie had to leave for business today, and she took it very hard." Her voice transforms as she talks about Poppy, becoming softer, less pinched.

Charlie's departure must have been the situation that made Albert so late this evening, I realize.

"She'll be back from her ride at seven tomorrow morning," Mabel continues, "and you'll need to be downstairs to greet her."

"Her ride?" I ask.

"Yes. Her horseback ride. She takes one every morning."

"Even at a time like this?" I ask before I can stop myself.

Mabel sighs, putting her hand on her hip. Clearly answering my question is a terrible burden. "She needs routine. She can't be allowed to dwell on the situation." She speaks with an authoritative, clipped voice, as if she is the one in charge of Poppy's well-being.

"Is that what her brother thinks?"

"Of course it is!" she answers, her hand fluttering to her heart, clearly offended. "Now get to sleep. You'll have to be presentable tomorrow." She looks me up and down as if she doubts the possibility of that, and then shuts the door, sealing me off from the rest of the house.

I sink into the bed, kicking off my shoes and stretching out. I couldn't sleep on the plane, too busy worrying about this new life I'm starting. About what I'm going to say to a girl who just lost both of her parents.

I remember the confusion and pain and horror of the weeks after my mother's death, when I was put in a group home and a lawyer and the government were deciding my fate. I remember the nights spent staring at the wall of my tiny bedroom at my aunt's house, trying to draw up every good memory of my mom that I had.

How on earth am I supposed to care for a girl who's going through the same thing?

My mother's voice doesn't whisper in my ear now to calm me. And even though I tell myself I don't want to hear her, terrified of what it means when I do, I wish I had some reassurance.

"Mama," I whisper into the air, "you have to help me."

I fall asleep with that prayer on my lips.

CHAPTER 2

Someone bangs on my door, and I startle up. It takes me a moment to realize that I'm in Scotland and another moment to realize that if I don't answer the door, the pounding won't stop.

I get up and fling it open to find the grim face of Mabel on the other side. "Miss Poppy is almost back from her ride. You must come meet her now." She takes me in, from the top of my out-of-control curls to the frayed bottom hems of the jeans I didn't bother to take off last night. "And for heaven's sake, lass, try to look somewhat respectable," she adds before whirling off down the hall.

I resist the urge to stick my tongue out at her and rush to my suitcase, pulling out my black pants and a soft cream-colored sweater. They're the nicest clothes I own, the ones my aunt begrudgingly helped me buy for my interview at the Buffalo Head Café. I throw them on, knowing that I'll have nothing better to wear tomorrow.

There's a mirror above the small sink in the corner of the room. I hurry to it, pulling a brush through my hair. It refuses to be tamed, however, and I do my best to wrestle it into a pony-tail. I splash some water on my pale face and take a deep breath.

I can't avoid it anymore. I have to go down and meet my fate.

I slip down the servants' staircase and try to retrace my steps from last night to get back to the front entrance. I must make a wrong turn, though, because suddenly I'm in a room with the grandest grand piano I've ever seen and a gilded harp tower-ing in the corner. Floor-to-ceiling bookshelves crammed with dark, ancient books line the walls. I admire them for a moment before stepping closer to the piano, unable to help myself.

Mom had been on her way to becoming a concert pianist when she met my father and her whole life got derailed. When I was a baby, she drew piano keys on a large piece of cardboard, and one of my earliest memories is of her teaching me how to play a silent scale. Some nights, I would creep out of bed, peek out of the cracked door to the living room, and watch her sit in front of that piece of cardboard, her eyes closed as her fingers flew like whispers across the imaginary keys. It was the only time

I saw her look so calm, as if that cardboard keyboard gave her utter peace, if only for a few hours.

When I was eight, Mom started working as a waitress at an upscale café in the South Congress neighborhood of Austin, near downtown. It was the nicest job she ever had, one that brought in more tips than she'd ever earned before. One day, she waited on an old woman, Mrs. Alvarez, who lived nearby and had a small piano. When she heard Mom could play, she immediately invited her over to practice on the baby grand. It would give her so much delight, Mrs. Alvarez insisted. So Mom brought me over to that little lime green bungalow, and for the first time, I played a real piano. It took me a few tries to get used to the feel of the keys, to feel comfortable pushing them down instead of brushing over them. But after a few months, I was playing Beethoven, Chopin, the old Scottish ballads Mom had taught me. My rhythm was completely off, and nothing sounded quite right, but I had never felt such joy.

Hearing my mother play that baby grand, I finally understood why the piano brought her so much peace, even in times when nothing else did. The music rushed from her fingertips, filling up the room with beauty. Beauty that made your breath catch in your throat, your eyes close, your whole world narrow down to the sound and the feel and the emotion of those notes.

I'm stuck in the daydream for several moments before I realize that I'm going to be late if I don't stop staring at the piano and get a move on. I hurry out of the room, opening the nearest door, and almost bump into a maid. She's around my age and wears a white lace cap that's only slightly smaller than Mabel's. We're in another room with a huge wooden desk and even more bookshelves. An office, not the hallway I expected to find.

"Watch it," she mutters, turning around to look at me. "You the new governess, then? Or au pair or whatever it is?" She has wide brown eyes, and the hair pinned neatly under her cap is only a shade more brown than red: the lovely subtle color I used to wish mine was. A shade that wouldn't make me stand out so much.

I nod and stick out my hand. "Fee."

She takes it, shaking it firmly. "I'm Alice," she says, her tone a little less harsh now. "Where are you trying to go?"

"I have to meet Poppy after her horseback ride."

Alice sighs. "I better take you. This house is a bit of a maze if you don't know it."

She moves past me out into the library. I have to scurry to keep up with her as she trots briskly through the house, winding through several rooms until we reach a set of glass doors that open up to a view that takes my breath away. "Poppy'll be down there, near the stables," she says with a nod before heading back to her chores.

I step outside, trying to take it all in. Green space stretches out in front of me, surrounded by a tall perimeter of hedges and marble statues of bare-chested men and slightly more decent women. Judging by their ancient robes and the occasional trident, they're gods and goddesses, beautiful and intimidating. A glistening dark green pool rests a few yards away, a large fountain in its center. Beyond the great lawn, a mountain looms, nearly completely covered with fog. I step out onto the wet, lush grass, the wind kinder than it was last night as it brushes against me and dances through the hedges. The land slopes gently down, and I hurry to catch up to Mabel, who's already at the bottom of the hill.

I reach her just as I see a girl on a horse, the two of them pacing toward us. I straighten my shoulders and try to fix a smile on my face to cover my nerves.

Poppy is in that awkward stage we all go through: all long, skinny limbs and frizzy blond hair. She fixes me with an impressive scowl as she slips off the horse and hands the reins to the guy who must run the stables, the large wooden building to our left. He leads the horse away as Poppy examines me. "Who's she?" she asks Mabel, who is trying not to smile at Poppy's obvious disapproval of me.

"She's your new governess, Miss Poppy. Fiona will be picking you up from school and tutoring you from now on."

Poppy takes her gloves off, her scowl now trained on them. "Why can't Charlie do it?" She means to sound dismissive, but I can hear the small prickle of disappointment in her voice.

Mabel reaches out and places a wrinkled hand on Poppy's shoulder, squeezing it reassuringly. It's such a motherly gesture that I can't help but frown in confusion. "Motherly" was about the last thing I expected this dour old woman to be.

She says softly, "Because Charlie's had to go to Glasgow for a couple of weeks to deal with the paper, you know that. Now I know this isn't ideal, but if you have any complaints, you only need to come to me and we'll find you a better governess, all right?"

There's the woman I expected. I try not to sneer at Mabel as Poppy turns her attention back to me. Mabel squeezes Poppy's shoulder once more and then walks off, and Poppy and I are alone.

She crosses her arms and watches me.

I take a deep breath and try not to put an ounce of pity in my voice. Pity is the last thing she needs right now, when she's so angry. "Look, I know this isn't what you wanted. That it's not even close. But I'm here for whatever you need."

"I don't *need* you," she counters.

"It'd be pretty lonely here with only Mabel and the others to talk to."

She shrugs. "I have friends. I'm fine."

I'm fine. The two words that became my mantra after Mom died. Any question anyone asked me could be answered by those words. And every time I spit them out, they tasted more and more bitter.

I take in her tightly crossed arms and the firm line of her mouth. She's not going to bend to me anytime soon. Not until she trusts me. And considering her whole world just got ripped out from underneath her, trust is something that is going to take a lot of time.

"Well, since I'm already here," I say finally, "why don't you show me your homework? Let me see what I can help you with."

She stares at me for a moment, then shrugs, clomping in her riding boots up toward the house without waiting to see if I'll follow.

I sigh and trudge up the soft green hill after her.

CHAPTER 3

Poppy and I spend the morning going over her homework and cautiously getting to know each other. We spread her assignments out in the fifth-floor room that has been designated as her study, right next to her bedroom, a place overwhelmed with pink and ruffles and glitter.

Poppy must be a girly girl. Or, at least, she might have been before her parents' death twisted her into this sullen version of herself.

She doesn't say anything as I examine the family portraits that clutter the top of her dresser: the family in ski gear on top of a pristine white mountain, the family in front of a gigantic Christmas tree, the family in front of the Eiffel Tower. I'm fascinated by the tall woman with the dyed blond pixie cut and calm smile in each of the photos. I've seen plenty of photos of Lily in the *Daily Mail* and on other gossip sites, and she's elegant and striking from every angle. I can't imagine her being friends with my mother, the woman with hair as wild and untamed as mine and no trace of makeup, who preferred long, flowing cotton skirts over the power-woman sheaths that seemed to have been Lily's uniform.

It takes me a moment to realize that I recognize the tall boy in some of the more recent photos, the bored teenager standing next to his father. He must be Charlie, now twenty-two and head of the family. That curly red-brown hair and new-leaf green of his eyes is horribly familiar.

He's the boy from the pub. The one who sat next to me by the fire and brushed off the girl who had every other guy eating out of the palm of her hand. The one whom I caught looking at me.

Oh my God. I was a total bitch to him. I used the voice Hex had taught me to combat mean girls and drunk boys in high school. He probably thinks I'm insane.

But what was he doing in town? He's supposed to be in Glasgow, doing something with the family paper. Not drinking all alone in a pub a few miles away.

I feel a blush creeping up into my cheeks and keep my head ducked so that Poppy won't see it.

A few hours later, we've gone through every subject and

identified what Poppy needs to work on: history and math. I'll have to brush up on my sixth-grade math skills—or, really, my eighth-grade math skills, since Poppy's school is much more advanced than mine was—but history has always been one of my favorites. Mostly because my mother had such a wonderful way of making the past come alive through her stories. During her good spells, at least.

Mabel knocks on the door just as I'm beginning to tell Poppy the story of William Wallace and the Battle of Stirling Bridge against the English. Poppy is rolling her eyes at my every word, it seems like, but at least she's listening.

"Lunch, Miss Poppy," Mabel says, her eyes snapping to me. Poppy and I are lying on our stomachs, Poppy's textbooks scattered around us, and it's clear from her pinched look that the prim housekeeper doesn't approve of such a slovenly method of learning.

Poppy pushes herself up and follows Mabel out into the hall. Neither of them looks back at me, but I get up and follow them anyway. We twist down the main staircase, with its perfectly polished wooden rail that I don't dare touch in case I smudge it.

Mabel leads Poppy to the dining room, where a plate with a sandwich and apple slices is waiting for her in front of an overflowing bouquet centerpiece. She turns to me after Poppy is settled. "Follow me," she says, starting out of the room.

I look back at Poppy, sitting alone and still at the large wooden table, surrounded by glittering silverware. She stares down at her plate, resolutely not looking at me, but her blank expression stops me. "I'll eat here with Poppy," I say, my tone more forceful than I'd meant it to be.

Poppy glances up at me, her expression carefully guarded, but before Mabel can protest, she nods. The old bat can do nothing but harrumph, very loudly, and saunter off to fetch me a sandwich.

We eat our lunch in silence, silence that seems to grow louder and louder as the minutes drip by. I'm about to start talking about William Wallace again, just to fill the dead air, when Poppy speaks.

"Why did my mum pick you to be my governess?"

I keep chewing for a moment, buying some time.

I could tell her that our mothers were friends, but that would raise more questions, ones I don't want to answer. How much do I want to reveal to this girl? My past is . . . complicated. Personal. And since I have my father's last name, Smith, I don't need to reveal my connection to this place to anybody. So I shrug. "I applied, and I guess she thought I was right for the job."

Poppy snorts. "Well, she thought wrong. And I don't need a governess anyway."

I fix my eyes on hers. "My mom died when I was just a bit older than you."

She looks surprised for a second. Then her guarded expression is back. "How?"

"An accident," I lie.

"What about your father?" she asks.

I circle my hand around the metal chalice that is much too fancy for well water, the condensation dripping over my fingers. "Never knew him."

She nods, considering this.

"So I know what you're going through," I say. "I know how mad you are, and I don't blame you for it."

She rolls her eyes. "You sound like my therapist."

I have to laugh. "Yeah, I probably do. The state only gave me one session with a therapist, to evaluate me, but it was memorable. It helped a bit, I think." Though it was mainly memorable because of the white-hot terror I had felt sitting in front of someone who might be able to see into my mind. Who might tell me that I was just as broken as I feared I was.

I shake the memory off. "How about you take me on a tour of this place after lunch? I'd like to start learning my way around."

"Have one of the other servants do it," she mutters, pushing her nearly empty plate away from her.

"I want you to do it," I say firmly, my tone permitting no arguments.

Again she rolls her eyes, her favorite reaction, but then stands up. "Fine."

She takes me on a whirlwind tour of the castle, through various guest bedrooms, the study where I bumped into Alice—a room filled with books and maps that used to be her father's and is now her brother's—the library with the grand piano, and other sitting rooms and parlors that I'll probably never be able to find again.

The core of the house is the square tower that was built in the early fourteenth century, Poppy tells me, when the first lord got his title. There are low doorways and half staircases leading to the other wings that were added by later generations, all jumbled together to create one rambling castle.

Next Poppy shows me the room that she says is the most important one in the castle, located directly underneath the medieval tower. She grabs an electric lantern from a shelf at the top of a tight spiral staircase before we inch down stones too shallow for my feet. I grasp the thick rope that serves as a bannister so hard that I'll probably get rope burn.

We enter a dark space, lit only by Poppy's lantern. There's nothing in the cavern but a spindly pole in the middle, and I look around, wondering what I'm missing.

"Mabs would be so mad if she saw you right now," Poppy says with a smirk.

Mabs? She calls Mabel *Mabs?* I almost laugh out loud at the nickname. At the idea that that stern, unpleasant woman would have a nickname at all.

"Don't you see what it is?" Poppy asks.

I look back at the pole and step toward it, realizing that it isn't a pole at all but the trunk of a tree. It curves a bit, this way and that, as it reaches from the ground up to the roof, where it ends abruptly.

"Why is there a tree in here?" I ask.

"The legend is that, when the first lord was exploring his new lands, he grew tired and fell asleep under this holly tree. He had a dream that he should build a castle here, and so he did, right around the tree. It's supposedly brought good luck to the family ever since."

I reach out to touch the smooth, knotted bark, but then pull my hand back after a moment. There's some strange feeling coursing through me, something I'm catching from the thick air of the room. It feels alive somehow. Crackling with energy, power. And watching me.

I shake my head, trying to jolt myself out of my sudden panic. *What's the matter with me?* It's just an old tree trunk, and

I'm a bit dizzy from that staircase, that's all. I'm fine. I straighten my shoulders and take a deep breath. *Fine.*

"So why would Mabel be mad at me for not knowing what it was?" I ask, trying to sound normal.

Poppy circles the tree in front of me, swinging the lantern in her hand, creating strange shadows on the wall. "Because she's obsessed with it. She always says we're a lucky family, blessed because of the tree. Anything from surviving a battle to getting a good grade on a test is due to this tree, according to her. It's like she worships it or something."

I wouldn't have suspected grim, dour Mabel to have such an impractical belief, but then again, there's something about this centuries-old tree trunk in the middle of this night-dark room . . . some unsettling feeling it gives off.

Poppy moves toward the staircase, taking the light with her, and I scurry after her. I don't want to be swallowed up in the shadows.

We climb back up the staircase, and I breathe out all of the unnerving air from the strange room below.

We make our way out of the medieval part of the castle and into a wing built in the seventeenth century, where I find a long, dark corridor lined with dusty portraits, some the size of my head, others larger than life. I spend a few minutes examining the depictions of men with kilts and women in frothy dresses.

Poppy points to one of a grumpy old man with a top hat and a cane. "My great-great-grandfather," she says, her voice a startling spark in the cold hall.

"He looks very . . . forbidding." I frown right back at him.

"My favorite is the Grey Lady," she says, beckoning me to another portrait. It's one I passed before but didn't pay much attention to: a woman in a soft gray dress, her skin almost the same pale color as the ruffled confection she wears, in front of a mountain landscape backdrop. At first glance I judged her as boring—her pale eyes are blank and stare just past the viewer, it seems. But I notice now a sadness in her slightly parted lips, a haunted look in those eyes that moments before I'd thought to be devoid of character.

"Who was she?" I ask Poppy.

"A great-great-great-aunt or something. I think she lived here in the early eighteen hundreds. She fell in love with a farmer, but her father made her break it off with him since he wasn't a duke or whatever. So she jumped off the roof onto the courtyard and killed herself."

"You're kidding."

"No. There have been stories about her ghost haunting this house ever since."

"Every creaky old house needs a ghost, I guess," I say with a shrug. For a moment, I imagine this lovesick girl stepping out of her painting and roaming the halls, wringing her hands and sobbing.

Poppy starts walking again, and I pull myself away from the disquieting portrait. She opens a big set of double doors at the end of the hall, and we enter an honest-to-goodness ballroom, a huge space with floor-to-ceiling windows, a shiny parquet floor, and gold-framed mirrors along the walls. I move slowly to the center of the room, my eyes wide as I try to take it all in. My mother used to read Jane Austen novels aloud to me, and whenever there was a scene at a ball, I pictured the ballrooms almost exactly like this. I look up to find a fresco painted on the ceiling, a vision of Aphrodite rising from her clamshell, ringed by cupids and cherubs. The goddess of love, presiding over the most romantic room I've ever seen.

"Mum hosted three balls a year in here for her different charities," Poppy tells me. "I would hide behind one of the plants," she says, pointing to a cluster of potted trees and ferns in one corner with a green velvet bench in front of them, "and watch all the women in their ball gowns and all the men in their tuxedos. My mum always threw the most glamorous parties."

I realize then that, for Poppy, there is no part of this house that isn't filled with ghosts.

She leads me back into the medieval tower and up the stair-case to the fifth floor, with her suite of rooms. "This is the family floor," she says. "Charlie's room is at that end." She points to the left. "And my parents' room is at that end." She points to the right. Both of us stare for a moment at the closed double doors at the end of the hall.

"And that's the tour," she says, flouncing back into her room.

"All right, then. Thank you," I tell her, but she refuses to look at me. "So what do you usually do on Saturday afternoons?" I ask, making my voice painfully bright and cheery.

She shrugs. "Usually more homework. Or read. Or ride Copperfield, if I have time. I have a big show in a couple of months, so I'm practicing all the jumps with him."

"How about you introduce me to Copperfield?" I ask. "I've never ridden a horse before."

"Never?" she asks.

I shake my head with a smile. Despite growing up in a West Texas town with an annual rodeo and more livestock than people, I always managed to avoid horses, scared off by their size and unpredictability. I've never even touched one before.

She almost smiles back, then catches herself. But that brief slip gives me hope.

"I guess we can go see him," she says with a shrug.

She bounds through the halls and out a back door, hurtling down the hill past various sheds and a tall wall of hedges. "That's the maze," she says, pointing to it as she strides past.

"A maze?" I ask. I approach the opening in the hedges and see more shrubbery walls inside, and a path leading into the depths. The walls are at least four feet taller than I am. *A place where someone could get thoroughly lost*, I think, and shiver.

"Yeah. My great-great-grandfather or something had it built because he wanted a place he could hide with his mistresses where no one could find him."

"Charming," I snort, and Poppy murmurs in agreement.

Finally, we reach a large wooden barn, which looks much newer than anything else on the property. "Dad built this for me when he gave me Copperfield," Poppy explains as we walk into the large, shadowed space. It takes a moment for my eyes to adjust and see the horses in their stalls.

A guy who looks only a few years older than I am is brushing down a horse with silky rust-colored hair, the one Poppy was riding earlier, and Poppy leads me to him. "I'll take that, Gareth," she says. He surrenders the brush to Poppy with a smile and nods his head at me, and I realize that he was the one who helped her off the horse earlier this morning.

"I'm Fee," I say, holding out my hand.

He shakes my hand slowly, lingering in the motion. "Gareth.

And I ken who ye are right enough. This place is small." His brogue is so thick, with such wildly rolling *R*s, that I can barely understand him. I try to translate the words in my head, but his wide, knowing smile is easy enough to interpret. I pull my hand out of his grasp, but I can't bite back my own smile. He chuckles a bit and pats Copperfield's side before stepping out of the stall. "It'll be too much fog for riding this afternoon, miss," he tells Poppy.

She nods. "I'll just brush her down then. Fee's never ridden a horse before."

Gareth turns his deep brown eyes to me, eyebrows raised in surprise. "Really now?"

"Not much of a horse person," I explain, reaching out a tentative hand to pat the neck of the absolutely massive horse in front of me. His hair is more bristly than I expected, and I can feel the thick, powerful muscles underneath it.

"Well, Poppy here knows everything about horses. She can teach you whatever you need to know. Or I can, if you'd rather." He offers me another flirtatious grin, and I shake my head at his lack of subtlety. There's something endearing about how open he is, though. It's completely harmless flirting, which makes it all too easy to respond to. And he's cute enough, too, with messy muddy-brown hair and broad shoulders.

"I'll make sure she does," I say, smiling at Poppy. There's a faint hint of a blush on her cheeks and a pleased smile playing on her mouth.

Gareth nods at me before grabbing a bucket and heading out of the barn.

"He's dating Alice, one of the maids," Poppy whispers to me as soon as he's gone. "And they think we don't all know about it."

I'm surprised, but I try not to show it. I can't imagine practical, blunt Alice with someone like Gareth. And he was way too flirtatious with me, even if it didn't mean anything. "Why is it a secret?" I whisper back.

"Mabs doesn't approve of staff relationships."

"*Mabs* doesn't seem to approve of much of anything," I say, and there it is again: Poppy's almost-smile. She catches herself at the last moment, and her face smooths out into its usual expression of sullen boredom. But for that brief moment, she completely brightened.

Once Poppy's cleaned Copperfield's colossal hooves and settled him in for the night, we head back to the house. A dense fog has come in, rolling off from the mountain. "Is it always like this?" I ask Poppy, waving my hand around in the thickening air.

"This time of year, yes. Dad used to call this the witching hour, when the ghosts and fairies would come out and walk among us, just out of sight."

It sounds like the kind of story my mom used to tell me. I

shudder, my eyes darting around, as if I'm actually expecting to see an apparition rippling through the fog. I don't relax until we reach the castle door.

Poppy's done enough homework for a Saturday, so I ask the cook if she'll send dinner for the two of us up to Poppy's sitting room, where we curl up in blankets and watch some mindless English romantic comedy that makes Poppy almost-laugh a few times. That positive development makes up for Mabel's cold stare of disapproval when she brings up our bowls of beef stew and thick hunks of brown bread. No matter what she thinks, I think Poppy and I will work together just fine.

CHAPTER 4

Once Poppy has gone to bed, I'm left to confront the one thing that has been bothering me all day: the lie I told Poppy. Or, rather, what I *didn't* tell her. I try to busy myself by unpacking my suitcase, taking a long shower in the bathroom down the hall that I share with the maids and female kitchen staff, checking my email on the computer in the servants' common room. Hex wrote begging for information about Scotland, reminding me of the boring details of her job at the Buffalo Head Café, the most popular of the three illustrious dining options in Mulespur. She writes about how lucky I am to have escaped the monotony of serving endless chicken-fried steaks to drunk fans after every Friday night football game, and tells me she sort of misses me. I send her a long, rambling email back, telling her about Poppy and the castle and Mabel and Albert and everything else that makes up this place I've found myself in.

No matter what I do, though, I can't stop thinking about my mother and, after a while, I don't have the energy to try. I give up and go to my closet to get the shoebox, the most important possession that traveled with me from Austin to Mulespur. The vessel that holds my past.

I open it and remove the photos and the note, letting memory take me over.

I told Poppy that my mother died in an accident. It's what I tell everyone, except Hex, who knows the more complicated truth.

I was almost seven when I realized that there was something wrong with Mom. I'd gone with her to the supermarket in East Austin to find something cheap for dinner. We were standing in the cereal aisle, and I was impatient because my mother was comparing prices. We were surrounded by other shoppers, everyone delicately maneuvering their carts in the small space, faces blank and tired as they scanned the contents of the shelves.

All of a sudden, my mother grabbed my arm and pulled me to her.

"Stay away from her!" she yelled as I fought to escape her viselike grip. It took me a second to realize that she was talking to an old man near us. He looked up in surprise, his watery blue eyes flicking from me to my mother. He couldn't have looked more harmless if he'd tried: his back hunched over, his white hair covered by a newsboy cap, his face inundated with wrinkles.

"You can't have her!" my mother screamed, over and over, clutching me to her so tightly that I would have fingerprint bruises on my arms for weeks.

A security guard in an ill-fitting uniform had to escort us out of the market. I could feel everyone's eyes following us as my mother continued screaming that the man was trying to take me away from her.

She'd displayed paranoiac tendencies before, often convinced that someone was following us or listening in on our conversations in the apartment. But she had never reacted so violently, so publicly before. I finally realized that other people's mothers didn't act that way, that most kids didn't have to triple-check that the front door was bolted and the shades of the windows were drawn at all times.

When we got home, she slept for hours.

"I'm so sorry, sweetheart," she told me the next day. "I don't mean to be that way." And most of the time, she wasn't. Most of the time, she was my charming mother, who told me stories and made me eat my vegetables and tucked me into bed every night.

But after a while, her episodes started getting worse and

worse. She told me that if she told a doctor, they would put her on medication and take me away from her. I learned how to be very careful around my school friends, to make sure they never knew what was happening in my tiny garage apartment.

Then, one afternoon, she wouldn't let me into the apartment after school. She was supposed to be on shift at the café, but instead she was holed up inside. I unlocked the door, but she'd pushed her bed and my futon and everything else we owned up against it, and I could only get it open a crack. But I could hear her raving through the wall. "Get out!" she screamed. "You can't take me away! Get out!"

"Mama?" I said. It came out as a whimper. I hadn't called her "Mama" in years, not since I was a baby. "Mama, it's me. It's just me."

"You'll hurt me, I know you'll hurt me. You seem so nice and soft, but it's all deceit, I know it is. I know it now!"

"Mama, I just want to come in. I'll make you dinner. It will all be fine, you'll see."

"No!" she screamed, like someone was attacking her. "You can't take me!" And then there was a bang—a gunshot, I knew right away—and she stopped ranting.

I must have screamed. I must have screamed loudly and for a long while, because by the time the neighbors came home and came up to see what was wrong, my throat was scratched and my voice was gone. And so was my mother.

The social worker they put in charge of me asked, "Why didn't you call an ambulance when you first got home?" She was a woman of soft smiles and reassuring hand-squeezes, but I could see the judgment in her eyes.

"She always told me not to call anyone," I answered, my voice hardly more than a whisper. "She said it would pass, that I should just wait it out. If I called an ambulance, they would have taken me away from her."

I know now that I should have fought Mom, that I should have done whatever I could have to bring her to a hospital years before. But I was too scared, too young to know what was really going on, and it all happened so fast. I thought she would recover, the way she'd always recovered from her episodes.

Instead, I moved to the middle of nowhere with an aunt I'd never met, who only took me in out of obligation. She kept me fed and left me alone, and I know I should have been grateful. But every now and then, I would catch her watching me, her eyes piercing my skin as though she could see the darkness within me. Waiting for the crazy to come out.

Because I know I'm at risk for the same disease my mother had. And that if I have it, the symptoms will start to show up soon. It's why I was so terrified when I started hearing my mother's lilting Scottish voice in my head, years after she died.

But that voice is a product of grief, not schizophrenia. I don't have any other symptoms. I don't see or hear things that aren't really there. I don't have delusions of grandeur or paranoia. I straighten my shoulders and take a deep breath, the habit I developed to pull me out of my darker thoughts. It's the same ritual I perform before I play the piano, and it makes me feel calmer. Peaceful. Normal. *I'm not my mother. I'm not going to become schizophrenic.* I repeat that over and over again. Maybe someday I'll truly believe it.

I stare at the photos in front of me, the only images I have of my beautiful, once-joyful mother. In my favorite one, she has her curly red hair flung over her shoulder, her head tipped back in laughter, one hand resting on her hip and the other on her heart as happiness overtakes her. I can't remember what I said to make her laugh like that, but I can remember the sound of her laughter, deep and rich and irresistible, as I took the photo.

I press my eyes closed, trying to stop the tears, but it doesn't work. It never works.

I unfold the note, the one she wrote me during one of her last lucid spells. I've read it so many times that the edges of the paper—the blank side of an order slip from her café—are soft and frayed.

I love you. Always remember that I love you.

I fall asleep clutching that note, willing myself to dream something happy.

I try to get to know Poppy better over the next few days. I help her with her homework, discussing the Hundred Years' War and *Ivanhoe* with her and quizzing her on math problems that I barely remember how to do.

She still makes sure to let me know how very unwanted I am. Along with the constant eye-rolling, she typically refuses to respond to any of my attempts at friendliness. I ask about their family vacations, about her horseback riding, about her school friends, and all I get is silence.

I don't blame her. But she needs someone to talk to. She needs an outlet for all that anger and grief I know she's got bottled up inside her.

When she's at school, the hours seem to drag on. I make cautious friends with the gruff cook, Mrs. Mackenzie. She doesn't seem to like me, exactly—she doesn't seem to like any-body. She's too busy for anything resembling small talk, and whenever I walk into the kitchen, she fixes me with this look that demands I spit out whatever request I have and then get out of her way. But when I ask her to recommend some kind of tea that will help me sleep, she brews a cup of her special heather chamomile tea and shows me the tin, so I can make myself a cup of it every night.

During the day, I tend to secret myself away on the window seat in the library, where there are soft pillows and books to distract me from the memories that bombard me when I'm alone. There I can hide myself away from the rest of the world behind a thick curtain and look out over the back of the house. The land slopes down below me, and I can barely see the stable beyond the hedge maze and the trees. It's magical.

But after about a week or so, as the chill of early October begins to take over, I'm restless for something new. Poppy rides Copperfield every afternoon after school, so she doesn't return until dinnertime. There are too many hours and not enough to fill them with in this old, damp castle.

One morning, I decide to follow Alice around like a lost puppy, helping her with her housework in exchange for information.

We're cleaning one of the dozens of spare bedrooms when I finally ask the question I've been wondering about most.

"What's Charlie like?" I say as she hands me a feather duster.

She raises her eyebrows, then sighs. "That's—well, it's complicated."

"Why?" I'm trying not to sound too interested, but I can tell from her quick, hard glance that I'm not successful.

"Because he's changed so much since his parents died. He used to be something of a playboy, a partier. The lord and lady managed to keep his antics out of the papers, but he spent most of his time at university getting into trouble. Only graduated this year because his parents kept donating money. He had a girlfriend at St. Andrews for a while, Blair. But he'd cheat on her every time he came back home, with whatever local girl he could find. They all fall all over him." There's a hefty amount of disgust in her voice that catches my attention.

"Did you and he . . . ?" I ask.

She scoffs. "Not on your life. He's broken a few of my friends' hearts, though."

"You said he's changed since his parents died?"

Alice nods. "He had to. He couldn't be the irresponsible spoiled brat anymore, not when he had to take care of Poppy and his father's company. Now he's serious all the time, a completely different person."

"No more cheating on his girlfriend?" I ask.

"No more *girlfriend*," she answers, taking the duster from me and cleaning the mantelpiece and the antique dueling pistols hanging on the wall above it herself. "Or at least she didn't come to the funeral."

"And he's in Glasgow now?" I ask.

"He left the day you arrived. Had to show the board that he was ready to take over as CEO."

I nod, throwing the used dust rags into a basket and picking it up.

Alice stops me before I can walk out of the room. "When you meet him, just be careful, okay?" she says, her eyes intent on mine. "He has this way of sweeping girls off their feet, but once a heartbreaker, always a heartbreaker."

I laugh, shifting the bin from one hip to the other. "Players really aren't my type. Don't worry about me." It hits me how ironic it is that she's lecturing me about staying away from players when she's dating the flirt from the stables. But Poppy said it was supposed to be a secret, and I don't want to betray her tentative trust.

Alice nods, but there are still traces of doubt in her eyes as we leave the room together.

I think of the guy from the pub with the red-brown curls and the icy green gaze, wondering how he could cause Alice such concern. He must have been much more charming before his parents died, I decide.

Half the boys in my high school thought they were insanely irresistible, so I'm used to players and their practiced charm. When I was a sophomore, a senior boy named Matt spent the better part of fall semester hanging around my locker, asking me to parties and dates and football games. He used honeyed, well-rehearsed words and clichéd moves—tucking a lock of hair behind my ear, taking my books from me and walking me to class before I could protest. I would have been tempted, because he was undeniably cute, but I'd watched him use those same moves on three other girls in my grade, making them go all soft and giggly and then breaking their hearts once he'd grown bored with them. I refused to turn into one of those girls, and I rejected him every time, but he wouldn't take the hint, and finally Hex told me I needed to "woman up" and grow a backbone. So the next time he tried to grab my books from me, I gave him a flirtatious smile and told him, sweetly, "Not a chance in hell."

The memory makes me smile. Both of us were so embarrassed by the whole thing that we spent the rest of the year hiding from each other.

My smile fades when I hear stomping behind me, and when I turn around, I find Mabel bearing down on me, her eyes flashing. I assume she's mad because I've been helping Alice, who scurries off without even a goodbye.

"Where's Poppy?" she demands.

I stare at her for a moment, frozen. "It's not four yet, is it?" I sputter out. "She's still at school."

"The school just called. Poppy has been missing classes for the past week, and today she didn't even show up at all."

"But—Albert and I dropped her off this morning. I saw her walk into the building."

Mabel points her finger at me. "She's not answering her mobile, and no one knows where she is. It's *your* responsibility to make sure she's where she's supposed to be. You need to find her. And if she's hurt because of your negligence, you will find yourself fired immediately."

Her voice is nearly shaking with anger. She marches away from me, and I watch her go, my mouth open in shock.

I try to think. Where would Poppy go? I don't know anything about this girl. I don't know if she has a favorite place on campus to escape to or has friends who do this kind of thing.

I need help. I sprint out to the garage, a separate building several yards from the side of the castle. Albert lives in the apartment above, and I climb the rickety spiral staircase and knock on his front door.

He opens it, a napkin tucked into his shirt collar and a questioning look on his face.

"Poppy's missing. She didn't go to school today," I say in a rush before he can ask what's wrong.

He sighs, as if he's not entirely surprised. "Where do you think she's gone?" he asks, pulling the napkin out of his collar and gesturing me out the door.

"I don't know," I say, grasping the bannister tightly as I descend. "She couldn't have gone far from the school, right?"

"Unless she had a friend's parent drive her someplace. She's friendly with a couple of other day-student girls."

I look back at him as we hurry for the car. He must see the growing horror on my face, because he smiles reassuringly. "Och, lass, I'm sure she's fine. Not much trouble to get up to in these parts."

I can think of plenty of trouble someone could get up to anywhere, but I don't say anything as we buckle up and head for the school. Poppy's young and grieving, but she seems pretty smart. I can't see her shoplifting or smoking a pack of cigarettes or something crazy like that.

I pick at the cuticle of my left index finger, bouncing my knees as we wend our way through the hills to the school. I can't keep still. I can't focus on anything out the window. All I can see is Poppy's face, the grief and hurt always present underneath the surface. I see her in the back of a stranger's car, lost in the woods somewhere, her broken body at the bottom of a cliff.

I tell myself to stop, but the images keep coming.

I'm out of the car before Albert even comes to a full stop in front of Bardwill, Poppy's school. It's two in the afternoon, and all of the girls are still in class. Safe, where they're supposed to be.

You're not going to find her, I think, and then I freeze. Because my mind did not create that thought. It seemed to come from a voice in my head. A stranger's voice, like the ones my mother used to complain about, two hands pressed against her temples like she could squeeze them out. It's the first time I've heard a voice that wasn't my mother's.

I close my eyes, straighten my shoulders, and take a deep breath. *It's just me. Just my thoughts. I'm worried about Poppy, that's all.*

The guard at the front recognizes me from drop-off, and he takes me to the headmistress's office while Albert searches the grounds outside the school.

The hallway that I step into is ornate, beautiful. Nothing like the cold linoleum and buzzing, harsh fluorescent light of my Texas public schools. Paintings and photos of distinguished-looking women line the hallways, their knowing countenances radiating confidence and superiority. I keep my head down as we climb the stairs to the third floor.

The headmistress's assistant, a woman with a dark gray bun and a kind smile, ushers me right into the office. "Headmistress Callahan will be with you in just a few moments," she assures me. "Let me know if you need anything at all."

She closes the door, and I'm alone. I sink into one of the chairs and bury my head in my hands. Albert isn't too worried about Poppy, so I shouldn't be either. She just wanted to ditch school. She'll probably be home for dinner.

I try to take a deep breath, but I keep hearing the echo of that strange voice in my head. The air feels stuffy, so I spring up out of my chair and move to the window, where I can at least see some open space. It looks out on the back of the school below, old brick dorms and the huge new science center, its metallic sides and modern lines standing out like a goth among cheerleaders.

The door clicks behind me, and I turn to see the headmistress, who is much younger than I was expecting. She must be in her late thirties or early forties, and her dark brown hair is pulled back in a sleek ponytail.

"You must be Poppy's caretaker," she says, shaking my hand. Her voice is high-pitched and nasally, discordant with her chic appearance.

"I'm Fee," I say and release her hand quickly. "Do you know where she might have gone?"

The headmistress gestures me back to my seat, and I sit down reluctantly as she settles behind her desk. "Poppy is a very bright young girl who is going through a rough transition right now," she says.

A rough transition? One of the worst euphemisms for losing your parents that I've ever heard, and I've heard plenty. I resist the urge to clench my teeth. "I'm still getting to know Poppy," I say, my words clipped, "so I can't yet guess where she might have gone. But I would really, really like to find her."

The headmistress gives me this smile that drips with sympathy and condescension, and I understand immediately why Poppy would be eager to run away from this place. "I don't know where she might have gone, but I do know that Poppy is a very special girl who needs a lot of attention right now. And we're all worried about her here at Bardwill."

I stand up. "I'm worried about her, too. So if you'll excuse me, I'm going to go try to find her."

She finally seems to catch on to the fact that I can't stand her, because there's the slightest purse in her lips as she rises from her desk. "Of course," she says. "But once this situation has been resolved, I'd like to talk to you about how we can best help Poppy going forward."

I nod quickly before hurrying out the door.

Students have filled the halls, scurrying off to their last class of the day. I push my way through the clusters and out into the yard, more anxious than ever about finding Poppy.

Where would I go if I were her? Nowhere within that claustrophobic building with teachers and other students looking at me like I'm suddenly different, like tragedy has stamped a tattoo across my forehead. Where would I go to be free?

I realize exactly where I would go just as I spot Albert wait-ing by the car. "No luck," he calls. "You?"

I shake my head. "We should go back to the house. I think I know where she is."

We drive for what feels like hours until we're finally head-ing back through the cathedral of trees and up the road to the familiar gray stone castle. As soon as Albert stops the car, I hop out and head straight for the stables.

Gareth is shoveling hay into one of the stalls. It's quiet, save for the soft nickering of horses. I peer around the stable, but there's no sign of Poppy. Or Copperfield.

"Can I help you?" Gareth asks, leaning on his shovel. I can't help but notice the corded muscles of his forearms before I look away.

"Sorry," I say. "I thought Poppy might be here."

"Not for hours. She and Copperfield are out for a bit of a wander now."

"You've been helping her ditch school," I say with a sigh, my suspicions confirmed.

He shrugs. "She needed to get away. She needs space and time to grieve, and no one else is giving it to her."

"She's eleven!" I say, stepping even closer to him so that he can see the exasperation in my eyes. "She can't be traipsing around the country on her own!"

"She knows this part of the country almost as well as I do, and she mostly keeps to the estate anyway. She'll be fine." He pauses, looking down at me seriously. "You need to let her breathe."

I want to keep yelling at him the way that Mabel yelled at me, but I know he's right. All of the fight evaporates right out of me. "I don't know how to get through to her," I say, sitting down on a bench outside the stall he's been working in.

He sits beside me carefully, resting his back against the stall door and stretching his long legs out in front of him. "I think you're doing a fine job."

I snort. "What makes you think that?"

He catches my eyes. "She told me so. She told me that you lost your mother when you were young, too. She'll open up to you, if you give her time to keep learning to trust you."

I lean back against the wall, my shoulder brushing against his. "I hope so," I mutter.

It takes me a moment to realize that he's still watching me, and when I look over to meet his gaze, there's an easy smirk on his lips, a spark in those dark brown eyes that makes me blink.

I push myself up. "I should get back to the house. I've been helping Alice." I didn't mean to add that last part, but as soon as the words leave my mouth I know that I said them because I wanted to see his reaction to her name.

"That's nice of you," he says simply. Those dark brown eyes don't change, still intent on mine.

"She's very nice."

He finally reacts, dropping the smirk and raising his eyebrows.

"Well, she's not *nice*, really," I amend, officially babbling now. "She's not, like, the warmest person ever. But she's the only one in the house besides Albert who doesn't make me feel like I'm beneath them or that I'm bothering them or . . . or something."

"Did someone tell you that Alice and I are together?" Gareth asks, standing up.

"Yes," I confess, though I don't tell him it was Poppy, so I can pretend that I'm not breaking her trust.

"Well, we're not. We used to be."

"What happened?"

He shrugs. "Didn't fit," he says, like it's so simple.

"And what does she think about that?" I ask.

He looks away, and I have my answer. I can't keep this flirtation up. I'm not even truly into him, and he's not worth losing my tentative friendship with Alice.

"Yeah, well, look, I've got to go. Can you send Poppy inside when she gets back?"

He nods slowly and sits back down on the bench when I leave him.

I start to head to the house, but the thought of going back there, to the cold air and Mabel's disapproving scowl, makes me feel like I can't breathe. Instead, I let my feet lead me out beyond the stables, into the lush fields of grass. Poppy won't come back until she's good and ready, and I can talk with her then.

The wind lashes violently around me, and I wrap my arms around myself, pushing on. I wander around the castle, staying in this orbit so I don't get lost. The mud and bracken squelch beneath my tennis shoes. The afternoon fades into evening, the sun slipping behind the mountains. The air grows colder, unfriendlier, as the fog rolls in. This place is harsh, suited only for people with rugged souls and weathered faces. Or people like the Moffats, who are wealthy enough to build a fortress and surround themselves with soft, warm things.

My mother could have had that kind of shelter here. It was the life she was destined for, before she abandoned it all for my father.

Would she have lived if she hadn't followed that mad love and instead stayed here and married Lord Harold, like she was supposed to? Would she have had people to care for her without judgment, to make sure she was on her medication and didn't harm herself? People who would have helped her more than I did?

There's another letter in the secret box in my closet. An email, from Lily to my mother, which Mom had printed out and saved, that I found after she died. It was well worn, as if my mother had read it and reread it hundreds of times. It was dated three months after I was born, long after my dad left us.

I'll keep your secrets, Lily wrote. *I promise that I won't tell your parents anything you tell me. But you have to let me know how you're doing. I want you to know you can trust me and that you can always tell me anything.*

Even though Mom's own parents ignored her in the years before they died, Lily never did. She cared about my mother, and it meant so much to her that she printed out that email and read it over and over, the way I do with her note telling me she would always love me.

I sigh. Dusk has fallen. "The witching hour," Poppy called it. I feel as if the fog and my dark thoughts will consume me if I give them the chance. I need to head back before I'm late for dinner, but now I'm actually looking forward to being inside.

The fog is so thick that I can barely see. I hold my hands out as if I can feel my way through the air, stepping carefully so that I don't slip on the rocks or the wet grass below. There's a snap of a branch to my right, and I freeze. Hold my breath. The evening around me is still again. "Hello?" I whisper.

There's a rustle. Or did I imagine it? A quiver runs down my spine.

And then, out of the corner of my eye, I see movement—a dark shadow, disappearing into the fog.

I yelp, and my feet are moving before I even realize it. I'm running toward the hazy outline of the castle, breaking through well-ordered shrubs in my mad dash.

I stop when I reach a gnarled tree in the immediate castle yard. I lean against it, taking deep gulps of breath.

What did I just see? It was—it looked almost like a person. A woman, with long hair. Was someone out here with me? Was someone watching me?

No, I tell myself firmly. It was nothing. Just some animal, or a trick of the fog, and I overreacted.

Poppy's tales of the Grey Lady and the witching hour must have really gotten into my head. Because that rustle—I swear it sounded like the swish of a long skirt.

I think of my mother's tales of the *bean nighe*, a type of banshee. In the legends, she washes the clothes of those about to die, foretelling their doom. She can be an old hag or a stunningly beautiful young woman, whichever she pleases, and seeing her is a portent of impending death. I used to think those stories, which Mom would whisper to me in the dark, were wonderfully terrifying. But then she had an episode and thought she saw a *bean nighe* washing her clothes in the middle of an Austin street. She said she saw a beautiful woman in a long dress, her gaze locked on Mom as she wrung the blood from her grave clothes. Mom raved that she could see the cold gleam in the woman's eyes, hear the rustle of her skirt, above all the street noise.

I straighten up against the tree, shaking my head at myself and laughing a little. I certainly didn't just see a *bean nighe*, or a ghost, or anything. A squirrel, probably, or a fox, or whatever they have here. Nothing to get upset about. I should just forget it. That would be the normal thing to do.

I set my shoulders back and march toward the door.

CHAPTER 5

When I reach the house, I find Alice running through the hallways in a frenzy. "What's going on?" I call to her, but she waves me off as she bolts up the main staircase. Whatever it is, it must be important enough for her to break protocol.

I hurry to the kitchen, where Mrs. Mackenzie is flitting from the stove to the ovens and back again. "What happened?" I ask.

"Charlie's back two days early, that's what happened," she says, her voice almost a yell as she slams a pot down on the range. "And now it's all a-scramble to make sure everything's ready for him. I suggest you stay out of Mabel's way tonight, if you know what's good for you."

I take her advice immediately, hurrying up the staircase and checking the hallway outside before scurrying down to the library. If I have to hide, I'd prefer to hide with a good book. I don't know who I'm more afraid of running into: Mabel or Charlie.

Once I'm safe in the library, I stand over the piano, trailing my fingers across the tops of the keys as I try to calm my rapidly rising breath. I bet he doesn't even remember me. I was just some random girl who was rude to him. A girl with an American accent who showed up in a tiny town unused to strangers. Sure. No way he remembers me.

I groan.

"Do you play?"

I whirl around to find the guy from the pub, tall with tousled red-brown hair, leaning against the doorway. His eyes seem unnaturally bright as they watch me.

"You," I breathe out.

"Me," he answers simply.

"What are you doing here?" I ask, realizing how ridiculous I sound even as the words leave my mouth.

He must see that realization on my face, because he doesn't say anything. Instead, he offers me a smile that suggests genuine amusement.

I feel a blush spread over my face, and I look back to the piano to hide it. "I mean, no, I don't play. I used to. A long time ago."

"Sorry," he says, stepping closer to me. "I should probably do the gentlemanly thing and introduce myself. I'm Charlie."

I turn to him and take his outstretched hand. His skin is a bit rough, unlike what I would have expected of a boy who grew up in this kind of house. He smiles again, as if he can tell what I'm thinking, and I feel all of the breath leave my body. Because his eyes aren't icy at all. They're a warm shade of green, bright as the first shoots of grass in spring.

"Fee," I say finally, much too late. "My name's Fee."

"The new governess."

"Au pair," I correct before I can stop myself. I bite my lip.

Charlie's smile fades a bit, becomes softer. "My mum liked to say *au pair* instead of governess. She thought it sounded more sophisticated."

"I'm sorry," I whisper.

He watches me, those warm green eyes intent on mine. "Poppy told me you lost your mother, too."

I nod, breaking my gaze from his. "I know there's nothing anyone can say that can make you feel better. Or isn't awkward or annoying."

"Yeah, I'm starting to get that." He runs a hand across the top of the piano, his eyes following its progress. We both watch it, the seconds slipping past us.

"I'm sorry I was rude to you," I burst out when I can't stand the silence anymore. "At the pub, I mean."

He looks up, surprised. "I'm sorry I stared at you," he says. And he does look sorry. Even though he's staring at me now, so intently that I feel my cheeks start to flame.

He drops his gaze, finally, then glances at the door. "Come on, dinner should be ready soon."

"Oh, I think I'm supposed—I mean, I think Mabel expects me to eat with the servants now that you're back."

Charlie studies me for a moment. I fcel as if he can see every ounce of insecurity within me, and I want to look away. But I can't. How does he do that?

"Mabel has some outdated ideas about how this house should be run," he says finally. "You'll eat with Poppy and me. If you don't mind."

I shake my head. "I don't mind."

His smile is back, and it makes my breath catch in my throat. "Good, come on, then." He turns and walks out of the room, clearly expecting me to follow.

We walk into the dining room to find Mabel setting the table. She looks up at me, a mixture of surprise and scandal on her face. I lift my chin and stare right back at her, and her surprise morphs quickly into a glare.

"Set an extra place, would you, Mabs?" Charlie asks as he settles into his chair. "Fee is going to be joining us for dinner from now on."

"Of course, Lord Moffat," Mabel says, her voice pleasantly soft. I have to bite back a smile.

Once she's hustled out of the room, I turn back to Charlie. "She's going to spit in my food," I whisper. "And maybe yours, for arranging this."

"No she won't," he says with a smile. "She loves me, and she cares too much about being the perfect housekeeper to spit in anyone's food, no matter how much she hates them."

"I don't know what I did to make her hate me," I say, examining the door Mabel just disappeared behind.

"She's a peculiar bird," Charlie answers. "She'll warm up to you in time." When I raise my eyebrows at him, he nearly laughs. "Okay, maybe not." Mabel hurries back in with an extra setting of china and silver, sets it up, and hurries out again.

I sink into the chair across from Charlie. The head and foot of the table are conspicuously bare.

"You've met Charlie, then?" says Poppy, entering the room and settling down in the chair next to me. I raise my eyebrows at her with a sardonic smile. I know Gareth didn't drive her back to school for me to pick her up, so he must have told her that her ditching school hadn't gone unnoticed. She sends me an apologetic smile in return.

"Yes," Charlie says softly, and I can feel his eyes on me, ready to capture mine. I refuse to look at him. He's got me on edge, hyperaware of his presence, and I don't know what to make of it.

I fix Poppy with a knowing look and say, "You've been up in your room for hours now. How's the math homework going?"

She nods, picking up on the fact that I'm providing her with an alibi and that I won't tell Charlie she skipped school today. As long as it doesn't happen again, at least. "Slowly," she says. "But I think I'm almost done."

"Want me to take a look at it?" Charlie asks, grabbing one of the rolls that Mabel brings out with the dinner plates.

"No," Poppy answers lightly. "Fee's better at explaining it to me than you are."

He scoffs, and I try not to gape at the unexpected praise. "I'm brilliant at maths!" Charlie protests.

"Yeah, so brilliant that I never understand a word you're saying," Poppy teases.

A smile stretches across his face to echo hers. "It's good to see you smile again," he says softly.

I look down at my plate, trying to shrink away from the private moment they're sharing. It's easy to tell how much Charlie loves his sister: His entire demeanor changed the moment she walked into the room, turning from intense and slightly dark to bright and charismatic. I don't know what to make of him, but I can't deny that he's clearly a loving brother.

It's disarming.

The rest of dinner—overcooked meat and potatoes, apparently Charlie's favorite—passes rather smoothly, with Charlie asking Poppy questions about school and Copperfield and her friends. Her best girl friends are named Natalie and Imogen, but when Charlie asks how they're doing, Poppy just shrugs. "Fine, I guess," she says. "We don't have any classes together this year, so I just see them at lunch."

"What about inviting them over here for a sleepover or something?" Charlie suggests. "Like you used to."

Poppy shrugs again. "Maybe," she says, but she sounds anything but excited about the idea.

For dessert, Mabel brings out cranachan, a tower of oats, whipped cream, heather honey, raspberries, and "just a touch of whisky," as Mabel assures Charlie as she places one before Poppy. Each one is served in a little glass, and Mabel sets mine down just a bit harder than necessary.

Charlie digs right into his, shoving a big spoonful in his mouth. "Delicious, Mabs," he says with a nod to her. "Tell Mrs.

Mackenzie that I couldn't find anything like her cranachan in Glasgow, and I missed it."

I notice Poppy scowl down at her glass at his words, but Charlie seems oblivious. He looks to me, beaming. "Ever had cranachan before?"

I'm about to answer that my mother always tried to make it for my birthday, when she could afford the ingredients, when Poppy interjects, "Dad always tried to work from home so he didn't have to go to Glasgow so much."

Charlie's smile drops, and his jaw tightens. "I told you, I had to go in person to show the board I'm ready to take over the company."

"Right," she says, rolling her eyes.

"I know you're mad," he says, his voice low. "But you don't understand what's happening in the newspaper industry. You don't understand what it's like being a grown-up."

I almost wince. He couldn't have picked more perfectly condescending words to enrage an eleven-year-old girl if he'd tried.

Poppy grits her teeth. "You just couldn't wait to leave," she spits out. "You don't want to be here with me." Before he can answer, she pushes her chair back from the table violently, throwing her napkin down and stomping out of the room.

I glance at Charlie. His eyes are closed, his jaw clenched.

"I'm sorry," he says. "Lately my sister and I can't spend much time together without flying at each other's throats." He sighs. "I would have been right *bealing* if my dad said something like that to me, though, I guess." By his tone when he says it, I'm assuming "bealing" means furious. "Can't help making a mess of things," he adds, almost to himself.

I consider saying something comforting, something along the lines of "She'll get over it" or "This kind of thing is always hard," but when I open my mouth, a question I was never intending to ask comes flying out. "Why were you at the pub the night I came in?" I've been wondering this since I discovered who he was. He was supposed to be on a train to Glasgow. Why had he stayed?

"It doesn't matter," he says, staring out the door after his sister.

I look down at my half-empty cranachan glass, horrified that I asked him such a personal question. *He's my boss*, I remind myself. I should keep my mouth shut, no matter how curious I am. No matter how disarming he is.

But instead of getting angry, he changes the subject. "Do you have any siblings?" he asks, turning to me.

"No."

"So when your mum died, you were all alone."

The empathy in his tone makes my chest constrict, tears threatening to build in my eyes. I bite the inside of my cheek and nod.

"I should go check on her," he says after a small silence.

I nearly jump out of my chair, the legs scraping harshly along the stone floor. "I'll do it."

He sighs. "Yeah. Probably better."

I hurry out of the dining room without looking at him.

Mabel is on the other side of the door, glowering at me as I hurry past her. As if it's my fault her welcome-home-Charlie dinner has been ruined.

Enough. I've had enough of that woman's simmering disapproval. If nothing I do is right, I might as well just do what I want. I march defiantly up the main staircase to Poppy's room.

I knock at her door, but there's no answer. When I press my ear to the heavy wood, I can just barely hear the sound of muffled sobbing. I try the knob, but it's locked. "Poppy?" I call out. "It's me. Can you let me in?"

"Go away!" Her yell comes through clearly enough.

As much as I don't want to, I think back to those weeks after my mother died. I was angry, scared, and lonely, forced to move away from everything I knew, losing all sense of home. What would I have wanted to hear then? I take a deep breath. "For me, the worst part was feeling alone," I say through the door. "So I'm going to be here, on the other side of this door, until you feel like opening it. I'll be right here. Okay?"

She doesn't respond, which I'll take as a good sign. So I settle down onto the cold wood floor, my back against the wall and my knees up to my chest, and wait.

I wait for almost an hour until the muffled sobbing dies down, and then I hear the floorboards creak and finally the click of the lock. She opens the door slowly and stares down at me for a moment, her eyes red and puffy. Then she closes the door behind her and sinks down beside me.

For a few minutes, she doesn't speak and neither do I. Finally, she sighs and looks over at me. "Did you have someone to do that for you? After your mum died?"

I shake my head. "Not for years. Not until I met my friend Hex when I was fifteen."

"Her name is *Hex*?" Poppy asks, her eyes wide.

"No. Her real name is Delilah. But she hates it because her mom had named her, and when she was thirteen, her mom left because her boyfriends started paying too much attention to Hex. So Hex lives with her grandmother now and doesn't want anything from her mother."

"Why did she pick Hex?"

"Because she wanted to scare people. Hex is beautiful, really tall and stunning. People notice her, especially guys, but she doesn't want them to. So she shaved off all her hair and pierced her lip and eyebrow and learned to growl at people so they would stay away. And she picked the name Hex to warn people away, too."

"But she was nice to you."

I let a small smile slip. "Not at first. We went to the same school, shared the same classes, and it was three months before she even said one word to me. She found me crying in the bathroom one morning before school, and she accused me of getting upset over something silly, like a boy or a bad grade, totally prepared to start mocking me mercilessly. When I told her it was because I missed my mom, she stayed with me until I was done crying, and after that, she became my best friend. My only friend."

"Where is she now?" Poppy asks, her voice soft.

"She's back in Texas."

"Do you miss her?"

I nod. "Every day."

"I'm sorry I've been so awful to you," Poppy says after a moment.

"It's okay," I say, and I look right at her so she knows I mean it. "Charlie's sorry, too, you know. That he had to leave you."

She looks back down at the floor. "I know."

73

We sit there quietly for a few minutes until Poppy pushes herself back up. "I should probably shower before bed. I still smell like horse."

I stand up, too. "About that. Try to make it to school tomorrow, okay? Or Mabel might skin me alive."

Poppy snorts. "Okay."

CHAPTER 6

That night, I'm too excited to sleep, so happy that I finally made it through to Poppy. So I go down to the library and curl up behind the curtain on the window seat. I've started reading *Rebecca* by Daphne du Maurier, about a woman who's married a widower and moved into his big house on the English coast, a place with fog and secrets swirling in the air.

Suddenly, the door to the library swings open and bangs against the wall. I scream, the book dropping from my hand.

"Oh, God," a voice says. A voice I know.

I push myself off the window seat, drawing back the curtains that hide me until I see Charlie standing in the doorway, his face white with shock, staring at me like I'm a ghost. "You scared the bloody hell out of me," he says. He's lost his suit jacket and tie, and his white button-down hangs open, revealing a lean chest with lines of definition down to his low-slung pants.

"You scared *me*," I whisper, unable to stop staring.

"I'm sorry." His voice is low, deep, and he braces himself against the doorway, pressing his hands against the frame like he needs something to hold himself up. Or like, if he weren't grasping the sides of the doorway, he'd be launching himself forward. At me.

He's looking at me with those warm green eyes again, his strong jaw tense.

I slip off the window seat, closing my book. "I'll get out of your way," I murmur.

"You don't have to leave," he says quickly.

I open my mouth, about to say something about how I should get to bed, when he interrupts me.

"I'm sorry about earlier. At dinner. Did Poppy—is she okay?"

"She will be," I say with more confidence than I feel. I take a few steps toward him, until I'm halfway across the room. "She's just hurting."

He laughs one short, bitter laugh. "I keep hurting everybody." I hear honesty, pain in his voice.

"What do you mean?" I ask, unable to stop myself.

He shakes his head and doesn't answer.

I step forward again. I feel as if I'm approaching a wounded animal, trying to soothe it into trusting me. So that I can fix it.

But I can't fix this, I remind myself. I don't have the cure for grief caused by losing your parents. I can't even cure myself.

Why is his shirt unbuttoned? It keeps distracting me.

He finally looks at me, his eyes trained on my lips, which I realize now are slightly parted.

And then, inexplicably, he starts laughing. Uncontrollably. "I'm sorry," he says, nearly doubled over. "It's just—"

"Are you drunk?"

He holds his thumb and index finger sideways in the air, the universal sign for "just a little bit," and I roll my eyes.

Plenty of my classmates back in Mulespur spent their nights hidden away on playing fields or in friends' barns, far from the prying eyes of parents, getting wasted on cheap beer. Then they'd show up to class hungover, if they showed up at all. I didn't care how they spent their time, but doing well in school was the only way I could make it out of Mulespur. I wasn't going to waste my life away night after night.

"Would you at least button your shirt?" I snap at Charlie.

He finally stops laughing and looks down, seemingly surprised to find himself so rumpled. When he looks back up at me, there's something new in those green eyes. Curiosity, maybe. An almost calculated interest. "Does it make you uncomfortable?" he asks, stepping toward me. Once. Twice. And then another long stride.

He must be really drunk, I realize, or he wouldn't have made such a suggestive remark. He wouldn't have stepped so close to me that I have to tilt my head to look him in the eyes.

This is the player version of Charlie that Alice warned me about. All charm and no substance.

I lean in slightly, watching with satisfaction as his eyes widen. Slowly, achingly slowly, I raise my lips to his ear. "Get some sleep and sober up, *Master Charlie*," I say, my tone full of fake deference.

I step back, a smile flitting across my lips, and step around him to leave. He says nothing, just lets me go.

Back in my room, all of my confidence fades away. I just told my boss to sober up. My *boss*. And I leaned in close to him, so close that I could smell the whisky on his breath and then, beneath that, a scent like rain and wood fire.

I shiver and fling myself on my bed, only pausing to take my shoes off before curling up under the blankets. Maybe I'll wake up tomorrow morning and it will all have been a dream. Or maybe it really did happen, but he was so drunk that he won't remember anything at all.

I hide my face in my pillow. How could I have lost control over myself? How could I have acted like that in front of my boss? No matter his behavior, I should have been able to keep up some kind of professional demeanor. It's what normal people would do.

There's a muffled sound of laughter from the other side of the wall. It almost sounds like it's coming from the left, but I'm in the last room in the hall, so it must be coming from Keira to my right. She's one of the maids, and she seems friendly enough when we cross paths around the castle. I hope she's not laughing because she heard me throwing myself on the bed.

I burrow back into my blankets and do my best to calm the whirling storm in my mind. I have to get a good night's sleep if I want to figure out how not to lose my job tomorrow.

I'm just about to slip into unconsciousness when a large bang on the other side of the wall jolts me upright. The left side, the outside wall. The room falls silent again, the only sound my staccato breathing.

But then there's another muffled sound, and I sit up, straining to hear. From the tinny sound of whispered conversation, it seems like someone to my left is watching TV. At two in the morning. There must be some weird acoustic thing happening to make it seem like the noises from Keira's room are coming from the other side.

I bury my face back in my pillows, but I can't block out the sound. I consider getting up and asking Keira to tone it down, but I don't want to offend her. Not when I'm still so new to the house.

Finally, after about an hour of indecipherable whispers, the room falls silent, and I fall asleep.

CHAPTER 7

I wake up the next morning groggy and tired, determined to avoid Charlie all day. If I don't see him, he can't fire me. But when I walk into the dining room with Poppy for breakfast, he's sitting at the table, not sleeping off his hangover as I was predicting. He winces when he sees me.

Poppy approaches him cautiously. "Sorry," she says, almost in a whisper, "about last night."

He raises his eyebrows, and his whole face brightens. "Me too," he says.

She nods, grabbing the dish of potato scones and sliding one onto her plate. Charlie looks over at me. "Thank you," he mouths, and I nod.

I grab a piece of shortbread and bite into it, just to have something to do, but as soon as it hits my mouth, I freeze.

Because it's not just any shortbread. It's my mother's short-bread, with a hint of cayenne pepper, just enough to shock the taste buds. She made it accidentally one day, when I was eight, after knocking a bit of cayenne into the batter. We liked it so much that, ever after, she made it the same way.

I nearly spit it out.

Mabel marches into the room, setting a plate piled with thick bacon and a fried egg in front of Charlie.

"Where did this recipe come from? For the shortbread?" I ask her.

She turns around and blinks at me. "Mrs. Mackenzie's been making it this way for years. Is it not to your taste?" she asks with a sneer.

"It has cayenne in it."

"What?" Mabel asks.

"What's *cayenne*?" Poppy asks. She's staring at me, too, now. My face must have gone white, and I know my eyes are round in horror.

Mabel lifts another piece of shortbread from the plate of them and takes a bite. "I don't taste anything strange," she says, narrowing her eyes at me, as if I'm just causing problems for the sake of it.

I swallow the last crumb of shortbread and sit down. Maybe my taste buds are off this morning, out of whack from lack of sleep or something. "Never mind," I murmur, and everyone goes back to their breakfast.

I stare down at the remainder of the shortbread. For that brief moment, I felt like I was little again, back in Austin with my mother, chatting and laughing over cookies. Have I just been missing her so much that my brain tricked me into thinking it was that same old taste? Still, I don't dare take another bite.

I opt for some fruit and keep my eyes on my plate for the rest of the meal, but I can barely taste a thing. Every time I open my mouth, it fills with the thick tension in the room, coating my tongue and nearly making me gag. He's looking at me. I can feel it.

I get up to leave as soon as Poppy is done. "Fee, can you wait a second?" Charlie asks before I can scurry out of the room.

Poppy waltzes away, and I have to face him.

He waits to speak until I finally meet his gaze. "I owe you an apology," he says. "I was guttered last night, and I acted inappropriately."

I breathe out, relieved. So I won't be fired, then. "I take it 'guttered' means really drunk?"

He almost smiles. "Yes."

"I thought you weren't a big partier anymore." I nearly bite my tongue. What's the matter with me?

"You've been asking about me?" he says, his brow raised in genuine surprise.

I shrug, trying to act unconcerned. "I just wanted to know what kind of man I was working for."

He nods with a sigh. "It was a . . . a hard day yesterday, and I didn't handle it the way I should have. I'm sorry you had to see me like that." He speaks formally, as if he's making a big effort to act the way he thinks he should. The way a grown-up would.

"I understand," I say.

"Do you? Because you've got this look—" he starts, but cuts himself off.

I blink. "What look?"

"Nothing," he says quickly. But he stares at me, as if he can see every single emotion racing across my features. As if he can see through my thin facade of normality.

"I should go make sure Poppy's ready for school," I say, breaking my gaze from his and skirting around him.

Alice finds me the next day roaming around the castle, strolling along the portrait gallery, trying not to linger too long in front of the gloomy stare of the Grey Lady. "Bored yet?" she asks, resting her vacuum against a doorframe.

"How'd you guess?" I say, my lips quirking up slightly.

"Wandering the halls is never a good sign."

"It's too stormy to wander outside," I say. It's been raining in blinding sheets all morning, dark clouds swirling above, a cold and gloomy October day that makes the castle feel small and suffocating. I've had a prickle on the back of my neck for hours, the sensation I get when I feel like I'm being watched. "It just feels so . . . isolated here."

"That's because it is. We're miles from any other house, any other family. It's our own little world out here." She lifts the heavy vacuum again. "Come on, I have to clean the family rooms."

I follow her up the stairs to the fifth floor. "Is that why you dated Gareth? Because he's the only guy nearby?" I ask with a lilt in my voice. I can't help my curiosity anymore.

She half smiles, half grimaces. "You heard about that, huh?"

I shrug, trying not to show how interested I am.

"I've known him since we were little," she says with a sigh. "We grew up in the same area. When he came to work here last year, it was easy to sort of . . . fall together. I think we were both just lonely and bored. At first, at least. And then, I don't know." She presses her lips together, glancing at me as if she's just remembered I'm here. "Ancient history at this point, anyway."

She watches me now, as if she knows all about that strange moment I had with Gareth in the stable. My breath grows shallow; there's not enough air in this room.

But then she speaks again, and it's not about Gareth at all. "So, Fee, what do you think of Charlie?"

I'm caught off guard, and I hope with all my might that I'm not blushing, but I'm sure I am. "He's not—well, I guess he's not what I expected him to be."

She tilts her head at me, disappointment falling across her expression. "I know he's charming. And he can make you feel like you're the only girl in the world. But it doesn't mean anything to him."

I take a deep breath. "What did he do? To your friends?" I ask.

"He slept with a few of them. Just one-night stands, nothing serious. Except it was serious to my friend Georgina. They fooled around once, and she thought it was turning into something more. She thought he would leave his girlfriend for her. But he was just using her while it was convenient for him, same as all the other girls. He has no idea the kind of damage he causes."

I'm about to assure her that I'll never give Charlie the chance to break my heart, when Alice unlocks and opens the door to Lord and Lady Moffat's bedroom. I follow her inside, taking in the splendor. Ancient, faded tapestries adorn the stone walls, and a glittering chandelier hangs from the ceiling above a soft ivory-colored couch and armchair gathered in front of a fireplace, which is directly across from a huge white, canopied bed. There are family photos everywhere: the mantel, coffee table, nightstands. Charlie and Poppy at various ages, in formal and relaxed settings. I trace a finger along a frame holding a photo of Charlie that must have been taken just a few years ago. His red-brown hair is longer, shaggier, and he beams out at the camera from the deck of a sailboat. Shirtless, in just a pair of swimming trunks. I swallow, loudly.

"The family sailed around the Mediterranean a few summers ago," Alice says, noticing my attention on the photograph with a curious mixture of disapproval and envy. "They tend to stay away from the castle in the summer, when it's open to the public."

"They open this place up to visitors?" I ask, surprised. "Why?"

"They need the money, of course. Taxes and upkeep on a place like this are murder. Lord Moffat's newspaper hasn't been doing well for a while now. Not well enough to keep up a place like this, anyway."

"Why not?"

She shrugs. "No one's buying newspapers anymore. Not in print, anyway. And their website is clunky, outdated. The lord kept the paper old-fashioned on purpose, keeping it a source of serious, in-depth news only. So it's got that dusty old reputation, which means it isn't selling well. Needs quite a bit of work,

I should think. And Lord Moffat had a life insurance policy, but it wasn't much, so Charlie doesn't have a lot to work with."

No wonder Charlie's been under so much stress lately. I try not to let the pity I'm feeling show on my face, but Alice catches it anyway and clucks her tongue at me.

"They're still plenty rich," she says. "But plenty rich may not be enough to keep a place like this. Now come on." She rolls the vacuum to a door and opens it to reveal a small room with a dark wooden desk with delicate scroll legs and a plush office chair. "This was Lady Moffat's office," she says, plugging in the vacuum. "She did all of her social planning and upkeep in here, writing letters and organizing dinners and balls and charity galas and things like that. Even when they could barely afford them."

Alice turns on the vacuum before I can ask more about what Lily was like, so I examine the desk instead. On top of it are even more framed pictures of Poppy and Charlie, and a slim laptop. There's a beautiful coffee table book on French interior design, too, set on the diagonal and hanging halfway off the desk, like someone dropped it there just for a moment.

"Everything in this master suite is still the way they left it," Alice says, turning off the vacuum and noticing what I'm looking at. "No one knows what to do with it, and no one wants to bother Charlie about it."

This room is a time capsule, then. Preserving all of Lily's secrets.

Who was this woman who used to be my mother's best friend? Who wrote to my mother, probably from this very desk, telling her she would be her confidante? Why did she ask me here after all those years I spent with my resentful aunt? Why did she trust the daughter of a schizophrenic to look after her own child? The questions scream in my head, and soon I find myself staring at the desk drawer underneath all those photographs. What secrets did she hide in there? As soon as Alice goes back into the main room, I hurry around the desk and try to pull the drawer open, but it's locked.

I snatch my hand back as if the knob has burned me. What was I thinking? I can't go snooping around in some dead woman's personal things just because she used to know my mother. Whatever's in there is meant for Charlie and Poppy to go through when they feel up to it. Why on earth would I have followed such a strange impulse? What kind of delusion is this?

I can feel the blood drain from my face. *What's the matter with me?*

I swallow, hard, and shake my head. I straighten my shoulders and take a deep breath. *Just forget it. Nothing's wrong.* I walk as steadily as I can back into the main room and, with a quick wave to Alice, make my way to the safety of my own room.

CHAPTER 8

Charlie finds me one morning a week later in my usual spot in the library. I'm reading through Poppy's most recent history test, which she got a C on, so I can go over her missteps with her this evening. It looks like we'll have to do a refresher course on Mary, Queen of Scots.

Charlie's been locked up in his office the past few days, emerging only for breakfast and dinner, and since I don't want to bother Alice too often, I've gotten used to being on my own during the day again. Seeing him here, now, makes me feel as if I've been caught doing something wrong. Or maybe that's just the way he's looking at me.

"I thought I'd find you here," he says. "You know there are other rooms in this house, right?"

"Yes, but none of them have free books," I say with a shrug.

I'm having trouble meeting his eyes, and I take a deep breath, remembering everything Alice told me. He's just a player. I know how to deal with players. Even the ones trying to turn a new leaf.

He leans against the bookshelf next to me, boxing me in. He wears a light blue dress shirt, the sleeves rolled up his forearms. It fits him perfectly.

"How do you like your new life so far?" he asks.

"It's a bit . . . confusing," I say, surprised at my honesty. Why does he care? Or, rather, why does he feel the need to make pointless conversation? He's probably just trying to be nice to his sister's nanny, I remind myself.

"How so?" he asks, his eyes narrowing in interest.

I try to formulate a response that won't make me sound like a complete idiot and finally settle on what Alice said. "This place is like its own little world out here."

"It can be a bit isolating," he agrees.

"But it seems like Poppy might tolerate me now, which is nice," I say with a wry smile.

"And what do you think of me?" he asks, surprising me.

"I don't know," I start, accustomed now to being so caught off guard. Accustomed to the way it makes me much too honest with him. "You're a bit . . . unknowable."

He wrinkles his forehead a little, as if he doesn't like that I find him unknowable, but he doesn't comment. "What do you do while Poppy's in school?" he asks after another suspended moment.

I look around, as if I'll find the answer among the shelves. "This," I answer.

"You don't play the piano?" he asks, nodding to it, and I remember how he found me hovering over the keys that first day.

I shake my head.

"Why not?"

As I try to think of a way to explain it, I realize how ridiculous it will sound. "It seems too beautiful for me to play it."

"It's *meant* to be played."

"By someone who knows what they're doing. Someone like my mom."

He frowns. "Come on," he says.

"Charlie—" I start to protest, but he takes my hand, and all words float out of my head.

"I have to hear you play," he insists, while I try to get my breathing under control. It's as if his touch sears right to the core of me, making my heart race. "How about this? For every song you play, I'll tell you a secret."

"A secret?" I repeat clumsily. He's still holding my hand.

"One secret for one song. Then maybe I won't seem so unknowable."

He pulls me down from the windowsill and lets go of my hand, placing his own on the small of my back to propel me forward. I want to lean into it, turn and slide my arms around his neck, pull him into me, caress his lips with mine.

The impulse shocks me, and I nearly stumble. Of course. *Of course* I'm attracted to the exact wrong person.

I can't help it. He makes me feel calm, quiets that doubting voice in my head. I feel settled, present in my own skin around him. He makes me feel unsettled, too, but in a good way.

I have to stop this, I think as he guides me toward the piano. These feelings will compromise my new life here if I let them go any further.

It's just a stupid crush, I tell myself. *It will pass.*

He stands behind me as I arrange myself on the piano bench. Gingerly, I place my fingers on the keys, wondering why the hell I thought I could do this. How am I supposed to play with him standing there, watching me? I close my eyes, take a deep breath, and before I can stop myself, the song begins. The notes of the first movement of Beethoven's *Moonlight Sonata* creep from the keys, filling the room with the language of longing and regret. A slow, quiet ache. It was the first song I ever heard my mother play, on that beautiful piano in Mrs. Alvarez's bungalow. That moment, that song and the emotion she put into it, changed my view of her forever. I understood, even then at such a young age, that her life held secrets I would never know. That, before she was my mother, she had known a whole world of passion and heartache.

It's only when the sound of the final note fades that I remember that Charlie is standing behind me. That I have opened up this most secret part of me to his judgment. The realization makes me release a stuttered gasp.

He says nothing, and I summon the courage to turn and look at him. In his bright green eyes, I can see the same loss, the same desperation that always fills me when I hear this song.

I stand, stepping around the piano bench so that there's nothing between us.

"You should play," he says finally. "Every day. This piano needs you." He breaks his gaze from mine, and I cross my arms over my chest.

"I was at the pub that day because I'm a coward," he says, and it takes me a moment to realize that he's telling me a secret, as promised. "I was supposed to catch the train to Glasgow a few hours earlier, but I couldn't."

"You were late?" I ask.

"No," he says. "I stood on the platform and watched it leave without me. I just—I couldn't leave home just yet. I didn't feel ready to face the world. So I ducked into the pub and caught the next train." He finally looks at me. "I must sound ridiculous."

"No," I say. "I can see how it would be hard to face all that responsibility after everything that happened."

"I hated leaving Poppy, too, even if she doesn't believe it. I still don't know if I made the right choice."

"You're here now."

He rubs a hand across his forehead. "I don't know if that makes it any better," he says. "And now that the board approves of me, I'll be going to Glasgow every few weeks. The paper's not doing very well—hasn't been for ages. I've got ideas on how to fix it, but that takes money we don't have, and the board's nervous. So I have to keep abandoning her."

"She'll understand," I say, though neither of us knows if that's true.

A knock from the open doorway startles us both, and we snap our heads to look. It's Mabel, clearing her throat, her eyes sharp as she examines both of us. "Someone at the door for you, Master Charlie," she says.

He glances at me only once before following her out into the hallway, and I collapse back onto the piano bench.

How could I have opened myself up to him like that? I've never played in front of anyone but my mother before. Even at school in Mulespur (which had the funds for a band only thanks to the football boosters, who couldn't bear the idea of their precious varsity players going out on the field without musical accompaniment), the music teacher let me play the piano after-hours, after everyone had gone home, so that I wouldn't have an audience.

But I can't help but admit that the brief moment when Charlie opened up to me made playing in front of him worth it. A secret for a song. I've never made such a thrilling deal.

I bury my head in my hands. I like him. I can't believe I didn't realize it before. But then again, I'd never experienced anything like that violent shiver I felt when he placed his hand on the small of my back. Everything with Charlie feels so . . . new. I don't know how I could have let this happen.

I push myself back up, determined to make it to my room before I start hyperventilating over my stupidity.

But when I hear raised voices as soon as I step out into the hall, I can't help but follow them to the front door.

Charlie stands with his back to me, facing a girl I can barely see behind his frame. But I hear her voice, loud and shrill in the empty space of the foyer. ". . . didn't mean for it to happen, but it did. And we need to deal with it."

"Deal with it *how*?" Charlie says, his voice low and strained. I press myself against the hallway wall, officially eavesdropping now. I try to feel guilty about that, but my curiosity is overpowering. Who could make Charlie this upset?

"I want to keep it, Charles," the girl answers, her voice softer, throatier now. *Charles?* Who would call him Charles? "I want *us* to keep it."

There's no question now about her meaning, whoever she is. She's pregnant, and Charlie is about to become a father.

I retreat as quietly as I can, tiptoeing back down the hall. I reach the servants' staircase and sprint all the way up, flinging myself into my room.

Who is she? Could that be Blair, the ex-girlfriend, or just some random local girl he slept with once and forgot about? What will he do? I barely know him, but somehow I think that, no matter who she is, he'll step up to his responsibility and be a father to their kid, the way he's stepped up to his responsibilities with Poppy. He just doesn't seem like the deadbeat-dad type, whatever his reputation.

But I don't know that for sure. I don't know him. And he's my *boss*, I remind myself for the millionth time. I can't be sad, because I haven't lost him. Because he was never mine to begin with. He's going to be a father, and he'll probably marry that girl, and I'll just remain the governess up in the attic who watches it all happen from the periphery. And then, at some point, I'll go back to my old life, and this flashing wound will be nothing but an amusing memory.

I hope.

CHAPTER 9

I manage to avoid the girl, whoever she is, for the entire morning. But when I go out to Albert's car to pick up Poppy from school in the afternoon, I nearly run right over her.

She's lying on her back in the stone courtyard in front of the castle, like a cat basking in the sun, her eyes closed, one hand resting on her flat stomach. She wears black skinny jeans and a loose light gray T-shirt, her dark hair spread out against the gray stones beneath her.

I must have stopped too short and noisily, because she moves her hand to shield her eyes from the sun and looks over at me. "Who are you?" she says, her voice disinterested despite the bluntness of her question. She's beautiful, in a feline sort of way. Her eyes—slate blue, a color I've never seen before— are narrow, almond-shaped, and the line of her nose is long and straight. Her brown hair is so dark it's almost black, and it shines in long, loose waves. I'm suddenly very conscious of the ever-present frizz in my red curls.

"I'm Fee," I say, my throat dry. I clear it. "I'm the au pair."

She props herself up a bit more, her eyes narrowing. "I've met the au pair. She's a sixty-year-old obese woman with pock-marks." The clipped, aristocratic tones of her accent nearly match Charlie's, but hers sounds more labored. Maybe I'm just imagining it. Or maybe it seems that way because talking to me is nothing more than a chore for her.

"I'm new," I answer, trying to match her bored tone but managing only to make my voice a bit breathier. There's something about the way she's looking at me, examining me, that makes me nervous. I resist the urge to fidget, to shift my weight from one foot to the other.

"Hmm," she says. "I'm Blair."

"Oh, of course," I say for lack of anything better. My suspicion has been confirmed. "It's nice to meet you."

"You've heard about me?" There's something lurking in her tone that makes me think very carefully about how I'm going to answer that question.

I decide on a simple "Yes."

She straightens her arm, lying back down and closing her eyes once more against the sun. "Nice to meet you, Dee," she says, deliberately misremembering my name, I'm almost positive.

I hurry to the car, feeling like I'm escaping the clutches of a tiger, and by the time I slide into the backseat, I'm shaking. How has she provoked such a response in me? Is it just because she was Charlie's girlfriend—scratch that, his *pregnant* girlfriend? Or was it the look in her eyes, sharp and stormy as they pierced through me?

Albert takes one look at me in the rearview mirror then turns to face me, his eyes crinkled in concern. "What's happened to you?"

I try to clear my expression with a light smile. "Nothing. I just nearly ran over Blair is all."

"She doing that lying-in-the-sun thing again?" he asks, starting the car and looking out his side mirror to see her, still there behind us. "Last time she came here was Christmas, bloody freezing, but she still spent half her time in the courtyard."

I nod. "She's not really what I expected." I press my lips closed, annoyed at myself. There I go again.

Albert just laughs. "She's a nice lass, kind to everyone," he says, pausing a moment before continuing. "We all like her."

I keep my lips pressed together, refusing to let any of my many questions spill out. Albert is too perceptive for me to let my guard down. He'd know in an instant that my interest in

Blair implies an interest in Charlie, and I don't really want to know what he would think—or do—about that.

We arrive at Bardwill to see a short woman in a stiff skirt suit waiting out front. It's not until we get closer that I see that it's Mabel, out of her traditional uniform and white lace cap. Albert pulls up in front of her, and she opens the passenger door.

"Mabel, I . . . what are you doing here?" I ask as politely as possible despite my surprise.

She glances at me once before settling into her seat. "I've just come from a meeting with Poppy's headmistress. She wanted to speak to her caretaker about her performance in school."

Right. I'd been meaning to set up that meeting. I'm certainly glad not to have to talk to that woman again, but I never expected Mabel to be the one to talk to her.

"Oh? And how did it go?" I ask coolly.

"I told her we care very much for Poppy," Mabel says, with a stiff neck and no eye contact, "and that we are doing everything we can to help her through this hard time."

I nod and keep quiet, but I'm still confused and a bit hurt. Mabel didn't even tell me about the appointment, let alone ask me to go in with her; she just assumed the responsibility for herself. I keep underestimating how close she is to Poppy.

Poppy doesn't seem at all surprised to see Mabel, in any case. As she skips over to the car with a group of girls, I see that she's getting closer to her friends again, opening herself back up. On the way home I learn that apparently Natalie has a mad crush on a boy named Logan from the boys' school, and Poppy finds it the most fascinating news ever. I let her prattle on with a smile on my face, though I'm still distracted by this new perspective I have on Mabel and her position in Poppy's life.

Back at the castle, I expect to run into Blair again after we wave goodbye to Albert and head back across the courtyard, but she's moved from her spot, and I don't see any trace of her inside.

When Poppy and I are set up in her study, going over a math problem, I ask her, as casually as possible, "What do you think of Blair?"

Poppy looks up from her workbook. "I don't really know her. I've only met her a couple of times. Charlie was never that big on bringing her home to meet Mum and Dad. She seemed really nice, though."

She must have been in a bad mood when I met her, then, because Albert had said the same thing. Maybe she really *is* nice. Maybe the pregnancy has her really stressed out. Or maybe I'm just being paranoid.

"How did she and Charlie meet?" I ask, trying my best to sound perfectly pleasant and merely curious.

Poppy shrugs. "University, I guess. They both went to St. Andrews." She pauses, then continues, her voice lower, "Mum asked Charlie about her once, a few months ago. She wanted to know why he hardly ever brought her home, you know? So she was asking all these things, like how they met, what she wanted to do after college, if she was from a good family. Charlie went mental, said why did it matter what kind of family she came from? Mum kept asking, like why was he so defensive? And then he said something about her dad, like he was a bad guy or something. And that Blair didn't talk to her family anymore, but that didn't make her a bad person. He said that *he* was her family now, and then just stormed off."

I raise my eyebrows but say nothing. I must have been wrong. If Charlie feels so strongly about her, she must not be too bad. And it sounds like her home life was a wreck.

Poppy taps the paper in front of her with the eraser of her pencil. "What's my next step?" she says. I turn my focus to the problem, but I can't seem to shake the thought of the strange feline girl with the unsettling eyes.

That night, I tell Poppy that I'm going to be eating with the other servants from now on. The thought of sitting at the table with Charlie and Blair makes my stomach clench, and I know I wouldn't be able to eat a bite. She only nods in response, but I can tell she's confused. Maybe even disappointed. I have to remind myself that Blair probably doesn't want me at the table anyway, since she can't even remember my name.

"You'll still have breakfast and lunch with us, though, right?" Poppy says.

"Sure," I say, unable to say no to that trace of pleading in her eyes. "Of course."

I'm slipping away from the kitchen and up to my room after dinner with the servants when Charlie catches me. I hear his footsteps behind me in the hallway before I see him, and I know I can't escape.

"Fee, hey," he says, his fingers brushing along my arm to stop me. I draw my arm away from his touch as subtly as I can as I turn to face him. "I'd like you to meet Blair."

He steps aside, and I see she's been standing behind him the whole time. I can see now that she's shorter than she seemed in the front hall this morning or in the courtyard this afternoon, a few inches shorter than I am. She offers me a broad smile, but I can feel those narrow blue eyes examine me carefully once more. "We've met," she says.

"Yes, good to see you again," I say with the barest suggestion of a smile.

She snuggles into Charlie's side, and he places an arm around her shoulders. They stand there, a unit. Indestructible. "Charlie says you've been great with Poppy," Blair says, her voice syrupy with politeness. What happened to the strange girl lying on the courtyard, who practically refused to remember my name?

"Well, Poppy—she's great," I stutter. "You know," I add quickly, "I was actually on my way up to go help her with her math homework. She's been doing so well, just got a B on a pop quiz today. I think she'll be able to pull her grade up nicely." I'm babbling and staring at Blair like an idiot, so I press my lips shut and shift my focus to Charlie.

"Thanks, Fee," he says softly, his expression inscrutable.

I hesitate for a moment, trying to read what he's feeling, but I snap myself out of it quickly and leave before I can make things any more awkward.

"So nice to meet you!" Blair calls brightly after me.

So maybe she is the sweet girl everyone says she is. But then I think of the calculating narrowness of her eyes as she looked at me. And Charlie's arm around her shoulder.

I need to stop thinking about her, so I dive into a night of helping Poppy with her homework. When it's Poppy's bedtime, I retreat to my room with a book about Mary, Queen of Scots, and try to lose myself in the sad tale of a woman who had terrible luck and made some of the worst decisions in life and love.

Hours later, the whole castle is sleeping and still, but I'm still awake, trying to focus on the murder of Lord Darnley, Mary's second husband. Suddenly, a strange scraping noise starts up, right next to my head. It comes from that outside wall, the same place that the loud bang came from a few nights ago. This time, it sounds as if someone is dragging some kind of metal or wire along the wall, slowly. It can't just be an errant tree branch or something, not with that metallic screech. It must be from Keira's room, I decide. Is someone moving furniture in there?

I turn my attention back to the book, but the scraping doesn't stop. It persists and persists, until the words below me swirl into unrecognizable shapes. I slam my book shut and swing my legs out of bed, trying to think of the politest way to ask my neighbor to quit doing whatever the hell she's doing.

Thankfully, though, as soon as I reach the door, the metallic scraping stops. But now it's been replaced by that muffled whispering noise, the one that I mistook for a TV on one of my first nights here. And it's definitely coming from that outside wall. I look around, bewildered, and catch sight of an air vent on the opposite wall, which I share with Keira. Could it be that the sounds are coming from there, through some weird acoustics caused by the castle's ventilation system?

I get out of bed again and pull my desk chair up to that wall. I stand on top of it and put my ear to the vent but hear nothing. The sounds are definitely coming from that stupid outside-facing wall.

I throw myself back in bed and pull the pillow over my ear. *Worry about it in the morning, Fee. For now, just try to fall asleep.*

CHAPTER 10

A few days later, when I can't battle the boredom anymore while Poppy's at school, I decide to run a few errands. After lunchtime, I ask Albert if he can drop me off at the village.

"Not a problem," he says. "I've got to visit someone at the hospital at Beasley, not too far from there."

"I'm sorry," I say, and he blinks at me, confused. "That your friend is in the hospital," I clarify.

Albert smiles slightly. "Thank you."

I nod, confused by his lack of reaction, and follow him silently out to the car.

Albert drops me off at the familiar intersection by the train station and tells me he'll pick me up in a couple of hours. I wave goodbye to him and take a moment to look around at the tiny cluster of stone buildings. This place is unusually sleepy, even for a Wednesday afternoon.

I decide to go to the store first. The whispering has continued every night, and even with the help of my heather chamomile tea, I'm having trouble ignoring it. It feels like I've only slept in snatches of time for the past few days. I'm hoping that a good pair of earplugs will bring me some peace. And I need a new phone, one that I can use in Scotland. With the bit of salary that's been put in my bank account, I buy the cheapest smartphone I can get and set up a plan. Just having it in my pocket makes me feel more independent.

I still have an hour until Albert comes back, so I head for the pub next, seeking shelter from the wind that seems to grow bitterer every day.

A group of old men sit at the bar, the pub's only patrons, but they fill the dark space with their good-natured laughing.

I cozy up to the bar, one seat over from the men, and order a Coke from the taciturn bartender. I'm eighteen, so I could order a beer or anything else I wanted here, but I want to keep a clear head. Though as I consider what I came here to do, I wonder if some liquid courage might help.

I promised myself that, once I got here, I would ask around about my mother's family. I want to know more about her parents, my grandparents, who died before I was born. I want to know what they were like.

The men beside me are glued to a soccer—football—match on the suspended TV, all agreeing very loudly that the referee is some kind of idiot.

Eventually, one of the men looks over and catches me watching them. "Anything I can do for you, lass?" he asks, sounding amused.

I take a deep breath and nod. "Yes, actually. Have you . . . did you ever happen to know a girl named Moira Cavendish? She lived here about twenty-five years ago."

"She of the fancy Cavendish people?" he asks, rubbing a hand against the back of his bald head. "Big house about half an hour from here? All that money from their wool mills?"

"Oh. I guess?" I say, surprised. I always got the impression that Mom's parents were well off, but his description makes it seem like it's much more than that. "Her parents were Angus and Greer Cavendish."

"Were? They're still alive, far as I know."

I grip the edge of the bar tightly with both hands. "I'm sorry, what? They're still alive?" I ask.

I feel the blood drain from my face, and the man leans a bit closer to me. "Are you all right, lass?"

How can they be alive? They can't be. Mom told me that

they died soon after she left Scotland. She wouldn't tell me how—she said it made her too sad.

Was she lying to me?

All of the men are staring at me now, and I take a deep breath. I can't freak out. Not now, not here.

I start ripping the damp napkin beneath my glass to shreds, focusing on the little decimated pieces as I ask my next question. "What are they like?"

Thankfully, they all lean back and start drinking again, probably just relieved that I didn't keel over or faint. "Haven't ever met them," says the first man. "But I bet Tommy knows— hey, Tommy, you know the Cavendishes?"

"Aye," Tommy says, dressed a bit more formally than the others, in a tweed jacket. "Did a bit of work on their toilets a few years back, over at Dunraven Manor."

Dunraven Manor. Is that where my mother grew up?

"Tommy's the best plumber in all the northwest," his companion boasts.

"Was," Tommy corrects. "I'm retired now, which is why I can spend my days sipping whisky with you worthless lot."

As his companions laugh, Tommy looks to me. "I met the missus once. She was a frosty kind of woman. I was only too happy to work with the head housekeeper after that, believe me."

I nod, trying to look interested and not as nauseated as I feel.

"Do you know anyone who might know them? A bit, um, better?" I ask.

"We don't run with the fancy set. Better ask the Moffats up there at the castle or some such if you want to know about that sort."

I nod, taking a final sip of my Coke and hopping off the barstool. "Thank you," I say to the group as I slide the bartender a few pounds. The men all tip their caps at me as I walk out.

I look around the village, as if I'm seeing it for the first time. My grandparents. My grandparents are alive and not far from here. I have a family.

Why would Mom lie? Were my grandparents cruel to her? Did they disown her because of my dad? What happened all those years ago?

And why didn't Lily mention my grandparents in her emails to me? Did she assume I knew they were alive and just didn't think to mention it?

I don't understand any of this. Questions overwhelm me, and I shove the palms of my hands against my eyes.

I spend the rest of the afternoon wandering up and down the road, those questions banging around inside my head as I wait for Albert.

Beyond the image of my grandmother as a standoffish

upper-class woman, the men hadn't offered me much. They didn't know the Cavendishes, not really.

If I want to find out anything, I'm going to have to ask Charlie. But I can't ask him without revealing that my mother used to be one of the "fancy set," as Tommy called them. And if I reveal that, I could end up revealing everything: her schizophrenia, her suicide, the danger in my own genetic makeup.

I couldn't bear it. I couldn't bear for him to see me as I see myself: a ticking time bomb. I imagine him telling Blair, how she would look at me with those feline eyes and a grimace of distaste. They wouldn't understand. They would see my mother as damaged, as trash. They wouldn't see her as the woman who poured her soul into her music, who taught me Highland dance and the Texas two-step, who challenged me to sword fights with wooden serving spoons around the apartment until we both collapsed from giggling too hard.

I can't ever be Fiona Cavendish. I am Fiona Smith and will keep my father's name, like I've always done.

Charlie can never know.

My teeth are chattering by the time Albert finally pulls up, and I get into the heated car with a sigh of relief.

CHAPTER 11

I head for the stables at five that evening to meet Poppy after her ride. Gareth is nowhere to be found, the only sounds in the dark space the pawing and snorts of the horses.

The horse to my left, the smallest in the stable, looks up at me with calm eyes. I approach it cautiously, and it sticks its head out the door to meet my outstretched hand. I stroke its long snout, which is velvety-smooth beneath my fingertips.

"Hi," someone says behind me.

I whirl around, nearly falling into Gareth as I stumble over my own feet. I brace my hands against his strong chest until I regain my balance, and then a moment longer, as I look up to meet his eyes. "I'm here for Poppy," I say quickly, snatching my hands back.

He nods with mock solemnity, like he doesn't believe me, and I can't help but roll my eyes.

"It's okay," he says, planting the shovel he's carrying into the ground. "You can admit it. You just couldn't wait to see me again."

I should frown at him, shoot him down. He's using the same hollow charm that Charlie tried on me that night he was drunk. I think of Alice and know I should deflect this immediately.

But I can't help but laugh. This house is filled with so much grief and pain, and this news about my grandparents has made me feel so confused and off-balance. It feels good to laugh again, to flirt with a cute guy and not have it mean anything. So I bat my eyelashes dramatically at Gareth and coo, "Yes, I just can't stop thinking about you. You haunt my every thought or whatever."

He laughs, resting his arms on the shovel. "Poppy should be back in a few minutes. She and Copperfield were just having their therapy session."

"Their therapy session?" I repeat, my sarcasm falling away.

He smiles. "That's what I call it, anyway. Only time that girl relaxes is with that horse. I guess it's her way of working through the darkness."

"You understand what she's going through?" I ask, but it

comes out more like a statement. Because there's this tone in his voice that I recognize. A tinge of heartbreak.

He clears his throat, all traces of laughter now gone. "My pa was a drunk. Spent most of his life in the pub and ended it in a ditch. He'd tried to walk home in a snowstorm."

"And your mom?'

He looks away, down at the ground. "Ran away with a bloke from the village when I was six. He was married, left a wife and five kids. He came back a couple of years later, but my mum never did." He shrugs, like it means nothing, but I can tell what it's costing him to tell me this. I know that talking about all that pain can feel like reliving it.

The small horse snorts, and I realize that we're standing too close together, my body leaning too much toward his. I blink and step back as casually as I can.

"I'm sorry," I say, because it's the only way a person can respond to a confession like that.

He nods. "Me too. About your mum."

My breath stutters in my throat until I realize that he just means that he's sorry that she died. He doesn't know about her illness. "Thanks," I breathe out.

Suddenly I'm tired. I'm tired of feeling confused and scared and sad all the time. I want to be free of it all, if just for a moment. I want to feel brave and in control. I want to work through the darkness, the way Poppy is.

I look back at the horse whose snorting interrupted us, and, before I can second-guess myself, I ask Gareth, "Can you teach me how to ride one of these things?"

When I look back at him, his eyes are wide with surprise, and a warm smile is growing on his face.

"You can ride Oliver here," he says, grabbing a saddle and heading toward a huge gray horse in a stall a few spaces down.

"Oliver?" I ask.

"Oliver Twist. Got him last year with Copperfield, when Poppy was going through a Charles Dickens phase."

A ten-year-old who loved Dickens. No wonder Poppy's not having any trouble with English class.

"What about the small one?" I ask, pointing at the snorting horse I'd been petting.

"Nessie? She'd bite your hand off as soon as look at you. Oliver's a safer beastie."

I pull my hand away from Nessie immediately.

I watch Gareth expertly saddle Oliver and lead him out to the yard, and my stomach begins twisting in knots. I liked the idea of riding a horse much better when it was safely in a stall, calm and still. Now that I'm thinking it through, I have no desire to get up onto the back of one, especially one as big as Oliver, who seemed a much smaller, more docile creature back in his stall.

Gareth must be able to see the tremendous doubt on my face. "Oliver's a big softie, aren't you?" he says, rubbing the massive creature's neck like they're old friends. "He'll be a good horse to learn on," he assures me, holding out his hand.

I stare at his outstretched hand for a second, unable to move. *Take a chance, Fee,* I tell myself firmly. It's what Hex used to say to me whenever I'd get too much inside my own head. She was always encouraging me to step out of my comfort zone and take control of my own life. She thought I let my fears rule me, and I knew she was right.

So I pretend to be brave and take Gareth's hand. He clasps mine firmly. "Put your left foot in the stirrup here," he instructs.

I'm just about to when Oliver nickers and shifts his feet, and I back up hastily.

Gareth pats Oliver's neck again, watching me. "Come on, then," he says.

I look into his eyes and see the challenge there, and so I march back up to that damn horse and put my left foot in the stirrup. Gareth hands me the reins and shifts behind me, placing his hands on my waist. Before I can react to his touch, he's lifted me up, my right leg swinging over Oliver's broad back to find the other stirrup. And I am officially on a horse.

I've seen plenty of people do this before—the rodeo in our town was the biggest annual tradition, and some families had a horse or two tied up in pastures on their property. But those people, and of course Poppy, look natural up there. I don't think anything about me hesitantly perched upon Oliver looks natural.

I glance down at Gareth as he adjusts my stirrups and catch the remnants of the smirk on his lips. "What do I do now?" I ask, my voice at a much higher pitch than usual.

He takes the reins from my hand. "Why don't I just lead him around a bit so you can get used to the feel of him?"

I nod. I can handle that. I think.

Gareth clucks at Oliver and pulls him forward. The beast follows, and it's as if a massive, solid wave is rolling underneath me. It's strange, but not as terrifying as I was sure it would be. Before I know it, I'm actually smiling.

Poppy and Copperfield canter over as Gareth and I are circling around the yard.

"Not bad," Poppy says, casually slinging herself off Copperfield. I try to square my shoulders and stop looking as unsettled as I feel.

I hear a delighted laugh behind me, and I shift to see Blair walking over to us from the castle, her slate blue eyes shining as she watches me. "Oh, sorry," she says, covering her smile with her hand. "Is this your first time on a horse?"

I blink. "Yes," I say.

"Well, good for you for trying," she says brightly, and I instantly want to get off this horse and hide under a rock somewhere. I frown down at my hands so that I don't frown at her.

"I think that's enough for today," I tell Gareth quietly. He nods, looking from Blair back up at me, a frown on his face as well.

"Swing your right leg back over," he says. I slide down into his arms, grateful to be back on solid ground.

His hands linger on my waist for a moment, and I look anywhere but at him. Which is how I see Blair watching us carefully, that calculating look on her face. It's only there for a second, until she meets my gaze and replaces it with an expression of bland politeness.

"Come on, Poppy," I say quickly, stepping out of Gareth's grasp. "Let's get started on your homework."

That night, I wrap myself up in a blanket on my bed, warding off the pervasive chill of the attic. I type "Dunraven Manor" into the map app on my phone and study the route I would need to take from the closest village, Perthton, not too far from here. My grandparents are there. So close to me.

I press my fingertips to my temples, rubbing circles there as if I could clear my thoughts, but that's not going to be enough to get me to sleep. So I slip out of my blanket and patter down to the kitchen to make a mug of chamomile tea.

I'm just putting the kettle on the stove when I see Mabel scurrying past the doorway, holding an electric lantern in her hand. Like the electric lantern that Poppy used to show me the strange room below with the tree in the middle of it.

I can't help it. I go to the door, peek out, and see her disappear down the hall that leads to the heart of the tower and that terrifying spiral staircase. I sneak down the hall to see the reflection from her lantern cascading down the steps, then hear the scrape of the door closing behind her at the bottom of the stairs.

What is she doing down there? I strain to hear something, but all I get is silence.

The thought of her down there, in that room with its strange crackling air and that spindly tree trunk . . . it makes me tremble. Does she truly believe the tree has some kind of magical power?

What would I find if I crept down that narrow staircase and opened the door?

My pulse races at the thought of it, and an unnerving sensation creeps over my skin. I hurry back to the kitchen, where the kettle is screaming bloody murder. I take it off the burner and run back up to my room without my usual cup of tea.

CHAPTER 12

The whispering starts again that night, but the ear-plugs do the trick, and I finally get some good sleep. The next morning at breakfast, I linger in the dining room longer than I usually do. Since Poppy made me promise to join her and Charlie and Blair in the mornings, I've been rushing through the meal, too uncomfortable to eat much around Blair. But today, I get a second cup of tea and pay close attention to Mabel as she rushes in and out, serving the large platters of food for all of us. But I see nothing different about her. She is still the same short, slightly stocky woman in a stiffly ironed apron. She has her hair in the same neat, dark gray bun, the same hard glint in her eyes, the same pursed lips. She doesn't look at all like she did last night, scurrying around frantically, heading to the underground heart of the castle to worship an ancient tree.

Breakfast ends, Poppy goes to school, and now my thoughts are once again occupied by my grandparents. And Dunraven Manor, which is so close. So after Albert and I drop Poppy off at school, I casually ask him to drive me to Perthton.

"Perthton? Why do you want to go *there*?" he asks, turning around in the driver's seat so that he can look me in the eye. "There are closer villages for shopping."

I shrug, trying not to squirm under his curious gaze. "I saw there was a yarn store there," I say. The search I did on Perthton said it was the largest yarn store in the Highlands. "I thought I could take up knitting while Poppy's at school."

He still looks at me, as if unconvinced, but agrees and starts the car anyway.

Should I just tell him? I could reveal that I'm the long-lost granddaughter of the Cavendish family. He's lived around here his whole life and has been working for the Moffats since his twenties—he probably knows the Cavendishes. But I don't want to talk about it, not even with someone as understanding as Albert. Not until I know more about all these family secrets.

Thankfully, Albert doesn't say another word as he drives me to Perthton. It's a much larger town than Almsley, though that's not saying much. It has a couple of shops and pubs and even a small hotel on its main square.

I promise to call Albert when I'm ready to be picked up and step out onto the sidewalk. I walk into the yarn shop, a much tinier place than its website led me to believe, and pretend to browse the shelves for a few moments until the car disappears down the road.

According to the map, Dunraven is only a couple of miles from the village. I find the two-lane highway that will take me there and start walking.

It's warmer than it's been in weeks, and the sun's even trying to peek through the clouds. After a few minutes, I shrug off the heavy coat that I borrowed from Alice and sling it over my arm.

There's no sidewalk, and only about two inches between the edge of the road and the low-lying stone wall that runs alongside it, which separates me from fields of rolled-up bales of hay and shaggy cows. So every time a car comes by, I have to hop up onto the wall to let it pass. Luckily, though, there's not too much traffic on this stretch of road.

I try to enjoy the walk, the feel of sunshine through my thin sweater, the comical Highland cows with their curious stares. But today is one of those days when the sadness has a terrible weight, and it presses down more heavily than usual. Some days it seems the grief is closer for no particular reason. Perhaps it's not the best day to seek out my mother's childhood home, but I can't stay at the castle when I know exactly where my grandparents are.

I try to ignore the grief, but soon all I can feel is the churning anxiety in my stomach. The sunshine disappears, and a misting rain starts to fall, the wind growing more forceful, pulling at my clothes like it's warning me to turn back.

I don't have to go looking for my grandparents now, I tell myself. I could just see the house where my mother grew up, then leave. I'll just look at it and hurry back to the village and wait for Albert. There's nothing to worry about.

Finally, the low stone wall grows higher, more protective, and eventually I reach a road on the left. It's blocked off by an ornate wrought-iron gate, and a plaque on the front reads DUNRAVEN MANOR, PRIVATE PROPERTY.

There's a security camera at the gate, but it's pointed down at the road to identify any incoming cars. After a quick glance over my shoulder to make sure there are no cars passing by, I climb up the chin-high wall and swing myself over it.

I pause. If those men in the pub were right, that means I'm standing on my family's land. This place is my mother's history. My history.

The thought of it is too big to comprehend, and I don't

take the time to try. Instead, I start walking. I don't see a house, though the entrance road stretches far into the distance in front of me until it disappears down a hill.

I walk the path through these beautiful acres of wild land, which are growing with lush fir trees and healthy heather despite the chilly fall weather. I pass a placid flock of sheep, their wooly coats dirty and gray. They snip away at the grass with hardly a glance at me, and I continue on, careful where I place my feet. I should have worn boots, not these old Converses. The ground beneath me is rocky and treacherous, just like it is at the castle.

I realize as I walk deeper into the property that I'd been hoping to feel some kind of connection, some deeper sense that this place was my homeland, but it doesn't come. *Because you don't have a home*, that wicked voice in my head says. The nasty one that's not my mother. I stop for a moment and close my eyes, willing the voice to disappear.

The mist turns into rain, and then heavier rain, and before I know it, I'm soaked through. I should call Albert, but if I leave now I don't know if I'll have the courage to come back. I at least want to see the house.

I follow the path up and down a few more hills before I finally catch sight of a sprawling manor in a valley below. And the sight of it takes my breath away.

I wouldn't have thought that a manor house would be as large as a castle, but as far as I can tell, it's even bigger. It's made of a similar gray stone, but it doesn't look as ancient as Fintair Castle does. It's not a fortress, meant to protect the inhabitants against invaders, but a palace, built to be pretty and proportional, a huge rectangle with wings on either side stretching longwise, making an H-shape. There are more windows and chimneys than I can count.

I hardly have time to marvel at it, though, before I hear someone clear his throat behind me.

I whirl around to find a man standing a few feet away, frowning at me through the rain. He wears a patched wool jacket and sturdy boots and has one of those weathered faces that make it impossible to tell if he's thirty or fifty.

"You're trespassing, lass," he says. He crosses his arms in front of him, which makes him look even broader and more intimidating, which must be his goal.

"I'm so sorry," I say, my words tumbling over each other. "I must have gotten lost. I didn't mean to, I'm sorry."

"Gotten lost after climbing over a stone wall into private property?" he says with a snort. "There are cameras all over. We've been watching you snooping around for the past ten minutes. Come with me."

"I'm not snooping!" I protest.

"Aye, right! Are you going to come with me willingly, or am I going to have to drag you, lass?"

My shoulders slump. "Lead the way," I mutter.

I wasn't even sure I wanted to meet my grandparents today, and now I'm going to be dragged before them like a criminal. I follow behind the man like a scolded puppy. He takes me down the hill to a side door of the manor house, and despite my somersaulting stomach, I can't help but gasp at the sight of the place up close. It towers above me and seems to stretch on forever. Why did Mom never tell me how exquisite and expansive her childhood home was?

But when we walk through the front door, I realize that she did. Because way up on the ceiling of this glittering entryway, there's a fresco of a fire-breathing dragon, its scales blue and green and gold. I know immediately from its colors and menacing expression that it's the same dragon Mom described in her stories. In those tales, the princess who slew dragons lived in a giant palace with so many rooms that the king and queen had run out of uses for them.

We enter some kind of den or study, with stiff-looking couches and towering walls of old books. Normally I'd be awestruck by a room like this, but all sense of wonder escapes me when I see an older woman standing in front of me with her hands clasped, watching me as I drip water onto the polished wood floor. Her hair is dark gray and spun into a low bun at the nape of her neck. Her dress is the same dark gray, and her lips are pressed into a thin line. My grandmother?

"Who are you?" she asks.

"Are you Mrs. Cavendish?" I ask, nearly breathless.

That provokes a reaction: a quick quirk of her eyebrow. "No. I'm Mrs. Drummond, head of household. Mr. and Mrs. Cavendish do not concern themselves with such trivial matters as voyeuristic intruders."

I breathe out a sigh of relief. "My name is Fee," I say quietly, hoping she's never heard my name mentioned before. "Fee Smith. I'm an au pair for the Moffat family."

"And what are you doing here?" she asks, with a slightly less glacial tone.

"I'm sorry, I didn't want to disturb the Cavendishes—I just wanted to see this place. Everyone's told me how beautiful Dunraven Manor is. I'm so sorry I've caused so much trouble." There. That didn't sound so crazy. Did it?

Mrs. Drummond gazes at me for an extended moment, and I begin to doubt myself.

"Well," she says finally. Her form softens, losing most of its fearsome disapproval. "No harm done, I suppose. And if you really are the Moffats' au pair, you'll be able to call Albert and have him pick you up, yes?"

"Yes. Yes, of course. I'll call him right now." I take my phone out and dial his number. He answers on the first ring, and when I tell him where I am, he promises to come get me immediately.

Mrs. Drummond nods at the man who apprehended me. "That will be all, Reggie. Thank you."

She fetches me a towel, which I use to dry off, and then waits with me for Albert. We sit there for a full half hour while questions about the Cavendishes bite at the tip of my tongue. Are they here right now? Could they walk in at any moment?

"Do you like working here?" I croak out finally.

"It's one of the most desirable posts in the country," she says without hesitation.

"What are the Cavendishes like?" I ask, my voice hardly louder than a whisper.

She considers me for a moment, her expression softening. "They are fine employers." She pauses. "They were very close to Lady Lillian Moffat, as a matter of fact. She came to visit them every week. She was almost like a daughter to them, and they are very distraught by her passing."

A *daughter*? I blink, absorbing the impact of her words, the unintentional cruelty they convey.

And that cruelty, combined with the grief that has been suffocating me all day, is too much. I try to swallow the sudden lump in my throat, but it only grows larger. In a few moments, I know I'll be sobbing.

Luckily, Mrs. Drummond gets up to look at something out the window. "Albert's here," she says, opening the door for me.

I hurry out into the heavy rain and to the car, not even stopping to thank Mrs. Drummond. I can't speak.

"Everything okay?" Albert asks, swiveling around in his seat to look at me. "What were you doing out here?" I think he means to sound concerned, but it comes out harshly. "Fee?" he says when I don't answer. I can't help it. I start crying ugly, heaving sobs, my entire body crumpling over across the backseat.

I just want him to start the car and get us out of here, but instead, he opens his door and hurries out into the rain, toward the house. I'm weeping into the soft leather of the backseat. I can't stop. I want to go home. Why can't we just go home?

It's an eternity until Albert comes back, and the engine finally roars. "Put on your seat belt, lass, and I'll get us out of here," he says softly.

I struggle to get the stupid seat belt into the stupid clasp as Albert, my savior, speeds us right out past the gate.

I hate them. I don't even know the Cavendishes, but I hate them. How could they be so affected by Lily's death but not at all by Mom's? How could they treat Lily as a daughter when they never cared about their own? Mom may have run away, but they clearly didn't try too hard to look for her. What kind of monsters would do something like that? Ignore their own family, ignore *me*, while I've spent years yearning for one?

I pull my knees up to my chest and press them against my eyes, but I can't stem the tears.

I can't stop crying. *Why can't I stop crying?* A rational person would have calmed herself down by now. When Mom was really getting worse, she would cry for hours at a time, over nothing. I half expect to hear her voice in my head right now, telling me that everything will be all right. But for once, she's silent.

Is this what it was like for Mom?

That thought only makes me cry harder, and by the time we get home, I'm practically hysterical. Albert swerves to a stop in front of the castle, where someone I can't make out through the rain or my tears is standing. Albert gets out of the car to meet them, and I hope with everything I have left that it's not Mabel. Or Blair. I don't want either of them to see me like this.

The car door across from me opens, and all of a sudden Charlie is sitting beside me, unbuckling my seat belt and pulling me to him. I'm hiccupping, trying to apologize, and I try to move my tear-soaked face from his shirt, but he just presses me closer.

"It's okay, Fiona," he murmurs in my ear. "It's okay."

It's the first time he's used my full name. His arm is wrapped firmly around my waist as he smooths down my hair with his other hand. Over and over again, as if I'm a wild animal he's soothing. No one's held me like this, not since Mom. Gradually, finally, the tears stop. That familiar feeling of calm and peace settles over me, the way it always does when I'm with him.

I breathe a few shaky breaths before I find the strength to push myself up and look him in the eye. I'm about to apologize, but he places a finger against my lips and shakes his head.

"You don't have to explain," he says. "Let's just get you inside."

He's still touching my lips. He realizes it at the same time I do, and he drops his hand back on his lap.

I open the car door and stumble out onto the driveway on shaky legs. The rain has let up, and I take a deep breath of fresh air before turning back to the castle.

Blair is standing in the doorway, watching us. How much did she see?

I can't look at her as I pass her, but I can feel her eyes on me.

"What's wrong with her?" she whispers, and Charlie whips his head around to glare at her.

"Nothing. She's fine," he says in a warning tone.

"Sorry," she murmurs. "If there's anything I can do, Fee . . ." she says, her words trailing after me as I head for the kitchen and the servants' staircase. I need to hide away for a while, wash my face, get myself under control.

Charlie's making to follow me, so I turn suddenly to face him, nearly causing him to collide with me. Part of me—most of me—wishes he had. That I were brave enough to wrap my arms around him and let him hold me some more.

I make myself look up into those warm green eyes. "I'm okay," I tell him. "I just need some time alone."

For a second, it seems like he might argue. But instead he presses his lips together and nods. "Of course," he says before walking away.

"Thank you," I call after him, but I don't know if he hears me. I can't help but feel like I hurt his feelings when all I did was let him off the hook so that he didn't have to comfort the crazy crying girl. I decide he's probably grateful but is too polite to let me see it. I decide I didn't hurt him at all.

CHAPTER 13

I go through the motions for the rest of the day. I leave with Albert to pick Poppy up from school then help her with her homework before dinner, but I don't speak to anyone else. As soon as it's finally acceptable for me to return to my room, I take up a mug of tea, put in my earplugs, and immediately fall into a deep and dreamless sleep.

The next morning I wake up embarrassed but energized. When I go down for breakfast, Charlie says hello to me like he does every morning, and I'm grateful for it. He's offering me the chance to sweep yesterday under the rug and to let everything go back to normal, and that's exactly what I need.

After I drop Poppy off at school, I come back to the castle to find Alice wheeling her cleaning cart into the master bedroom.

"You okay?" she asks, assessing me frankly, momentarily

reminding me of Hex. Blunt, no nonsense. I used to complain to Hex about my aunt—how she insisted that I pay her rent as soon as I turned sixteen, how she made me eat in my room and never in the kitchen with her, how she refused to do the dishes or laundry or anything else that she could make me do instead. Hex would always listen for a while and then tell me to shut up and work harder, so that I could get out of Mulespur as soon as I turned eighteen.

"I'm fine," I say, my words quick and clipped.

"You want to talk about it?" she asks anyway.

"No."

She nods. "Fine." She unhooks the broom from her cart and begins sweeping the floor in quick, practiced arcs.

I look over at the locked desk drawer in Lily's office, tempted, but then tell myself to forget it. I wander to the table in the middle of the room. There are family photographs in every room of the house, but none have more than this one.

"What was Lady Lillian like?" I ask, looking at a photo of her and Poppy that must have been taken only a few years earlier. They're standing on a busy street, their arms laden with shopping bags. Poppy looks so different in the photo, but not because she was younger. It's the smile that stretches from ear to ear, carefree and innocent, that I don't know if she'll ever have again.

Lily wears a more guarded expression, her eyes covered by dark sunglasses.

"She loved her children," Alice says after a moment. "That was the first thing you learned about her. Poppy always had an au pair, but Lady Lillian mostly took care of her herself, with Mabel's help. And Charlie, even when he messed up or came home drunk or whatever—he could do no wrong. She doted on them both."

"What was she like with everyone else?"

Alice considers the question. "She wasn't mean or anything. She just sort of . . . ignored us. Everyone but Mabel, at least."

"Mabel? Really?" I ask, surprised.

"Yeah," Alice says. "Strange, right? The two of them were almost . . . I don't know if 'friends' is the right word, but they spent a lot of time together. Mabel had been with the lady since she was a baby. She helped raise her, so they were very close."

"Wow," I say, pulling a bucket of dust rags out of Alice's cart and delicately dusting the tops of the frames. "I can't picture Mabel as the mothering type." Then again, I couldn't picture her as the tree-worshiping type either. Apparently she contains multitudes. I remember that first time I met Poppy, how Mabel squeezed her shoulder reassuringly, like a mother would.

"I know," Alice says with a snort. "But she was devoted to Lady Lillian. Just like she's devoted to Charlie and Poppy now.

That's why they call her 'Mabs,' what Lady Lillian called her when she was a little girl, and not 'Mabel' or 'Ms. Faraday,' because she's like one of the family."

Huh. Maybe she isn't so bad after all, I think, lingering over a photo of Charlie and Poppy posing in front of a waterfall, Charlie holding on to his baby sister with a huge smile on his face.

The door behind me opens, and I jump back like I've just been caught doing something wrong. Blair sticks her head in, then purses her lips ever so slightly.

"Oh, I'm so sorry," she says, her eyes flicking from me to Alice and back again. "I didn't mean to interrupt you. I was looking for Charlie."

"In his parents' room?" I ask before I can stop myself.

She raises an eyebrow at me, and I feel the sudden urge to duck my head. Instead I keep my eyes fixed on hers until they water.

"If you see Charlie," she says finally, "would you please remind him that we're going out for dinner tonight, and Albert will have the car ready at eight."

"Of course," Alice says when it's clear I'm not going to respond.

Blair shoots her a faint smile before turning and gliding out the door.

"What was that about?" Alice asks, her tone almost amused.

"Right?" I ask with a huff. "It was like she was challenging me."

"Not her, I meant you," Alice says, pointing at me with the broom. "You were completely icy to her."

"Just matching her," I say with a shrug, but a flush of embarrassment and confusion rises to my cheeks.

"She seemed perfectly fine to me," Alice says, her brow furrowed. "You were the weird one."

I shrug again, staring out the door. Was that true? Was I imagining her strange behavior?

Of course I was. Why would Blair need to challenge me? I don't pose any threat to her. It's not like I stand any chance of getting between her and Charlie, especially not after yesterday's mortifying meltdown. I can still hear her words in my head. *What's wrong with her?*

It's all in my head. A paranoid delusion. The thought makes the room spin.

I put the dust rag down and hand the bucket back to Alice, suddenly craving the quiet and solitude of my own room.

I'm imagining things, I tell myself as I trudge up the stairs. I want Blair to be awful and evil, so I'm projecting that onto her, just like any stupid girl with a crush would do. It's not a sign of anything more . . . serious. I can fix this. I have to start being nice to Blair if I want to stay here.

If I want to stay near him.

I bury my head in my pillow. How did everything get so completely screwed up?

I'm reading on the windowsill in the library a few days later when Charlie finds me again. He stalks toward me as if he expects me to run from him. His bright green eyes draw me in, as they always do, and I couldn't run even if I wanted to.

"Hi. I haven't had a chance to see you alone since—" He stops himself. "I know you probably don't want to talk about it. But if you ever do, you know . . . you can. With me."

I nod. *He's just trying to be nice,* I remind myself. *Don't read too much into it.* "Thank you for the other day," I say lightly, trying to put on a bright, carefree expression. "That was really nice of you."

He stares at me, the real me, hidden underneath this ridiculous mask. How does he do that? Strip away every ounce of pretense until he can truly see me? Why do I let him?

"Play me a song, Fiona," he says, using my full name again. Back in Mulespur, people would overpronounce "Fiona," stretching out its syllables to make fun of its fanciness. I started introducing myself as Fee quickly enough. But somehow, on his lips, my name sounds like a caress.

"A song for a secret?" I ask, dropping the cheerful act.

He nods, and I can't resist. I make my way to the piano,

settling onto the bench and straightening my shoulders like Mom taught me, then place my fingers on the keys, wrists up.

The notes of Franz Liszt's Liebestraum no. 3 glide between us. I spent a month learning this piece in Mrs. Alvarez's lime green bungalow. Mom told me the title meant "Dreams of Love" in German, and I remember thinking, when she played it for me for the first time, that it was the most beautiful, true thing I had ever heard. I could picture myself dancing in the arms of a man I loved one day, the two of us floating above the earth, happy and complete. I had to master it.

I lose myself in the ethereal melody, not returning to reality until the song is over and I lift my fingers from the keys.

I can feel Charlie breathing behind me, but I can't find the courage to turn around and face him. If I do, he'll see the want and longing that I know is etched on my face.

"What secret do you want me to tell?" he asks softly.

I don't want a secret, a voice screams in my head. *I just want you.*

This is so much more than just a crush.

The realization scares the hell out of me. I get up, still not looking at him, and go back to the window seat, settling into it with my eyes firmly on my hands in my lap.

"Fiona?" he says. He can tell something's wrong; I have to look at him.

I take a deep breath and lift my chin until my eyes meet

his, knowing he can see the secrets they hold. "Tell me who you used to be," I demand, surprising myself with the strength in my voice.

He swallows, then clears his throat. This question is my attempt to distance myself from him, and I wonder if he knows it. I need to remind myself of who he was, of why I shouldn't feel this much for him.

"I was nothing," he says, his voice barely louder than a whisper. "I was worse than nothing. I hurt people, I disappointed people, and I didn't care. I spent money like it was nothing, on parties and stupid things I didn't need. I surrounded myself with friends who were as reckless and selfish as I was." He pauses, shaking his head. "I cheated on Blair. I used everybody I ever met."

I hate this. Watching him confess all this to me—I can feel how much it hurts him. I wish I could take back my stupid question, snatch it right from the air.

But this is what I need to hear. Just a few months ago, he was an entirely different person. One I wouldn't have even liked.

Charlie steps closer to me and continues. "And then I got this call in the middle of the night, from Mabs, telling me that both of my parents had died in a car crash. And I knew instantly that I was now responsible for my sister. So I changed. In that moment, I changed everything." He steps closer again, and suddenly it feels as if there's less oxygen in the room. "Fiona, I'm not that guy. Not anymore. At least, I'm trying like hell not to be."

"I know," I whisper.

"Why don't you come to dinner with us anymore?" he asks. He's standing so close that I can see the flecks of blue in his green eyes, and every single dark lash that frames them.

I scoot back on the seat until my back touches the window, trying to create some distance between us. "I figured I'd leave you be so you could all eat together. Just the family."

"Family?" he says, and I nearly wince. He steps forward once more, closing the distance I've tried to create between us, his knee brushing against mine. I stifle a gasp. His touch is agony. I think about the two of us in the car: his arms around me, his hand in my hair, his lips next to my ear, letting me cry. I barely hear him when he asks, "You know, don't you?"

I consider playing dumb, but only for a moment. "Congratulations," I say instead, trying to make my tone as bright as possible. "You'll be a wonderful father."

It's as if a curtain falls over his face, and his inscrutable expression is back. "Thank you," he says blandly. He opens his mouth slightly, as if there's something more he wants to say, but then closes it again and stalks out of the room without another word.

I close my eyes and try to ignore the tears that threaten to form. I spring off the window seat and shut the door behind him, hoping to block out most of the sound. I throw myself into a furiously happy rendition of Vivaldi's "Spring" from *The Four Seasons,* but it comes out sounding like a dirge.

I stop, resting my hands on the keys and my forehead on the smooth wood of the upturned fall.

I need air. I tiptoe down the hall and out the back door into the bracing chill of the autumn night. I start to jog toward the lights of the stables and the warmth I know I'll find there.

I unlatch the door and open it with a warning creak. "Hello?"

I open the door further to see Gareth standing in a stall opposite. "Bit late for a ride, isn't it?" he says.

"I needed some fresh air."

He raises his eyebrows and looks around, and I pick up on the warm scent of horses and hay. Not exactly fresh.

So I add, "But it was cold outside, so I came here."

He steps out of the stall and peels off his heavy work gloves. "Come on, then," he says. He brushes past me and out the door, and I follow.

He leads me to a cottage behind the barn, pulling the unlocked door open and gesturing me inside. He flips on a lamp. In its dim light, I see a bed covered in rumpled white sheets, a desk with nothing on it, and a kitchen equipped with a tiny fridge, oven, and sink. There's an overstuffed armchair drawn close to the fireplace.

"This is where you live?" I say.

He nods. With a small smile, he crouches in front of the fireplace, striking a match and setting bits of newspaper on fire until it catches on the wooden logs stacked on top. We huddle close to the flames until we both stop shivering.

We stay standing side by side, facing the fire. After a few minutes, I shift so that my shoulder rests against his arm. That touch makes my heartbeat speed up until I grow a bit dizzy. And then I press closer to him.

Slowly, he turns to face me, a daring look in his eyes.

We pivot toward each other. He locks his arms around my waist, and my hands tangle in his soft hair, his lips on mine. *God, his lips on mine.* We kiss like we're fighting for our last breath. As if we'll die if we stop.

He pushes me backward, gently, until my back meets the wooden slats of the wall. But nothing else about his kiss or the hands running down my body is gentle. And it feels so. Damn. Good.

There's a howl somewhere inside me, and then the image of Charlie looking down at me, begging me to believe that he's not the player he used to be, invades my mind, and I break from

Gareth's lips with a gasp. "We can't," I say, pushing myself out of his arms.

He shoves a hand through his hair. "Why not?" he asks. His eyes are wild with want, and I have to back up again as if it's contagious.

"Mabel," I say finally. "Staff relationships aren't allowed."

"Fee," he says. He steps toward me, and I step back again, reaching behind me for the door handle.

"I need this job," I say, trying to sound determined, unshakable. "I can't, I'm sorry."

I pull the door open and rush out before I can change my mind.

I run back to my room, getting in bed and trying not to scream out into my pillow. I can't believe what I just did. I want to erase the feeling of Gareth's lips on mine.

What the hell was I thinking?

CHAPTER 14

I wake up with a headache and one hell of a guilty conscience. The whispers were louder than usual last night, penetrating the earplugs as if they were berating me for being such an idiot. How could I have gone to Gareth like that? I was upset about Charlie, so I acted on impulse instead of staying calm and thinking things through. Just like my mother used to do.

When I was ten, Mom told me we were moving to the country. I came home from school, and she'd already packed up all our belongings. "We need a new life," she said, handing me my suitcase and nearly shoving me out the door. "We need to get away from this noisy, polluted city. We need clean air to *think*."

I was so confused, and I protested the entire way down the stairs and once we were out on the street. I had school. I had

Mrs. Alvarez's piano. My whole life was here, in Austin. We couldn't just *leave*.

We made it to the first major intersection, where I watched as her will collapsed at the sight of speeding cars and the busy reality of the street. She shuffled backward a few steps and crouched down, frightened. "I think—I think I want to go back," she whimpered.

She looked so small, fragile, looking up at me as if I was the one in charge. As if I was the only one who could save her.

I put my arm under hers, letting her lean on me, and walked slowly with her back to our home. Once inside, she shut herself in the bedroom for days, only leaving to go to work.

I shudder at the memory and pull the covers up to my chin. I can't take out my frustration on Gareth ever again. Aside from all the other things wrong with it, including the fact that I betrayed Alice, my only friend here, last night wasn't fair to him, and it's leading me down a road I don't want to be on.

I grab my phone from the nightstand and check my email. There's another message from Hex, a sarcastically funny and bright summary of her daily life, including details about ornery café customers and how hard she's working to get out of Mulespur.

I hit reply and try to think of what I should say. Should I

launch into everything that's going on with Charlie? Blair? My grandparents? What happened last night with Gareth?

I think I'm going crazy, I begin. I stare at the cursor blinking beside those words, then press down, hard, on the backspace key.

I sit up, straighten my shoulders, and take a deep breath. Normal. I just need to be normal. I put on my nicest outfit, brush the frenzy out of my red curls, and swipe some blush across my cheeks to bring some healthy color to my pale face. Once I'm presentable, I make my way down to the dining room for a nice, normal breakfast.

Before I make it to the table, I run into Blair outside the door. We both stop, a moment of awkward silence settling over us. She looks at me, cocking her head to the side as if puzzled. "You've worn that sweater three times this week," she says softly.

I can feel the blush rise into my cheeks. "Alice does laundry daily," I say.

"Oh," she says, still examining me. Finally, she turns and heads into the dining room, and all I can do is follow. Charlie is sitting at his usual spot on the long side of the table with his laptop in front of him. He stops typing and looks up when we enter, his gaze passing over Blair to land on me. I look away before his eyes can snare mine; I can't let him see the guilt and confusion there. I feel Gareth's lips on mine again, and I feel sick. Why did I think, even for a second, that kissing him would make me feel better?

Now I see that everyone, not just Charlie, is looking at me. I glance at Poppy, and she smiles, amused. "Didn't you hear? Blair just suggested we all go on a shopping trip," she tells me. "What's the matter with you this morning?"

I smile at Poppy. "Oh, I just didn't get much sleep last night," I say, heading for the sideboard with the selection of cereals. I stay far away from the shortbread, like I do every morning.

"Would you like to go shopping with us, Fee?" Blair asks sweetly.

"I don't think so, but thank you," I say.

I pretend to be mulling over the cereal choices as Poppy comes to my elbow. "It could be fun," she says, her voice hopeful.

"Yes, you have to come, Fee," Blair says. I finally turn to look at her. "You can get some new clothes."

It feels as if my cheeks must be permanently stained red, but I keep my eyes locked on hers. I can feel Charlie watching me.

"There are some decent-enough shops in the villages around here," Blair continues. "I'm sure we can find you something. On Charles's tab, of course."

"I can pay," I manage.

"Of course you can, darling, but he's your employer. He should pay for the things you need."

"Of course," Charlie says easily.

"Good! That's settled. We'll go tomorrow. Sound like a plan, Poppy?" she says with an inviting smile.

Poppy beams and nods, then looks at her brother. "If it's all right with you?"

"Absolutely," he says with much more enthusiasm, smiling gratefully at Blair. Maybe he wasn't ever looking at me at all.

"I'll see you tomorrow, then," I say to no one in particular before hurrying out of the room. It's only when I reach Albert's car and wait for Poppy that I realize I didn't even have a bite of my cereal. So much for a nice, normal morning.

I spend a few hours browsing the shelves in the library, desperate for a new book to distract me. I reject dozens of novels and biographies after reading a chapter or two, finding myself uninterested in the tragic, romantic lives of characters and historical figures. That's how I finally find a thick tome on a bottom shelf with *Families and Clans of the Highlands* written in gold on the spine. I carefully pull it from the shelf and lug it over to a comfy armchair. The book is old, its leather case wearing thin and its pages yellowed. A waft of musty air rises as I open it.

It's a history of important Scottish families, and I flip

through entries for hundreds of surnames, skimming stories of famous family members throughout history. I look up this branch of the Moffat family and find a detailed account of them fighting for King George II in the Jacobite rising in 1745. I read about Moffats who founded schools and hospitals around the area, Moffats who hosted fine balls and expanded their elaborate castle as the centuries wore on.

There's even a mention of the Grey Lady:

> *The youngest daughter of the eighth lord fell to her death from her window at Fintair Castle. It's said that she had formed an attachment to a local farmer and was distraught when her father discovered it. Guests and neighbours of the castle since that time have reported witnessing a mysterious apparition roaming among the hills of the property: a Grey Lady, searching for her lost love.*

I look out the window to the hills, and I can't help but remember that strange rustling shadow I saw when I got lost in the fog heading back to the castle the night Charlie arrived. That noise that sounded so much like the swish of a long skirt.

I tell myself again that it was probably just an animal, that I was scared and my mind was playing tricks on me.

I bring my focus back to the book and, with a deep breath, flip over to the section on the Cavendish family.

There's hardly enough information on them to fill a page, and there are no accounts of anything that happened after the early twentieth century, when this book must have been printed. They don't hold any titles and didn't seem to own Dunraven Manor back then. I read a paragraph about a group of Cavendishes who fought against King George II's army at the Battle of Culloden in 1746 and one about a man named Dougal who was well known for singing Scottish ballads in pubs and who became a schoolteacher in the village of Perthton. *He had a voice like wind through the heather, the townsfolk said, and a fair hand at the fiddle.*

A musician, like my mother. I brush my fingers along the words, as if I can absorb them into my skin. This man was my family. I have roots here, a family that stretches back for centuries.

By the time I have to go pick Poppy up from school, I've almost forgotten all about my mortification at the breakfast table.

I'm woken up in the middle of the night by a noise on the other side of the outside wall, loud enough to penetrate my earplugs.

It's not the tinny TV whispering this time. Instead, it's a real, unmistakably human whisper. Or maybe two different whispers in dialogue. One soft, the other gravelly, having a conversation right next to my head. Six stories up, in midair.

I can't make out a word, but I can tell from the cadence and tenor that something is wrong. "Hello?" I whisper, my voice sounding loud and intrusive in the chilly air. But the whispers continue without a pause. "Hello?" I say again, louder. Still no break. Instead, the whispers seem to grow even louder, though I still can't make out any words.

"Who's there?" I ask.

There's a creak like a footstep on an old floorboard, and then the whispers continue. "Hey!" I shout. "What do you want?" My voice is wild, terrified.

The whispers grow louder still, until finally I can make out the words.

"Go home, little bird," the soft one says.

"You're not wanted here," the gravelly one says.

I gasp. The door to my room flings open, and I shriek. A shriek that seems to go on and on.

It takes a moment for me to realize that Alice is in my room, sitting on my bed, her hands on my shoulders. "Fee," she says firmly. "Fee, wake up. You're having a nightmare."

I press a fist to my mouth to stop the shrieking. There are a few girls from the kitchen in the doorway, watching me. "A nightmare?" I say.

"You were talking in your sleep," Keira says. "I'm in the room next to yours. I could hear you."

"So you heard the whispers, too? Two people, whispering?"

She shakes her head slowly. "No. Just you."

I stare down at my hands. Have I been dreaming this whole time? "I'm sorry. It must have—you're right, it must have been a nightmare."

The girls drift away from the door, and Alice stands up. "Are you okay?" she asks.

"I'm fine," I say, trying to match her firm tone, willing my heart to stop racing. "Just a stupid dream." *That's all it was*, I tell myself. *A dream.*

But what if it wasn't? What if it was a delusion?

I bite down on my lip, hard, so that I don't let out a whimper. Alice nods. "Get some sleep."

I curl back into my sheets as she closes the door behind her.

It must have been a dream. Those lines: "Go home, little bird. You're not wanted here." They're from my mother's story about the little bluebird princess whose sister was kidnapped by an evil crow. All the male birds in the kingdom flew to the crow's castle to fight, and, one by one, all of them died, their broken bodies littering the floor of the mighty fortress. So one night the bluebird princess herself flew under the cover of darkness to the crow's castle. She soared above the bodies of all the boy birds up to the throne room, where the crow was watching over her caged sister.

The crow took one look at the bluebird princess and scoffed. "Go home, little bird. You're not wanted here."

"I'm not a little bird," she cried. "I'm a mighty warrior!" And with that, she flew high up to the ceiling, snipped the rope of the chandelier with her beak, and sent it crashing down on the crow, killing him instantly. She freed her sister and returned home a hero.

It was one of my favorite stories, and I would make my mother tell it over and over again. And now those words are haunting me.

The room is silent now. No whispers. Still, for hours as the night stretches on, I strain my ears listening for them. I can't make myself stop, can't fall asleep. I'm still awake when the dark black of night turns into deep blue and then the gray of early morning, and it's time to get up.

CHAPTER 15

I come down to breakfast a few hours after the sun has finally risen. Blair and Poppy are eating their last bites of cereal and have already sent for Albert and the car. "I know it's early, but we're just so excited to go shopping," Blair explains, grinning at Poppy.

"It's fine, I'm ready," I say, grabbing a piece of toast and wolfing it down on the way to the car. Mabel's probably going to crucify me later for the trail of crumbs I'm leaving.

"Let's go to Perthton, Albert," Blair says, and I snap to attention. "It has the best stores, I think."

She's not looking at me, but I still shiver. Does she know I went to Perthton that day? Albert glances at me with a curious expression as he starts the car.

The whole way there, Blair and Poppy chat giddily about new styles and what Poppy would wear to school if she didn't have a uniform. Poppy is brighter and more open than I've ever seen her, and for the briefest moment, I have to be grateful to Blair for that. Even if her sugared sweetness sets my teeth on edge. I watch her, with her broad smiles and overly dramatic hand gestures. I feel like all of that is just a veneer, a carefully polished affect.

She's trying to win over her boyfriend's sister, and she's doing a very good job of it.

Yawning, I lean my head against the window and try to stay awake as they continue on.

Albert drops us off in Perthton, and Poppy and Blair are practically squealing as they head to the high street. My legs feel full of lead as I follow them, trying not to let my bad mood spoil Poppy's fun.

Poppy slows down at the street corner and stops in front of a small house. "This was Mum's house. Where she grew up," she says softly.

I look at the two-story stone house that looks as if it's been standing on this corner for centuries. It's maybe only thirty feet wide, with five windows on its front side and a tiny garden with thorny bushes. "She grew up here?" I ask, surprised. It's nice, certainly, but it's a far cry from a castle. Or Dunraven Manor. I can't imagine the perfectly coiffed Lily from the photos living here.

Poppy nods. "My grandparents ran the pharmacy in town. I never knew them—they were both dead by the time I was born. Mum said they worked hard, but they weren't very loving. She couldn't remember her dad ever hugging her, and her mum hardly ever said she loved her." She takes in a deep breath and lets it out. "So she wanted Charlie and me to always know that she loved us."

Her words remind me of the well-worn note from my mom telling me to always remember that she loved me. Maybe Mom's parents were like Lily's, I think, and suddenly, their friendship makes sense.

"And Mabel took care of her?" I ask.

"From the day she was born," Poppy says. Her voice is heavy with sadness, and I squeeze her shoulder to let her know I'm there.

"Well, come on," Blair says, her smile soft but her voice sharp. "Let's get shopping!"

Poppy follows her, but I hang back to take in the house for an extra moment. Lily and Mabel moved from here to a castle on a huge estate. Of course Mom was right when she said that Lily would appreciate that life more than she would have.

I have to walk quickly to catch up to Blair and Poppy, who are on their way into a cute little boutique filled with brightly colored clothes that seem determined to dispel the gloomy autumn weather outside. I run my hands over the soft fabrics, watching Blair and Poppy out of the corner of my eye. Blair is pulling different shirts and dresses from the racks with girlish giggles, piling them onto a saleswoman's outstretched arms. "This would look *fabulous* on you," Blair exclaims to Poppy over and over.

Watching her dote on Poppy, I find myself wondering how far along she is now in the pregnancy. She's not showing yet; it must be the first trimester.

I realize that I'm staring at her stomach, so I look down at the price tag of the dark plum-colored dress in my hand, then let go quickly. A hundred pounds? No way a single dress could be worth that much money.

Blair ushers Poppy into a dressing room piled with the heaps of clothes they've pulled.

"Anything catch your eye?" she says lightly once Poppy is behind the curtain.

I snatch the much-too-expensive dress off the rack. "This one," I say.

She cocks an eyebrow at it. "That's not really the best color for you," she says, but the tone of her voice tells me she thinks just the opposite.

"I'll try it on just in case," I say steadily as I brush past her to the available dressing room, swiping the curtain shut behind me. Behind the curtain, my hands fumble with the delicate zipper, and I take a deep breath. It's just a dress, and I'm not the one paying for it. I don't know why I'm suddenly so uneasy.

I step into it, do up the zipper, and close my eyes for a moment before I turn to face the full-length mirror.

It's knee-length and made of swishy fabric, with a sweetheart neckline that's definitely low, but not too revealing. It's gathered at the waist, then falls in a cute, flouncy skirt. Blair was wrong: The color makes my red curls gleam, and my breath catches in my chest.

I look exactly like my mother. She always wore longish dresses, and though her favorite color was dark green, this rich plum shade still reminds me of her. As does my hair, which has always been so much like hers . . .

Am I happy or sad to see this resemblance? Maybe a little bit of both. And a little bit scared, too.

I step closer to the mirror and look into my own dark brown eyes. The same color as my mother's, the same shape. I remember, suddenly, vividly, the way her eyes would flash and roll when she was in the middle of one of her bad spells.

I step back, swallowing the sudden lump in my throat and smoothing down the skirt with my hands. "Let's see it!" Poppy calls from the other side of the curtain, so I draw it back to show her.

She's wearing cute pink slacks and a silky white shirt printed with tiny horses, and I can't help but smile. The outfit is perfect for her. She reflects my smile right back at me. "It's beautiful!" she says, clapping her hands together in excitement. "You have to get it."

I've never seen her so enthusiastic and undeniably girly, and my smile grows wider.

Blair is watching me carefully, taking me in with those impenetrable slate blue eyes. I straighten my shoulders. "She's right. You do have to get it," she says, but there's no enthusiasm in her voice.

Poppy's already hurrying around the store, pulling out other items for me to try on, when the bell on the front door jingles. I look over to see Mrs. Drummond, the housekeeper from Dunraven Manor, enter the shop.

I freeze. What am I supposed to do if she sees me and mentions the other day in front of Blair and Poppy?

Thankfully, my legs start working again, and I dart behind the dressing room curtain. I draw it back a bit and watch Blair approaching Mrs. Drummond.

What is she doing?

Poppy follows her over, and when Mrs. Drummond turns

around, she utters an exclamation of surprise. "Well, what a treat!" she says, a smile flung across her face. "Ms. Rifely," she says, nodding at Blair.

How does Blair know Mrs. Drummond? Does she know my grandparents, too?

I feel sick. Of course Blair knows the grandparents I've never met. She probably went to introduce herself as Charlie's girlfriend or something, and they probably loved her. Just like they loved Lily.

I let the curtain fall back and sink to my knees, nauseated.

I listen as Mrs. Drummond and Blair talk about the cold weather and the shortening autumn days. "And how are Mr. and Mrs. Cavendish?" Blair asks.

"Well enough. They had a touch of the flu that's been going around, but they seem to be on the mend."

"Oh no," Blair says, sounding concerned. "I'll have Mrs. Mackenzie send over some of her famous chicken soup."

Suddenly, Poppy's at my curtain. "Fee?" she calls. "Are you ready to go?"

"Almost," I say as loudly as I dare. "I just need to change. I'll be right out."

The conversation has died off, thank goodness, and I don't hear Mrs. Drummond's voice anywhere else in the store. By the time I change into my regular clothes and peek out of the dressing room curtain, she's gone, and I can breathe again.

Blair taps her foot impatiently but feigns brightness as she asks, "Ready?"

I nod. This girl knows my grandparents. She worries about their health and makes pleasantries with their housekeeper. I'm hit by a wave of hatred so strong that it makes my knees shake.

It's not rational, I tell myself. She hasn't done anything wrong. She's dismissive and fake, maybe. That's it.

But I don't care. I hate her.

We spend the rest of the day flitting from village to village, hitting every boutique we spot, and I learn to ignore the price tags on everything Poppy shoves into my arms. Soon enough the car is piled with our shopping bags, and it's time to go home.

That evening, just before dinner, I spot Alice pulling her cart out of Charlie's room just as I step out of Poppy's. "Alice, hi!" I call.

She glances up at me in surprise, and then her whole face clouds over. She looks shadowy and menacing, like the chilling approach of a thunderstorm. "What is it?" I ask, stepping toward her, the smile falling off my face.

She takes out her cell phone and hands it to me. I look down at the screen to see a picture of me. With Gareth.

My arms are around his neck, and we're pressed against the wall of his cabin, our mouths locked together. It's unbearably intimate, and I almost want to look away, as if I've just interrupted a pair of strangers.

"Where did you get this?" I ask.

"Someone emailed it to me. Anonymously. Said they didn't want to get involved, but they thought I should know."

I can feel the blood draining from my face. "Alice," I say quickly, looking up at her, but she snatches the phone back and shakes her head.

"It's fine. Be with him if you want to."

"I don't want to be with him," I say, my voice too loud and high.

She looks at me, her mouth open in disgust. "Then what the hell are you doing?"

I open my mouth to explain, but I can't. I don't even know how to explain it to myself.

She bites her lip and shakes her head again as she watches me. "He's a good guy," she says finally. "I mean, he seems easygoing and funny and all that, but he's had a really hard life, and he cares more than he lets on. He deserves a lot better than that."

"I know," I say, dropping my head.

"Look," she says with a sigh, and I look up hopefully. "We have to live in the same house, so I'm not going to keep being mean to you. But from now on, we're not friends. I don't trust you. Don't talk to me unless you have to, and I'll do the same."

"Alice," I say, but she's already gone down the hall.

Someone was outside the window of Gareth's cottage that night, watching us. And I think I know who it must have been.

But why would Blair give a picture like that to Alice unless she specifically wanted to ruin our friendship?

Despite my lack of sleep, I feel wired, every nerve ending in my body sparking. I wrap my new overlarge teal cardigan closer around me, shivering. What's her endgame?

I hurry down the stairs toward the library but stop when I see light shining from the cracked door of the office next door. I peek in to find Charlie sitting behind the desk. No sign of Blair.

I should keep walking. I shouldn't disturb him—or have anything to do with him. But I'm mad, and talking to Charlie is the one surefire way to show Blair any type of defiance. And if I'm being honest with myself, I don't think it would be physically possible for me to walk past this room and the opportunity to talk to him alone.

I take a breath, determined to appear and feel normal, and push the door open.

It's only when I'm inside that I notice how his head is propped up by his hands, and there's a large crystal bottle of golden whisky on the desk in front of him.

"Oh, sorry," I say, immediately beginning to back out.

He snaps his head up. "No, please, come in," he insists. "Close the door."

Something in his tone gives me pause, but I do as he says. "Join me," he says, pouring a bit of whisky from the decanter into a fresh crystal tumbler, then holding it out to me. "Unless you think I'm being horribly inappropriate again."

He probably is. I should have followed my first instinct and walked away. But I've just lost the one real friend I had here, after spending the day with a girl who seems to hate me and is carrying the baby of the guy I can't stop thinking about. And that guy is here in front of me offering me the chance to forget all of that for a few moments. So I quiet my thoughts, move in closer, and take the tumbler.

"What has you drinking this time?" I ask, settling down on the couch across from him, tucking my legs underneath me.

He watches me as I take a small sip of the powerful drink. It burns in my throat, and I try not to wince. "I shouldn't be talking about this with you," he says softly. "Since I'm your employer and all that."

I shrug and take a larger sip. Having his eyes on me makes my stomach twist. "You need someone to talk to."

I wonder for a moment if he'll insist that I play another piece on the piano before he reveals this new secret, but there's no teasing in his voice tonight.

He sighs. "I should be talking to Blair."

"Why aren't you?" I whisper. I'm afraid of startling him, as if speaking too loudly will remind him that he shouldn't be telling me so much. "Why are you here, alone, drinking?"

"Because she's why I'm drinking."

I circle my hands around the tumbler. I can think of plenty of reasons why Blair would drive him to drink, but I know there's probably only one thing he's truly worried about. "You know, you're a father already in all the ways that count," I say softly. "You'll be a wonderful father for that baby."

He groans and buries his head in his hands. "I feel like I'm acting. Like I'm just pretending to be a good father figure for Poppy when really I have no idea what I'm doing. I'm terrified I'm going to mess everything up and everyone's going to see right through me—"

"Hey," I interrupt. "You're doing a great job, even if it feels like pretending to you."

He doesn't lift his head. "I thought things between Blair

and me were over. I hurt her so much when we were together—
that's why I broke it off with her. I told her I didn't want to be
that guy anymore and that being alone was the only way to start
fresh."

"You don't seem like that guy to me."

"Yeah, well, you didn't know me then."

I nod, knowing I probably wouldn't have liked the Charlie
he was then. "No, but I know you now," I say. I don't know if it's
the whisky coming on sudden and strong or just that it's been
such a long, hellish day, but the words keep pouring out. "And
just like you said, you've changed. You're not a *boy* anymore.
You're a man. And you're the type of man who would never
hurt someone he cared about."

He looks up at me with a tortured expression, but then
drops his eyes back down to his glass before I can react. "Thank
you," he says quietly.

I take another deep swallow, and it burns less now as it goes
down.

I hate that he doubts himself so much. I hate that he can't
see how much he's changed, how good he is to Poppy, how
much he cares. Does no one tell him that? Does Blair not tell
him that?

"I told you a secret," he says, his voice lower. Deeper. "Now
you owe me a song."

Just when I thought we were done with games. "No piano in here," I point out.

"Then you'll have to tell me a secret of your own."

My eyes widen in shock and nervousness, and he laughs. "It's only fair," he says.

A secret. Which secret could I tell him? This predicament definitely makes it seem easier to play the piano instead, to open up to him that way, rather than to say something out loud.

I consider telling him something small and unimportant, like the name of my favorite song (the "Skye Boat Song" that Mom used to sing to me whenever she felt haunted by the memories of her homeland) or my earliest memory (climbing the stairs up to the Austin apartment with my mom, her voice bright and encouraging as I eased myself up the tall steps).

But I don't. I find that I actually want to tell him something real. I just don't know what.

"What do you want to know?" I ask finally.

He thinks for a second. "What do you want from the future?"

His question is deceptively simple, but for me it's a minefield. Because what I want most from the future is something I can't reveal: that I don't want to end up like my mother. I don't want her disease, her sadness, her fragile, breaking mind.

So I give him the less dangerous answer.

"I want a family," I say. "I want people around me who are

part of my blood and part of my heart. I want to be part of a unit that looks toward the future together." I pause, wondering if what I'm saying is making any sense to Charlie, who grew up with all of these things as givens. But when I look at him, I see a mix of sorrow and admiration in his eyes that lets me know he understands. And I think I see something more in his gaze, too. Something so wonderful I'm afraid to hope for it. "I just don't want to be so alone anymore," I say anyway, looking right into the wonder in those eyes.

"Fiona," he says. I blink, trying to stave off the tears I feel coming.

Everything before me is swimming in a blur, and I realize my tumbler is nearly empty. Charlie notices it, too, and he grabs the decanter and stands up. He walks to me, and I don't break my gaze from his. He stands over me for a long moment, the intensity in his eyes reflecting onto mine, then pours a bit more whisky into my glass. "You're too easy to talk to," he says. He kneels in front of me, and the change in perspective makes me see stars at the edge of my vision. Somehow, I've forgotten to breathe. "It must be your eyes," he says. "They invite all sorts of secrets."

He brings his hand up to my face, and the stars at my periphery burn brighter. *I need to breathe*, I scream to myself and take one shaky breath, in and out. His hand cradles my chin, his thumb brushing my cheek. He catches a tear in its tracks.

"You're crying," he says. "Why?"

I couldn't answer him even if I wanted to. All I can do is stare as he brushes his thumb over my mouth, pressing gently on my lower lip. When I part my lips, I hear him take a harsh breath in.

Suddenly he stands and walks back to his chair, as if that moment—that wonderful and dizzying moment—never happened. But I can still taste the salt of my tear on my lips.

My head is spinning as I look down at my glass. I finish the rest of my drink in one gulp and stand, swaying only slightly. "I should let you get back to work," I say.

"Fiona?" he says. He stands up, but before I can find out why, I skirt around the couch and practically hurl myself out of the room.

I go upstairs and curl up in bed, trying to clear my head of anything at all, hoping to fall into a dreamless sleep, uninterrupted by any strange noises or whispers.

It doesn't work. I sleep in fits and bursts, stirred awake every few minutes by every creak and crack of the floorboards and walls. By every loud, garbled whisper, words I can't make out.

But despite all of that, the loudest sound I hear is the echo of my own voice telling Charlie that I don't want to be alone anymore. And all I can feel is the echo of his thumb pressing against my lip.

CHAPTER 16

Over the next few weeks, Alice proves that she's a girl of her word. When we pass each other in the hallways, she smiles and says hello to Poppy, but she hardly even looks at me. It's like I'm a ghost. Like I don't even exist to her.

The house feels a lot colder now.

Poppy and I spend a lot of time in her room, gearing up for midterms. She's in good shape for every subject except math, so we do equations for hours until we both want to curse whoever came up with algebra. I try to stay positive and enthusiastic about her progress, but I'm pretty sure she can see right through me.

One afternoon, Poppy's tackling yet another worksheet when I wander over to the window and see Blair, flung across the stones of the courtyard below, as if thrown. I have to press my palms against the window and get super close against the glass before I realize that she hasn't fallen to her death but is just lying there, relaxing. Even though there's no sun on this early November day, with its overcast skies and temperature that has crossed over from chilly to definitively cold.

The image of her lying there, her limbs at such violent angles, sends a shiver through me so strong that it feels like my blood has frozen under my skin. I blink a few times, as if she's a delusion that I might make disappear.

But no, she's there. She's real, and I'm just tired. Between the disembodied whispers and the persistence of my own black thoughts, I haven't had a real night's sleep in ages. The circles under my eyes are growing darker every day, and I have to drink cup after cup of coffee just to stay awake. This constant cycle of being both caffeine-wired and exhausted is taking its toll.

But who is this girl who lies outside on cloudy days and knows my grandparents? What does she do all day? She has to be doing *something* when Charlie's working; her weekly doctor appointments certainly don't take up all her time.

"Done!" Poppy calls.

I tear myself away from the window and the unsettling sight below and try to focus back on Poppy.

But it's no use. I pore over Poppy's careful work, but I can hardly make anything out.

A harsh copper taste, like I'm sucking on a penny, floods my mouth, and I feel like running fast and far away. Adrenaline. I remember reading about it in a psych book that I snuck out of the public library back home, too embarrassed to check it out. A hormone that courses through you when you when your fight-or-flight response has been triggered.

For a moment, I think about running. Quitting and going back to Texas. I could get back my old job at the Buffalo Head Café and work with Hex. I would be back among the familiar, living in some tiny, horned-toad-infested apartment with my friend, broke and directionless but relatively happy.

I linger in the fantasy for only a few seconds, but then forget it. I can't let Blair win. I can't let her drive me away. And then there are all the questions I have about my mother's past, about my grandparents. I can't leave before I find out what happened to my family and why they don't want anything to do with me.

So if I'm not fleeing, I might as well fight. Now I just have to plan how.

The next morning, while Poppy's at school, I decide I'm going to figure out what Blair does all day.

I find her in a first-floor sitting room that I've barely spent any time in. It's a grand, formal space, with ornate, centuries-old furniture, decorative baubles on every surface, and walls full of more portraits of dead kilted guys.

Blair lounges on a cushy crimson couch, staring at her laptop. She looks up at the sound of my creaking footstep in the doorway, and I try not to cower at the sudden venom in her gaze, which she quickly replaces with a look of indifference.

I step inside the room, determined not to retreat.

"Good morning," she says. There's a hint of a question in her tone, as if what she really wants me to do is say what I'm doing there and then get the hell out.

"Good morning," I say as casually as possible. I clasp my hands together to hide their shaking. "I was actually hoping to run into you. I wanted to thank you for the shopping trip this weekend."

She brightens, putting on her fake friendliness. "Of course! I had so much fun. I love getting to know Poppy better. She's such a special girl, you know?"

"Yeah, she is."

"She's so trusting. She believes whatever you tell her. And she clearly adores you."

Her words freeze me in place, and I just stand there, staring at her. *What does she mean by that?*

Her calm expression and bland smile give nothing away. "Oh," she adds, as if she's just remembered. "I need to tell Mrs. Mackenzie to send some of her chicken soup to the Cavendishes. I promised their housekeeper I would. They've been sick, poor things."

I can feel my eyes widen and the blood drain from my face. Does she know she's talking about my grandparents? Is she taunting me?

I study her for another moment before saying an awkward goodbye and excusing myself. Once I'm beyond the doorway, I hurry down the hall until I'm sure my footsteps are out of earshot, then lean against a wall and try to breathe. I can feel my pulse racing in my throat.

I can't get rid of the strange, sickening feeling in my gut. I don't know why, but I think that Blair is planning something . . . bad. Something that would affect not only me, but Poppy.

She wants Charlie all to herself, that much is obvious. But how far will she go to make that happen?

I try to keep a discreet eye on Blair for the rest of the day, but I don't want to do anything that would antagonize her further. All I gather is that she spends most of the morning on her laptop and then eats lunch in front of it in the dining room, alone.

After lunch, she meets Albert in the entry hall. "Ready?" he asks.

She hitches her purse up onto her shoulder, nods, and then they walk out the door together.

I should be upset that so far my efforts to figure out her game have been a bust. But the castle feels brighter as she drives away. All I want to do is take a nap, but I can't waste this rare opportunity to enjoy the rest of the day with a clear mind. I decide to brave the fierce November chill and swirling, pre-storm clouds and take a walk out to the woods.

I put on the rain boots that Poppy picked out for me—black with white polka dots, "Adorable *and* practical!" Poppy had exclaimed—and clomp through the bracken, muddy pine needles, and wet, dead leaves.

I pass by the entrance to the hedge maze and then skirt past the stables as quickly as I can. I'm still not ready to face Gareth, though I know I need to at some point. I need to apologize.

Later. For now, I just want to enjoy the afternoon. I wander out beyond the stables and the paddocks into the forest that the Moffats have purposefully left wild. The trees here are tall, some like overgrown Christmas trees and some with thick, soft-brown trunks that stretch up for a hundred feet before sprouting any branches. The air is fresh, with scents of soil and spicy pine swirling around me.

There's a hush in the air, a waiting quality. Mom used to tell me about the way nature likes to stop and hunker down when a storm is coming. She said she always knew she should get inside when the birds stopped singing.

Right now, I don't hear a peep from them. I shouldn't wander out too far.

The rain starts so gently that I hardly even notice it at first. But it builds steadily, and the wind picks up, stirring into a fury as I turn back for the castle. A few minutes pass, bringing lightning flashes in the sky, the boom of thunder responding.

And for the first time in weeks, I hear my mother's voice, shouting in my head: *Run, Fiona! Run! It's coming!*

I gasp, my feet stumbling into a run. What does she mean? Of course I know a storm is already here—so what else is coming? What's out here with me?

My boots feel heavy, and I stumble a few times, scratching my palms on the tree trunks I grab to brace myself. I'm soaked through, my clothes weighed down with water. The rain is now pouring sheets, and I can hardly see anything.

Am I going the right way? Or am I lost forever in this forest? All I can hear is the howl of the wind and the rain, angry as it pelts into me.

Something that feels almost like a human hand grazes the back of my head, and I nearly drop to my knees, suddenly dizzy. Was that a falling branch? I shake off my dizziness and sprint forward as fast as I can.

Limbs grasp at my coat, at my arms and legs, pulling at me, as if trying to drag me backward. They're just tree branches, I know this, but still I fight and shout and keep running. Everything out here is harsh, even harsher than my reality. Time seems to slow down, and as hard as I push forward, I feel like I'm not moving, as if this forest is pulling me back in.

I'm sobbing, terrified, scrambling wildly, until I'm finally out of the woods, back at the stables.

I'm so relieved that I'm crying, my tears mixing with the rain sliding down my cheeks. I don't stop running until I charge through the back door of the castle.

It's only when I'm inside that my pulse finally begins to slow. What just happened?

It doesn't matter, I tell myself, shrugging off my coat and stepping out of my boots, which have completely filled up with water. *I'm back home, and perfectly fine.*

I bend over, struggling to catch my breath, and then wring out my soaking red curls, careful to touch the back of my head gingerly. It's pretty sore—that branch struck me with surprising force—and I'll probably have a knot there by tomorrow. But at least it was just a tree, I'm sure of it. I shouldn't have let myself get caught in that crazy storm.

I'm almost laughing at myself, buzzing with relief, when I turn a corner and run smack into Charlie.

I yelp as he reaches out for my shoulders, bracing me. The heat of his hands travels through my sweater and into my skin before he pulls them away. "What happened?" he asks, looking me up and down.

I look down at myself as well, at my sweater and jeans that are now plastered to my skin. The sweater is black, so thankfully it's not see-through, but the way it clings to me doesn't leave much to the imagination. The texture of the lace of one of the new bras I bought is pretty clearly visible.

I cross my arms over my chest as he forces his eyes up to meet mine. "Are you okay?" he asks, his voice sounding almost . . . strangled, as if he's having a hard time focusing.

"I'm fine," I say, even as my teeth chatter and rainwater drips from me onto the carpet. "I just got caught in the storm, that's all. A hot shower and I'll be fine."

His eyes widen slightly, their green growing darker, and I feel the heat of a blush light up my cheeks. He backs away, nodding, as if he can't get away from me fast enough. "Okay," he says quietly, before turning and striding down the hall in the opposite direction.

I bite my lip, watching him go.

After a long, hot shower, I go out to meet Albert at the car. He's just come back from his outing with Blair to take me to Poppy's school. "Where's Blair?" I ask him.

He raises his eyebrows, as if surprised by the question. "I saw you two driving off a few hours ago," I explain as quickly and casually as possible as I slide into the backseat.

"She had a fair amount of errands to run in the village."

"Errands? In Almsley?" I ask. There's only one store in the village, and I can't imagine needing to spend longer than fifteen minutes inside it.

"No," he answers slowly. "Perthton."

I meet his eyes in the rearview mirror. "Perthton?" I repeat.

With my grandparents? I wonder. Is she there with them now, having tea while they coo over her and tell her she's the granddaughter they always wanted?

I close my eyes, trying to push down the sudden urge to throw something. Instead I pick at my fingernails until one of them bleeds as we start speeding away from the estate.

Albert must see me fidgeting with anger and stress, because he keeps glancing at me in the rearview mirror, his dark brown eyes examining me with curiosity.

"Anything you want to tell me, lass?" he asks.

"No," I say quickly. When I catch his eyes in the mirror, though, I can tell he knows I'm lying.

I feel a wave of relief once we reach Poppy's school. Soon her happy chatter fills the car on the ride home, and I can avoid Albert's questioning gaze.

Back at the castle, Poppy changes into her riding clothes, and I walk with her to the stables.

The storm has passed, leaving only puddles and dripping

trees in its wake, but I can't help but tremble as I look out at the woods. I can still hear my mother's urgent voice in my head.

Gareth is out front saddling Copperfield as we approach, and I can tell the exact moment he sees me. His hands go still for a second, but only for a second, before he finishes tightening the saddle belt and comes around to help Poppy mount.

"Here for another riding lesson?" he asks me. His tone is easy and teasing, but he doesn't look at me. Instead, he focuses on adjusting Poppy's stirrups and hands her the reins.

"No," I say quietly.

"It's muddy out there today," he tells Poppy. "Be careful where he steps. And make the jumps smooth."

Poppy nods solemnly and touches her heels to Copperfield's flank, guiding him over to the paddock where they've set up the jumps for her to train.

Gareth and I watch in uncomfortable silence as Poppy starts Copperfield at a trot, then brings him up to a canter. She expertly leads him over one jump, clearing two low bars. The next jump is higher and more difficult, two sets of three bars. My heart's in my throat as I watch her push Copperfield into a canter again, and then they soar over the jump in a graceful arc, Poppy's body melding into her horse's until they are one intention, one pure movement. They clear it easily, and I can breathe again.

Gareth's still not looking at me, but I can distinctly feel his awareness of me.

"She's really amazing, isn't she?" I say finally, trying to overcome the gap between us.

"Yes," he says simply. Still not looking at me.

I sigh. I have to tell him about the photo and that Alice knows what happened. "Look, Gareth—"

"I have to go check on the other horses," he says, cutting me off. "See you around, Fee."

He walks away, and I watch him until he disappears into the stables.

Why did I have to ruin everything? Now Alice hates me and Gareth can't even look at me, leaving me with exactly zero real friends here.

I trudge back to the castle, practically kicking myself as I go. This place is growing darker and colder to me by the day. And I can only imagine it's the opposite for Blair.

CHAPTER 17

I find him in the library the next afternoon. Charlie stands at the window, his back to me, looking out at the manicured garden. I know he hears me come in, but he doesn't turn around. Something about his posture, the way his shoulders are set, makes me close the door behind me, sealing us off from the rest of the house. "Are you okay?" I ask softly.

"I have to meet with the family lawyer today," he says after a small silence. "Make sure everything from the estate has been handled correctly."

I stay pressed against the door of the room, but every part of me wants to go to him, wrap my arms around him, bury my head in his chest, comfort him as he confronts the pain and grief of his parents' death all over again.

He finally turns to face me. "All I want to do is hide from it for a little while," he says, his voice raw and honest. I don't ask him what "it" means, though I wonder if it might include Blair.

I move toward the piano and sit down at the bench without another glance at him. I close my eyes, breathe, and begin playing the only song that can fit this situation.

Liszt's transcription of "Ave Maria." My mother was never much of a vocalist, but she used to sing this to me as a lullaby. For me, it's a song of comfort tinged with sadness, and it's overwhelmingly beautiful. It's a complicated piece that took me hours of practice in my high school's music room. But learning it was my way of remembering Mom, and I would play it until my wrists ached.

I'm nearing the end, building toward the climax, when the door bangs open. Blair stands in the threshold like a thunderstorm, her eyes flashing with lightning. I stop playing, and the notes hang in the air, unfinished and tangled. She looks from me, my hands still resting on the keys, to Charlie, who hasn't moved from the window. "What are you doing here?" she asks him, blinking. In that blink, the lightning fades from her eyes, as if it had never been there in the first place, leaving only concern and care. "The lawyer's been waiting for you for twenty minutes," she says.

I feel the heat on my cheeks, as if she's caught us doing something wrong, interrupted something intimate.

Maybe she has.

But then Charlie saunters around the piano, stops at the doorway to kiss Blair's forehead, and walks past her and into the hallway without a word, leaving Blair alone with me.

She looks to me, and though her expression is calm and mild enough, I swear I see the lightning return to her eyes. I try to keep my face blank and unconcerned, but she still stares at me, as if hopeful that her gaze will be able to pierce through my skin and leave me bleeding. Finally, she turns and follows Charlie, and I'm left alone.

My hands tremble on the keys, and I clasp them together to still them. Stupid, stupid girl. To think something was happening between Charlie and me, when he's about to have a baby with Blair.

But maybe . . . maybe I'm not so stupid. He just opened up to me because he couldn't talk to her. He confided in me that he wanted to go somewhere and hide. That has to mean something. Even if it's not everything I want it to mean.

And I can still feel the thrill, the memory of his thumb resting on my lips that day in his office.

Maybe Blair has a reason to be threatened after all.

That night, I make my tea and head up to my room. But as soon as I open the door, I'm hit with it: Highland Heather, a scent

I haven't smelled in years. My mom's perfume. It was her one luxury, which she special ordered because it reminded her of her childhood. Smelling it here, now . . . it's like she's inside this very room, waiting for me. I stand, rooted in the doorway, my pulse racing as my eyes dart around the empty space.

A door creaks open down the hall, startling me so much that I jump back against the hallway wall, dropping my mug with a crash. Hot tea splashes my hand and splatters down my leg, and I gasp at the sting of the burn. Alice steps out of her room, her eyebrows raised.

"I—I just . . ." I begin, but then realize there's nothing to say that would make any of this make any sense. *I smell my mother's perfume?*

But it doesn't matter. Alice isn't concerned about me; she brushes past me like I don't even exist.

I slump against the wall, sliding down until I'm sitting, and stare into my room. I know I need to go to bed, but my legs don't feel strong enough to hold me up anymore.

The smell is fading, or maybe I'm just getting used to it. Or maybe it's not even here at all.

I force myself up from the floor, pick up the broken pieces of my mug, and walk back to my room, breathing in through my nose and out through my mouth as I settle into bed. Curling up beneath the covers, I try not to think about the fact that this is the technique Mom used to use when she thought she might be spiraling down into one of her episodes.

But how many times can I brush aside these kinds of thoughts? How long can I keep telling myself it's nothing, that I'm still normal?

I need to sleep. So I do the only thing I can think of. I imagine my mother singing "Ave Maria" to me, and the soft, imaginary notes finally lull me into oblivion.

CHAPTER 18

A couple of days later, I leave Poppy with her home-work to grab some carrots and hummus, her favorite afternoon snack. When I get back to her room, I find Blair there, sitting on the floor beside Poppy.

I nearly drop the bowl of carrots, and as I recover I have to stop myself from warning Poppy to get away from her, the girl who everyone else sees as harmless and sweet.

"Poppy was just telling me about this history test she's got coming up," Blair says, smiling. I feel the air around me turning cold and tense.

We've been studying the Battle of Culloden Moor of 1746, when the Scottish Highlanders and their allies rebelled against the British crown in favor of Bonnie Prince Charlie, the grand-son of a former Stuart king who'd been kicked off the throne decades before. I've been trying to make it more engaging by including some facts I learned about her family from the old book in the library, that her branch of the Moffats was against the Jacobite side, many of them dying for King George II. There are so many names and maneuvers to memorize, though, that we're both going a bit cross-eyed.

"I could help, if you like," Blair says, tossing a long swath of her dark hair over her shoulder. "I did pretty well with the Jacobite revolutions in school."

"That's okay," I say quickly. "We've got it under control. Right, Poppy?"

"I guess so," she grumbles.

Blair rises slowly to her feet, smiling down at Poppy. "Well, I'll leave you two to it, then," she says. But before she leaves, she stops in front of me.

"Are you sleeping well?" Blair asks, her mysterious blue eyes examining me. "You have bags under your eyes, poor thing."

I resist the urge to run to the mirror, and stare straight ahead instead. "Just some noises that wake me up every now and then."

"Mmm," she murmurs. "The creaks of an old house." She shrugs. "I meant to tell you the other day, you play the piano beautifully."

"Thank you," I say quietly.

"I can see why Charles seemed so enchanted by it." She says it pleasantly enough, but I can hear barbs in her words.

I turn back to Poppy, ignoring the comment completely. "We should get back to the battle."

Poppy sighs and opens her textbook. Blair finally leaves the room as Poppy begins to read out loud, and I shiver in the cold air she leaves behind.

The next day, Poppy and I are returning from her riding lesson when we run into a construction crew coming out of Charlie's room.

"They must be almost finished with the nursery!" Poppy exclaims, running to the open door.

I follow after her, my feet moving as if by their own accord. I can't help my curiosity; I've never seen inside Charlie's room. *Blair* and Charlie's room.

His suite is as big and expansive as his sister's, and the first thing I see is an entire wall of bookshelves, spanning from floor to ceiling. I'm tempted to park myself in front of it and trail my fingers along the spines of the books, finding out what merits a spot in his private collection. Positioned in front of the shelves is his desk, which is covered with several large computer screens and tablets. I know he's always on his laptop, but I had no idea he was this into computers.

But then my eyes move from the desk, past the couch and armchairs arranged in front of the large fireplace, and go straight to the bed. It's ordinary enough: big and broad and covered with a soft, fluffy dark green cover. But this is the bed that he shares with Blair. I've spent a fair amount of energy trying not to imagine the two of them together in bed, but I can't avoid it now.

Strangely enough, the thought of them simply sleeping there beside each other, vulnerable and trusting, hurts just as much as the thought of them . . . not sleeping.

Turning away, I follow Poppy through a doorway into another, slightly smaller room. The nursery.

I have to will myself not to stop in my tracks. I need to see this, even if I desperately don't want to.

The room is painted a beautiful stormy blue, like the color of Blair's eyes. The wooden crib is painted white, matching the rest of the furniture. In the corner is a set of picture books stacked next to the tiniest armchair I've ever seen, and scattered across the walls are framed prints of illustrated giraffes and elephants.

Seeing all these charming little details that Blair must have been working on for weeks, it hits me. This baby is coming. She's been preparing for it. Her baby. His.

As I stand here in this family suite, so obviously different from my room in the servants' wing, I feel the color drain from my face.

Blair, Charlie, Poppy, the baby—they're all family. I have no place here.

There are footsteps behind us, and I turn around to find Charlie walking into the room, and every muscle in my body tenses.

"Charlie, I love all the new details!" Poppy squeals. She spins in the room, her arms wide open, and for a moment, despite my aching awareness of Charlie, I can't help but smile. "It's going to be so fun to have a baby in the house," she says, glowing, smiling widely at her brother.

He smiles, but his smile seems strained. "I'm glad you like it."

She swoons over the soft blankets and tiny clothes hanging in the closet while I feel the weight of Charlie's eyes on me.

"Poppy, can you give Fiona and me a second alone?" he says.

I look up at him, letting his eyes trap mine.

"Sure," she says, unconcerned. "I'm going to go get some snacks."

"Okay," I mumble, unable to break my gaze from Charlie's as she skips out the door.

"She's so much happier now," he says.

"She's excited for the baby," I say quickly.

"She's happier because of you, too," he adds. "Thank you for that."

I don't know what to say, so I keep my lips pressed firmly together.

"I hardly ever see you anymore," he says softly.

There's nothing for me to say to that, so I change the subject. "Congratulations, again, on the baby."

"Thank you," he says, looking around the room. "It's starting to feel more real now."

I can hear happiness, wonder, in his voice. He really wants this baby. He wants this family.

I like him more for it. Even as it pulls him further and further from me.

"Blair must be getting excited, too." I try not to sound as tense as I feel.

He looks into my eyes then back at the crib. "She is. She never used to see herself as a mothering type. Her mum . . . wasn't much of a mum. But she's been reading all these parenting books and planning and . . . I think she's going to be a great mother."

I remember what Poppy told me, that Charlie told his mother that Blair didn't talk to her family. That he was her family now. And she's his family. No wonder he's with her, no wonder he clings to her. She's giving him a family, just when he's lost most of his.

I swallow, hard, and try to keep my expression neutral.

"I didn't know you were so technologically inclined," I say, gesturing toward his desk in the other room.

He sighs. "It's always been a hobby. And if I could convince the board and find funding for it, I'd love to work on the newspaper's website. Make it accessible and more fast-paced, before it gets left behind. If we could hire more reporters, we could compete with breaking-news outlets, attract more readers. It could turn everything around. But no one wants to invest in newspapers now."

"I know you can do it," I say softly, and then he's looking back at me, and I can't meet his eyes. "Well, anyway, Poppy and I should get back to her homework," I say, turning for the door before he can reply. I walk back through his bedroom and out into the hallway, leaving him there in the nursery. I force myself to look away from that bed, but every detail of it is imprinted in my mind.

Maybe that's how it should be. Maybe I should finally do what I've been telling myself to do for weeks: Let him go.

I try my best to follow my own advice and lose this silly crush on Charlie over the next week. But it's embedded so deeply in me now. Any sleep I manage to catch is filled with dreams of him. I can't breathe when I run into him in the hallways, and when I come down for breakfast, all I can think about is seeing him in the dining room. I feel like my day doesn't start until the moment his eyes meet mine. When he leaves for another business trip to Glasgow, I don't know if I'm more disappointed or relieved.

The regional horse show is coming up, and Poppy spends more and more time with Copperfield, hardly focusing on her homework. Neither of us can talk of anything else, and when the Saturday of the competition finally comes, we're both twisted in knots of stress and hope.

Charlie promises to take the morning train back from Glasgow and meet us there, and when it's finally time to get Copperfield ready and go, Blair is waiting at the front door, wearing a white sheath dress and gray suede boots.

"I've decided to come along!" she declares cheerfully. "Everyone keeps talking about how phenomenal Poppy is, I have to see it for myself."

Poppy beams back at Blair, but Blair's smile fades quickly when she turns her gaze to me. "You can take the rest of the day off, Fee," she says. "You're not required this afternoon."

I blink at her. "Oh no," I protest. "I really want to come."

"Stay home," Blair orders sharply, though she covers it with a smile. "My future sister-in-law and I need some bonding time. I'm sure you understand."

Future sister-in-law? The words hit me like piercing claws, raking my chest and leaving me bleeding. Has he proposed? Or is she just assuming? My throat dries, and I can't speak.

Poppy opens her mouth and starts to speak up for me, but Blair interrupts. "You won't deprive Fee of her time off, will you, Poppy? I'm sure she's tired of taking care of you all day."

Poppy looks at me uncertainly. "You can stay home, Fee."

Blair's lips curve upward, now that she knows she's won. I should insist that I want to see Poppy compete in this event that means so much to her, but I know Blair will never let me go, no matter what I say. So I put on the best smile I can muster and tell Poppy, "Good luck."

Blair nearly pulls her out the door before she can respond, leaving me on the doorstep to watch as they drive off with Albert.

CHAPTER 19

I spend the next few hours berating myself for not fighting back, for not telling Blair and Poppy that nothing in this world would keep me from seeing Poppy triumph at her show. I hate that I let Blair win so easily. I'm in the library, unsuccessfully trying to concentrate on a book, when I hear someone approaching. Charlie is standing in the doorway.

"How did she do?" I ask him before he even has a chance to close the door behind him.

"She placed first, of course. Looked wonderful out there."

Hopping off the windowsill, I let out a sigh of relief and smile, but he doesn't.

"Where were you?" he asks, stepping forward. "Blair said you wanted the night off. But you were even more excited about that show than Poppy was."

"I know." I try to keep my mouth shut, but I can't help but admit at least a little bit of the truth. "Blair wanted time to bond with Poppy."

He nods, though the confusion doesn't leave his eyes. He picks up the book I'd been reading and examines the cover. "A history of the Black Death?" he asks softly. "So, light reading, then."

"Blair told me she wanted to bond with her future sister-in-law."

Charlie freezes, though his gaze is still intent on the book in his hand. I don't think he's even breathing. I know I'm not.

"Are you going to marry her?" I whisper before I can stop myself.

He turns toward me, setting the book down. The torture is plain in his green eyes, and suddenly his hands are on my shoulders, drawing me to him. For one dizzying moment, I let my eyes fall to his lips, and a strange buzzing sensation fills my entire body.

I pull my eyes back up to his to find that torture still twisting through them. He moves one hand from my shoulder to my cheekbone, brushing a finger along the line of it, then dipping that finger below my chin and lifting it up further.

My lips are a breath away from his, and I can't breathe.

All of a sudden, I feel myself stepping back, pulling away

from his touch. Someone gasps, and I'm pretty sure it's me. I spin and run out of the room, and he says nothing to stop me.

I nearly kissed him. He nearly kissed me. *He wants me,* I think as I hurtle myself up the stairs toward my room. The thought makes me glow.

But he's still going to marry her. I knew it when I saw the apology and torment in his eyes. I couldn't let him kiss me, not when I know how much more it would hurt when he still chooses her.

Charlie and I start to play the avoidance game with each other once again. I begin to grab breakfast from the kitchen in the morning, making excuses to Poppy so I can evade the dining room. I keep to my room during the day, reading books in bed instead of on the library windowsill. When Poppy and I study in her room, I scamper down the hall past the closed door of his bedroom, where he seems to be hiding away with his computers.

In a few days he heads back to Glasgow again, and I try to feel glad about that. I can't think clearly when we're in the same house, so maybe when he's gone I'll finally get my feelings under control. I haven't been able to sleep at night, knowing that he's only a floor below, in bed with her. The whispers continue, and some nights the voices are so vivid, as if they're speaking right into my ear. But even if they were to disappear, the whispers in my head would be loud enough to keep me awake. I'm so exhausted that my eyelids feel permanently heavy, and I've started falling asleep in the library during the day, dozing in the winter sun on the window seat.

A week after Charlie leaves for Glasgow, I'm reading on that window seat when Blair strides in. We haven't spoken a word to each other in about two weeks, but today it seems as if she's seeking me out. The curtain is open, so I know she sees me.

"I'm sorry to bother you, but have you seen Poppy?" she says. "I wanted to invite her out on another shopping trip."

"She's riding Copperfield."

"Oh, of course," she says, pausing and looking at me before continuing, "You should have seen her at the show. I can't stop thinking about it! It was as if she was born on a horse."

"I wish I could have seen her," I say quietly, trying to tamp down the anger boiling under the surface.

A shadow of a smile crosses her lips, though she does her best to hide it. "Well, if you see her before I do—"

I can't help it. "I won't let you do that to me again, you know," I say. My voice is deadly cool, and I can't believe I just said that. But now that the words are out there, now that she's heard them, I can't take them back.

"Do what?" she asks. The polished veneer has been rubbed right out of her voice, revealing only bitterness underneath.

I stand and turn around to face her. "I won't let you shove me out of the way so you can be closer to Poppy. So that you can be closer to Charlie."

"Who says you're *in* my way?" she asks, tossing her hair behind her shoulder and crossing her arms. "Do you actually think that Charles would ever choose *you* over *me*? The shabby governess over the mother of his child? Do you think he even *notices* you?"

It's been so obvious that Blair hates me, but I still can't believe it's out in the open. As mad as I am, at her and about this whole situation, I'm also relieved.

"I *know* he notices me." My voice sounds even, confident, but inside I'm shaking.

"You're delusional," she scoffs.

Her words hit me like a slap, but I try not to flinch. "And you won't win," I snarl. "Whatever game you're playing, you're going to lose."

"We'll see about that," she says with a growing smirk. She turns to leave, but just before she's out the door, she says, "The truth is in the lily pads."

"What?" I say, but she's already gone. *What the hell is that supposed to mean?*

My hands are shaking. I grab a pillow from the window seat and squeeze until my knuckles turn white. I want to run through the hallways, yelling that I was right about Blair—that she's a manipulative, psychotic bitch, just like I thought. But still no one would believe me. No one else seems to see past her facade, and I would be the one looking like a madwoman.

So what can I do? How can I fight, now that I know who the enemy is?

She's clearly trying to do whatever she can to get rid of me. Maybe she's even the one whispering at night, trying to annoy me, drive me out.

I'll have to return the favor.

CHAPTER 20

If I'm going to fight, I'm going to need allies.

The next day, I visit Mrs. Mackenzie in the kitchens and ask her what she thinks of Blair, pretending that I'm worried about keeping my job once she becomes mistress of the castle.

Mrs. Mackenzie fixes me with her usual no-nonsense look. "At least the girl doesn't come down here and ask me useless questions," she snaps. "Now either start helping with the pie for tonight or get out of my kitchen."

I check Mrs. Mackenzie off the list and decide to go find Albert. I head outside to the carriage house, and it takes me a few seconds to realize that I'm crunching through a thin layer of frost and a tiny powdering of snow. I've never seen real snow before, and I crouch down, touching the icy brittleness that lies over the grass. I smile, entranced for a moment by this beautiful cold. I stand up, and it hits me how far I've come from the red-dirt everyday sameness of Mulespur. I don't ever want to go back there. I walk on, more determined now than ever.

The snow doesn't seem to faze Albert, whom I find in the courtyard washing the car. He greets me cheerfully, but when I bring up Blair as casually as I can, he just sighs and looks at me with pity in his eyes.

"She seems to make the lord happy, lass. And he's probably going to marry her, so I don't worry myself too much wondering what I think of her."

"Well, that's exactly it—I worry about the lord. And Poppy, of course. You don't think she's a bit . . . fake?"

"No, but it sounds to me like you do," he says as he wipes down the passenger side mirror. "I've never seen her be anything but polite and kind myself. But I'm just an old man—everyone's nice to old men. What do I know?"

"You're right," I say, realizing that Albert's clearly not going to be any help. "Of course you're right. I'm sure I'm just reading too much into things."

"Happy to help, my dear." He nods, and I turn back to the castle, realizing that my list of potential allies has dwindled to about zero. The maids and kitchen staff have been useless, even though I did my best to sound like I was only looking for a bit of friendly gossip. The only one I haven't approached is Alice, who won't even talk to me.

There's only one other person I can think of, but I'm not sure if I can get him to talk to me either.

That afternoon, while Poppy is out on her ride, I pull my hood up against the wind and trudge through the glittering frost to the stables. The trek out there seems to take longer than usual, though I don't know if it's because of the freezing air or the dread I'm feeling about talking to Gareth.

My breath is coming out in puffs and my fingers are aching with cold by the time I make it to the warmth of the stables. Gareth is there, brushing down Oliver, stopping for only a moment when he spots me before going back to his task.

"Poppy's still out," he says. "Probably won't be back for another half hour, maybe twenty minutes if she gets cold."

"I'm here to talk to you, actually."

He sighs, puts the brush down, and comes out of the stall to face me. "What about?" he asks.

I start with the most important thing, even though I'm pretty sure he's already aware of it. "Well, first, Alice knows about us. About us, uh, kissing, I mean." I stick my hands in my coat pockets, not knowing what else to do with them.

He breathes out one short, ironic-sounding laugh. "Yeah,

she made that pretty clear a few weeks ago when she came out here, slapped me across the face, and stomped off," he says with a wry smile.

"She slapped you?" I ask, kind of impressed.

He nods. "Hard."

"I'm sorry."

"I deserved it. For that and for many other things."

I swallow, gathering my courage. "I'm also sorry that I kissed you. And then ran away. I didn't explain—"

"If this is one of those 'It's not you, it's me' speeches," he interjects, "I really don't need to hear it. I'd rather just pretend it never happened."

"Okay," I say, relieved. "That's fine with me."

But now he looks disappointed, and I want to kick myself. I'm only hurting him worse by being here. I shift to move past him, giving up on my quest for allies.

"Hey," he says, and I stop. "What else did you come here to talk about?"

"It doesn't matter."

"Just say it, Fee."

I take a deep breath. "This might sound random, but . . . I'm curious: What do you think of Blair?" I ask.

"What about her?" he asks, confused. Clearly he wasn't expecting this topic of conversation.

"Nothing," I say quickly, moving past him toward the exit. "I'm just—it's stupid, sorry."

"I think she does a very good job of pretending," he says, stopping me when I'm almost out the door.

I turn around, trying to hide the joy that I know has crept into my eyes. "You think she's fake?" It's only then that I realize I didn't really expect him to agree with me, that I was practically convinced that I really was the only one who saw her differently.

"I think everything about that girl is fake," he says, his eyes serious as he watches me. "And I think you should stay away from her if you want to keep your job."

"But I haven't done anything to her!" I cry, half out of anger and half out of joy, now that I've finally found someone who gets it. "She just seems to hate me for no reason." It's not quite the truth, but I can hardly bring up my piano sessions with Charlie.

Gareth steps closer to me. "Just be careful, Fee," he says.

I'm so relieved that I find myself dangerously close to flinging my arms around him and sobbing. I'm not crazy, I'm not alone. Someone else sees underneath her meticulous mask, too.

"I'll be fine," I promise.

Gareth is right. I need to stay away from Blair. She's got something planned, and now that she's shown me just how nasty she can be, now that she finally let that sweet-girl act slip, she's even more of a threat.

But as big as the castle is, it's not big enough to hide me. She finds me in the library again that night.

As soon as she pokes her head in the door, my heart stops. And then starts racing.

She enters the room with a smile. One of those carefully practiced smiles. Why is she smiling at me? "Hey, Fee. Have you seen Poppy?" she asks. Her voice is high, bright, unconcerned.

I stare at her. "Why are you talking to me?" I ask finally.

She blinks, her mouth slightly open in confusion. "What do you mean?" she asks.

I stand up from the window seat, trying to ignore how much my knees are shaking. "After what happened yesterday, you think you can just waltz in here and talk to me?"

"What? What happened yesterday?" she asks, her brow furrowing in a very good facsimile of a mystified expression.

"The fight," I say, not fooled by her innocent act and not backing down.

"What fight?" she asks. When I raise an eyebrow at her, she just shakes her head. "Fee, I'm sorry—I'm really sorry if I did something to offend you, but I have no idea what you're talking about."

I stare at her, trying to see past this perfectly executed semblance of ignorance. "You really don't remember?"

She shakes her head slowly. "We didn't have a fight, Fee. It's been days since I've even seen you." She pauses, shrugging her shoulders. "Maybe you dreamed it?" She sounds almost concerned.

I picture the fight again in my mind: the moment her polite veneer dropped, her disdain as she asked me if I thought Charlie even noticed me.

Could I have dreamed it? It happened in the middle of the afternoon; I wasn't sleeping. Unless I drifted off and didn't realize it? I've been so tired lately.

Or was it worse than a dream? Was the fight a delusion?

My blood turns to ice at the thought, freezing me from the inside out. No. Of course not. I remember it perfectly. She's just trying to confuse me so she can get away with everything.

"Fine," I say finally, lacking the energy or the focus to argue with her anymore. "Sorry. I'll tell Poppy you were looking for her."

"Thanks," she says, peering at me once more before turning for the door. As she turns, I think I catch a glimpse of a small smile gracing her lips.

I stare at the door for a long moment after she leaves, trying to puzzle everything out. Why would she deny that the fight ever happened? To avoid more confrontation? Because she had gone too far and shown too much of her hand and wanted to pull back?

One persistent memory nags at me: the odd comment she made at the end of our fight, about the truth being in the lily pads. That's the sort of nonsense I could only expect from a dream, isn't it? I've been catnapping on the window seat for days now. What if it really *was* a dream?

No, I decide, brushing that thought away. I remember the thunder in her blue eyes, the dizziness I felt when I finally told her what I thought about her. I couldn't have dreamed that. The lily pad comment was just another clever diversion to try to throw me off.

But this all seems so convoluted, even for someone as fake as Blair. Why not just persuade Charlie to fire me? He would choose her over me if she forced a decision like that on him. Why does she need to go to all this trouble?

Whatever the reason, I get the feeling she's planning something bigger. Like she's playing a long game, and I have to be ready for whatever's coming.

CHAPTER 21

Charlie comes back just in time for Christmas. The castle grounds are covered in a generous layer of snow, and fires are lit around the castle, making the air swirl with the scent of burning wood and Christmas trees.

Christmas was my mom's favorite holiday. Every winter she would fill our apartment with cinnamon, nutmeg, carols, and Christmas stories. We would stay up eating shortbread and singing until midnight on Christmas Eve, when we would exchange presents: homemade cards and poems from me, shoes or clothes or something else that I needed from her. She had this way of making everything about that time of year, about our little family and our ordinary home, so special and magical.

At Fintair Castle, most of the servants go home for the holiday. Only Mabel, Albert, and Gareth have stayed, and Albert tells me he has no family to go home to. "This place is my only home," he tells me after I ask him about his plans. "Has been for fifty years now. I don't plan to leave it anytime soon."

He goes to fetch Charlie from the train station the night before Christmas Eve, and I try to read a book in my room. But I can't keep my eye off the clock, and when I see that they'll be back soon, I creep downstairs to the kitchen, put the kettle on the stove for my nightly cup of tea, and pretend to be very interested in a cabinet of small knickknacks and photographs near the front door as I wait for the kettle to whistle.

I hear Charlie arrive just as I'm peeking my head into the entry hall, and I watch from the shadows as he shrugs his coat off his broad shoulders and looks around the room at all the decorations that have been carefully and sumptuously hung up in his absence. Suddenly he turns toward where I'm standing, and I sink back into the shadows before he can see me.

I'm not ready to face him yet.

Both of us are surprised when Blair comes running from the opposite hall, straight into his arms. "You're back!" she squeals as he hesitates a moment before wrapping his arms firmly around her, pressing her to him.

Of course I've seen them together before, but never in a private, unguarded moment like this. And I can't look away.

"Poppy's going to be so excited to see you," Blair says,

still holding him close. "She's been going on and on about Christmas and how much fun it will be to spend it together."

I haven't heard Poppy say anything like that, to me or to Blair.

Charlie smiles, steps back out of her embrace, and places a hand gently on her stomach. "And how are *you* doing?" he asks. I can hear how soft and full of love his voice is. But is it love for Blair or for the baby she's carrying?

Blair places her hand over his as they both look down at her stomach. It's still flat. How far along is she now? She's been here two months, so probably at least three. Wouldn't she have started showing by now, even if only a little bit? The sweater she wears is tight and unforgiving, and there's no hint of a bump.

The hazy form of the idea that she's just faking all this has been floating around in my head for days. But now that I've actually let myself think it, clearly and with her flat belly right in front of me, it sounds ridiculous. It would be too elaborate, let alone virtually impossible. To pretend to go to regular doctor's appointments, to spend all that time picking out patterns and toys for a nursery. No, there's no way even someone as petty as Blair would do something so drastic. She's skinny; she's probably just not showing yet.

"I'm fine," Blair says. "I just can't wait, you know? To feel it. Kicking or moving or . . . I just can't wait to meet our baby."

He leans down and kisses her, and I have to turn and walk away, back to the boiling teakettle. I've seen enough. I take my tea and go upstairs.

I lie awake all night. I'm restless, and I can't tune out the whispers. Usually it seems as though the whispers come from the other side of the walls, but tonight it feels like someone's in the room with me, mumbling nonsense into my ear. If I could only focus on it, if I could only understand . . .

I can't keep living like this. I'll have to find some kind of sleeping pill, I decide. But I don't know if there's a sleeping pill strong enough to knock the image of Charlie kissing Blair out of my mind.

Morning comes, Christmas Eve, and Poppy hardly says a word all day. Despite the cozy cheer of the warm, decorated house, we're all in a somber mood. It's their first Christmas without Lily and Lord Harold, and I can plainly see the ache and fresh grief that it causes Charlie and Poppy.

Poppy has a few papers to write over the holidays, so I spend some time with her on those to get her mind off her parents. But after a couple of hours of sitting next to her while she stares blankly at her computer, I suggest a movie marathon instead. We pass the rest of the day watching mindless romantic comedies and soapy period-piece dramas until she falls asleep.

I take our empty popcorn bowls down the main staircase, yawning as I head toward the kitchen. When I pass by the sitting room, I see Charlie and Blair sitting on that cushy crimson couch in front of the gigantic Christmas tree. The overhead lights are off, and the little white lights on the tree glint through the glass ornaments, creating a soft glow. Orchestral Christmas music plays from the old record player in the corner near me.

I freeze and tuck myself against the wall, peeking my head out to watch them. They are whispering intently, though I can't make out what they're saying above the music. Are they fighting? A butterfly of ridiculous hope flutters within me, then dies when I see her press her hand on top of his.

And then he swings himself off the couch and falls to one knee, still holding her hand.

I feel my mouth drop open, and I want so much to close my eyes, to pretend this isn't happening, but I can't help but watch as she hugs him tightly to her, her face a picture of triumph.

I slip as silently as I can down the hall and fling myself into the library, closing the door with the quietest click I can manage. He's going to marry her. Of course he's marrying her. I knew he'd propose eventually, I did, but actually seeing it happen . . .

She'll have his baby, and they'll be one happy little family, and then she'll kick me out. I'll move back to Texas and wait tables for the rest of my life, and I will never, ever see him again.

I cover my mouth to muffle the wild sob that leaps out of it.

I'm pacing the room frantically, hurrying from one side to the other. *Don't you realize what you're doing?* It's my mother's voice, soft but insistent in my head. I stop so suddenly that I nearly fall over. This is exactly what my mother used to do. She would rave and pace through the night, captured by some delusion.

I press my hands to either side of my forehead, squeezing hard, as if I can push these thoughts right out of my mind. But the voice keeps coming.

You're turning into me. You always knew you would.

What if I *am* turning into her? What if I have to live like my mother did at the end of her life, never knowing what was real and what was a delusion? She was so confused all the time. So scared. How can I live like that?

It takes every ounce of strength for me to ignore that voice, to press down the horror that it brings with it. I force myself to take a deep breath. I'm just stressed out and upset, that's all. Perfectly normal. And her voice in my head is just a reasonable manifestation of that.

I settle myself down on the piano bench and focus all my emotion and confusion and turmoil onto the keys.

Tchaikovsky's *Swan Lake* finale pours from my fingers, a melody of grief and regret filling the room.

I hear him open the door behind me, but I don't look up. My fingers keep flying over the keys, letting the swan breathe out her final breaths. The song is not as enchanting as it would be with a full orchestra, but the beauty of it still overwhelms me as it rushes from my fingertips. It still makes me want to weep. And with Charlie's almost tangible presence at my back, all my emotions are heightened. Everything in me is as tense as a bowstring.

I hear him step toward me slowly, until he's standing right behind me. Until I can nearly feel the warmth of his skin on mine. I close my eyes and breathe deep. Rain and wood fire, his scent.

A soft touch on my neck shocks my eyes open, and my fingers stutter on the keys. He runs the side of his finger slowly, sensuously up my neck and into my hair, then holds a long curl between two fingers and caresses it.

I've stopped playing, and the only sound in the room is our heated breaths, shallow and fast. And then he lets go, and all I hear are his footsteps as he walks away from me. He's gone, as if it were all a dream.

I don't move for the longest moment, trying to hold on to

the memory of his hand in my hair, of his breath rising with mine. I couldn't have imagined it.

I should be angry. He just proposed to another girl, to the mother of his child, and then he came to me. He can't toy with me like this. I'm not his to tease.

I push myself up off the bench and hurry for the back door, my anger rising with every step. *I'm not his*, I tell myself. *I'm not his.*

I'm still repeating those words in my head when I bang on the door to Gareth's cottage. He opens it, his chest bare and his eyes muddled with interrupted sleep and confusion. I fling myself into his arms, my hands pulling his face close, and I capture his lips in a kiss.

He's stunned for a moment, motionless. Then he's gently pushing me away and stepping out of my arms. "Fee," he says, his voice pained. "What are you doing?"

I open my mouth to answer him, but I can't think of anything to say.

"What happened?" he asks, crouching a bit so he can look into my eyes.

"Nothing," I lie. "Nothing, I'm sorry." I'm backing away, reaching behind me for the door. "I'm sorry," I say again, finding the handle and rushing outside.

What was I thinking? I was angry that Charlie was using me, so my perfect solution was to go and use Gareth? How on earth had I thought that was a good idea? Was I thinking at all? Alice was right, he deserves so much better than that.

I'm going crazy. The thought stops me in my tracks before I've reached the back door of the castle.

I gulp in a bracingly cold breath of fresh air and keep walking. I won't think about my mother now. Won't let myself remember how she'd grow increasingly irrational as she ramped up to each new breakdown. I can't.

I force myself to slow down, to move deliberately and methodically through the castle and up to my room. Once I'm there, I make myself go through my normal bedtime routine before I curl up in my sheets and do my best to go unconscious.

CHAPTER 22

Voices wake me up in the middle of the night. My eyes are startled open in the darkness. I hear murmuring on the other side of the wall right next to my head. The outside wall.

These are different from the usual whispers, the garbled mess pouring forth in the same tone of voice every night. Tonight I hear two distinct voices, two women, like I did the night before the shopping trip.

I still can't make out any words, but from the inflections, the tones, I conclude that it's an argument.

I peel off the covers as quietly as possible, straining to hear. I place my bare feet on the cold wood floor and tiptoe over to the door, pressing my ear against the wall. The voices definitely aren't coming from the hall. They are, like I thought, coming from outside. From right outside my wall, six stories up in the free air. Maybe there are people up on the roof?

A floorboard creaks underneath my foot, and the voices stop for a moment. As if they heard me, as if *I've* startled *them*. And when the voices rise again, I can finally hear what each of them is saying, the lines they repeat over and over:

"Go away, little bird."

"You're not wanted here."

They chant it again and again until they're nearly shouting.

My mouth falls open in a gasp, and I back away from the wall. I pinch my arm, but I don't wake up in my bed, safe. This is real.

It doesn't make sense. But I have to figure out what's going on, once and for all. I grab my coat, shove on my rain boots, then hurry out the door.

I make it downstairs and sprint out into the freezing rain, rounding the house until I'm on the side the whispers came from. But there's nothing here. Nothing but gray stone.

The roof above my room is shingled and steeply sloped and obviously clear of anything except for the December snow. Of course. Because why would there be a couple of people perched above the sixth floor of a castle? Why am I even out here?

My adrenaline fades, until all I am is tired. I'm so tired of all this. I can't think. I can't focus. And I can't keep living like this.

"Are you okay?" someone asks behind me. I whirl around with a small scream.

It's Gareth, his eyes concerned as he stares down at me. Rain streams down his face, darkening his hair and highlighting his cheekbones.

"Yes," I say, too loudly. "Yes, I'm fine. I just thought—nothing. I thought nothing," I finish in a mumble, looking back up at the bare wall outside my room.

"Look, Fee, I wanted to talk to you about earlier tonight," he says finally, shifting his weight from one foot to another. "I'm sorry I pushed you away. It just seemed like—"

"It's fine," I interrupt. "I'm sorry I, uh, attacked you."

He almost smiles. "I didn't mind, really. I was just worried about you." He pauses. "Still am."

"I'm okay. It was just—I don't know, it was stupid. And the last thing I wanted to do was confuse you."

It's as if a curtain falls over his expression, closing him off from me. "Right," he says.

"I'm sorry," I repeat once more. It's the only thing I can say.

"I'll see you around, then," he says, turning away. He turns back to face me before I can say good night. "You should get back inside. You're freezing."

It's only now that I notice how I've wrapped my arms around my body, that my teeth have started chattering. My wet hair is plastered to my head. I must look like a drowned kitten. Or a crazy person.

"Thanks," I say through numb lips before heading back toward the relative warmth of the castle.

Even when I'm back up in my bed, though, dried off and in fresh pajamas, I can't stop the shivers from running through me.

I try to push down the memory of those voices, ignore it, not think about it. *It doesn't mean what you think it means.*

But it's getting harder and harder to ignore.

I must have only been asleep for a couple of hours when a scream wakes me up. The sound is wild and guttural, and for one terrifying and wonderful moment, I think I am a child again, back in Austin with my mother.

The scream comes again, and I snap out of that daze. I wrench my door open and run into the hall. The scream must be coming from the floor below me, where Poppy and Charlie sleep. I rush down the stairs and head right to their hallway.

Poppy's door flings open, and I see her running down the dark hall toward the scream. It's coming from Charlie's room.

I reach her just as she reaches his door, but before we can push it open, Charlie bursts through. The guttural scream is coming from behind him—from Blair.

"I've called an ambulance," Charlie declares. "She's—there's something wrong with the baby."

He's wild with worry, his eyes hardly able to focus on us. I place my hands on Poppy's shoulders and draw her back. "Let's give them some space," I murmur.

She lets me pull her back and walk her to her door, but once we reach it, she cranes her neck around me and gasps. I turn to see Charlie, carrying Blair, cradled like a child, her arms hanging limply around his neck. She's wearing a fluttering white nightgown, and just before they disappear down the stairs, I see that the bottom of it is soaked red with blood.

Poppy looks up at me, wide-eyed. Her face is so pale, her hair so blond in this patch of moonlight streaming in from the window, that she looks as transparent as a ghost. "We should go to the hospital with them." Her voice comes out strong, confident, despite the horror of what we just witnessed.

"Poppy, Charlie would want you to stay here at home. There's nothing we can do for them at the hospital. Blair will be fine, I'm sure of it," I say, though I shiver as I remember that red, red blood. "We should get some sleep so we'll be rested enough to help in the morning, when they're back safe and sound."

"No," Poppy says firmly, raising her chin in determination.

"He's my family. He's my only family, besides the baby, who might be in trouble. We have to go to the hospital."

Family. The only family I've ever known was my mother, and I would have never let her go to the hospital alone. I would have fought to stay with her, too. "Okay," I say finally. "I'll put on some clothes and meet you downstairs. Albert can drive us. Remember your coat," I call, already hurrying for the servants' staircase.

By the time I make it down to the front door to meet Poppy, the ambulance is pulling into the driveway, the blaring lights and wailing siren especially jarring as they cut through the night's stillness. Charlie, Blair still limp in his arms, hurries to the back of it before the paramedics even have time to jump out and take Blair from him.

Mabel, Albert, Poppy, and I stand on the front steps as we watch the ambulance drive off with Charlie and Blair, the lights flashing through the dark hills until they finally disappear. Nodding at Poppy, I ask Albert for a ride, and he goes to get the car.

Mabel places a hand on Poppy's shoulder. "It's going to be all right," she whispers, her voice softer and kinder than I ever imagined it could be. "Blair's going to be just fine."

How are you so sure? a nasty voice inside of me mutters. *What if she dies and Charlie is finally free?*

The voice chills me, sending vicious trails of goose bumps up and down my skin. That nasty, intrusive voice. It's not my mother, and it's not me. I would never think something as awful as that. I don't want Blair—or anyone—to die. I close my eyes and swallow, sickened by the glee in that ugly little voice inside my head. I won't pay any attention to it. If I ignore it, it will go away.

Albert pulls the car around and jumps out to let Poppy and me in. "I don't think you should be taking her out of her bed at this time of night just to bring her to a frightening place like a hospital," Mabel says to me, the usual bitterness restored to her voice. "She needs her sleep." She glances at Poppy, her eyes full of concern.

"It's not your decision," I say, sliding into the car. "It's Poppy's."

Albert speeds us out of there before Mabel can reply.

During the long drive to the hospital, I can't focus on anything except Poppy's small hand clasped in mine—and on keeping the ugly voices out of my head. The three of us are silent as Albert drives, cutting through the dark night.

CHAPTER 23

When we finally get to the tiny hospital in Beasley, we find Charlie sitting in the waiting room, his head in his hands.

"What happened?" I ask.

He shakes his head. "I don't know. I woke up and she was screaming, and there was all this blood—so much blood!" He buries his head back in his hands. "She didn't want me in the hospital room. She kicked me out. No one's talking to me. I don't know—I don't know what's happening."

He's losing it, driven mad by worry and fear. He looks up and sees Poppy, as if noticing her for the first time, and I watch as he struggles to gain control over himself. "It's fine," he says to her. "It's going to be fine. These things happen."

Poppy nods and, letting go of my hand and reaching for his,

sits beside him. I sit down in the empty seat on his other side, Albert next to me, and the four of us wait in that blank space in silence, all of us trapped in our own thoughts.

I've managed to banish that ugly voice from my mind, and now all I'm left with is worry. Because despite everything I feel for Charlie, despite everything I think about Blair, he loves that baby. He's got to be hurting so much right now, and it kills me that there's nothing I can do to help.

Finally, a doctor comes out into the waiting room. He's young, probably just out of school. Which may explain why he looks so nervous as Charlie springs up from his chair.

"How is she?" Charlie all but shouts.

"She's fine," the doctor says, but there's a strangeness in his voice. A tone that tells me something's off.

"And the baby?"

The doctor hesitates, as if trying to choose his words carefully. Then, instead of speaking at all, he just shakes his head.

Charlie's expression falls, utterly and completely, and my heart breaks. I want to pull him to me, to wipe that mess of hurt and pain off his face, but I can't move. And he doesn't need me right now. He needs her.

"What happens now?" he asks, sounding so lost despite the courage in his tone. "What does Blair need?"

The doctor shakes his head again, clicking his pen open

and closed in an erratic rhythm. "She's perfectly fine. She can go home now."

"Already? She has to be in shock, or pain, or . . . something."

"She's just fine," the doctor repeats. "You can take her home now. In fact, that would be best for her. If you'll excuse me," he says, giving us an apologetic look before moving past us to the nurses' station, where he starts filling out some paperwork.

Charlie watches the doctor for a few seconds, stunned, before he walks back to find Blair. I put my hand on Poppy's shoulder, and she pivots to hug me tightly. She's crying, and I feel my T-shirt soak up her tears. "What about the nursery?" she asks in sobbing gasps.

I bend down to look her in the eye. "Hey, it's going to be okay. Charlie—and Blair—we'll get through it, okay?"

I hug her close to me again, and she nods. "I'm just so tired of having to get through things," she whispers, and I have to blink back sudden tears.

Because Poppy's lost yet another member of her family. And there's nothing I can do to help her either.

Albert drives all of us home. I'm up front with him; Poppy, Charlie, and a very quiet Blair sit in the back. Charlie is in the middle, a protective arm around his fiancée. No one talks. No one wants to disturb the grief-filled silence that's settled all around us.

When we get back to the castle, Charlie helps Blair out, handling her gingerly. She looks pale in the early morning mist, and there are dark circles under her eyes. She leans heavily on Charlie's arm but doesn't look at any of us. The two of them make their way up the stairs, leaving us below.

I don't remember that it's Christmas until my eyes land on the evergreen garlands lining the stair railing.

Mabel marches up to Poppy and me, her hair neat as always under her white cap, her eyes flashing with anger. "Poppy, go to bed at once," she says, then turns to me. "You've exhausted and upset her, taking her out to the hospital in the middle of the night," she spits.

"It was a family emergency," I say, staring her down. "She needed to be there, whether you understand that or not."

She lifts her chin defiantly at me. "If you think I don't care about this family, you're sorely mistaken."

"Poppy, go on upstairs," I say sweetly, ignoring Mabel. "Get some sleep."

Hardly able to keep her eyes open, Poppy nods and trudges up the stairs. I turn back to Mabel. "Enough," I say, my voice full of warning.

Mabel huffs, but retreats back toward the kitchen.

Soon I'm back in my room, trying to sleep that awful night and the morning away.

CHAPTER 24

Over the next week, it's as if a shroud has fallen over the house. Poppy can hardly muster a smile. Even the chipper kitchen girls seem less chatty.

The door to Charlie's office is closed most mornings, but I think he's really spending most of his time in his room with Blair, who hasn't left it since that night. Mabel sends all her meals up there.

I can't imagine the pain of losing a child that you wanted so much, so I don't blame Blair for becoming a recluse. But now I can't stop thinking about that doctor. Something about his behavior was so strange. Was he just nervous because he had to tell a father that his child didn't survive?

Or was I right all along to doubt Blair's pregnancy? And was the doctor somehow involved in the lie? Charlie had just proposed to her. If she were going to pretend to lose the baby, of course she would have chosen that moment to do it.

She couldn't be that cruel, could she? Then again . . . would Charlie have taken her back if she hadn't been pregnant?

And what will he do now that she's lost the baby, the only thing that was tying him to her?

But of course I know exactly what he'll do. He'll marry her, just like he promised he would. He wouldn't abandon her, especially not when she's just lost a baby. Their baby. Like I told him, he's not the type of guy who hurts people. Not on purpose, anyway.

He doesn't mean to hurt me, but he does anyway.

The garbled whispers are back, keeping me awake, with my head full of thoughts. The circles beneath my eyes grow darker, and most days I feel like I'm drifting through the house in a dream. Nothing feels quite real anymore.

Then, on New Year's Eve day, after a week of mourning, Blair reappears at breakfast, sitting at the head of the table in a peach silk dressing gown when I come in. I stop in the doorway, watching her as she butters her toast and smiles at Poppy. Poppy, clearly overjoyed to have her back, chatters about all the latest gossip from her friends and the jump she and Copperfield managed yesterday.

"Hi," I say to Blair, and she finally looks at me. I mean to sound welcoming and kind, but I can tell my voice comes out guarded.

She smiles blandly at me as I take my seat next to Poppy. "Good morning," she says, then turns away. "Oh, Charles, I forgot to tell you: Lady Thorne called me yesterday. It's almost time for the charity ball for the children's hospital in Beasley. She wanted to confirm some details. I'd almost forgotten that we'd agreed to host it, but the invitations are out. So I told her everything would be arranged."

"Are you sure you're up for that?" Charlie asks softly.

"Of course," she says lightly, looking down at her plate. "It's for charity. Besides, Mabs will help me, like she always helped your mum."

She still doesn't look at him, so she doesn't see him flinch at her casual mention of his mother. Suddenly, I want to hit her, despite everything she's just been through, and my hands shake with that wanting as I try to butter my own toast. Maybe I'm not a good person, or maybe just not when it comes to her. Not when it comes to protecting *him*.

"And anyway, this house could use a party," Blair continues, still oblivious.

"Could I come?" Poppy asks, looking hopefully at Charlie.

He nods hesitantly. And then his eyes shift to mine for the first time since I entered the room. I want to tell him everything that I'm thinking, but mostly that I'm so sorry. He must see it in my eyes, because he nods slightly and then turns his attention back to Blair as she starts listing everything they'll need to do to prepare for the ball.

That afternoon, I need fresh air and space to think. Even though it's bitterly cold outside, I pull on my thickest coat and head out for a walk.

I'm nearly to the hedge maze when I run into Charlie coming the opposite way, back to the house. "Hi," I say uncertainly. He's wearing a heavy gray coat and a green scarf that makes his eyes almost achingly bright. It's hard to look directly at him.

"Hello," he says. "Are you out on a walk?"

I nod.

"It's a good day for it," he says, sounding almost as awkward and stilted as I feel. "It's warmer in the woods than out in the open."

I can't help but shiver as I look over his shoulder at the line of tall fir trees beyond. I'm certainly not going back into the woods again. Even though I know it was just my imagination running on overdrive that day of the storm, I don't need to face that darkness again.

I look back at him, but he's looking past me, and I turn to see what's caught his eye. Mabel is standing at the back door of the castle, looking out at us. Even though I can't see them clearly, I can feel her dark eyes watching us, burning into us, like those of a wraith.

Charlie grabs my hand, and I whip my head back around to face him. He pulls me into the hedge maze, his hand as hot as fire on mine. What is he doing?

"Have you done the maze before?" he asks, dropping my hand as soon as we're hidden from view. His tone is casual, as if nothing happened. Is he not going to mention why we just ran from Mabel? Why he acted as though she caught us doing something wrong?

"No," I say faintly. He's stopped, and I realize after a long moment that he wants me to pick which way to go. I go left.

"Have you made any New Year's resolutions?" he asks as he follows me.

I can hardly focus on the maze, as I randomly turn at intersections. "I don't usually make resolutions."

"Why not?" he asks, sounding genuinely curious.

Because there's only one resolution that really matters to me every year: Don't inherit my mother's disease. And since I can't control that, resolutions seem pointless.

But I can't tell him that, so instead I say, "Because most New Year's resolutions end up abandoned by the end of January. Why put all that pressure on yourself?"

We've come to a dead end, and I stop, turning toward him. "I'm sorry," I say, looking up at him. "I'm so sorry about the baby."

"Thank you," he says softly.

I should keep walking past him. Pretend to find my way through this maze alone. But I can't move.

Until he steps closer to me, and I step backward, pressing myself into the dense row of hedges at my back.

He stops, and I don't think either of us is breathing.

"What are your New Year's resolutions?" I choke out.

His eyes trace a path from the top of my forehead down to my lips. "To stop wanting things I know I can't have," he whispers.

My lips part in surprise, but before I can say anything, he turns and walks off, leaving me lost in this stupid maze. My knees are shaking too much to follow, and I sink down to the ground, trying to catch my breath.

He's engaged, I tell myself. *He's just lost a baby.*

I don't care. I don't think I can ever stop wanting him.

I have to try. Or I might lose control of my mind. I can't torment myself like this.

I just don't know how to stop it.

I go to bed early, before midnight marks the New Year, sleeping as soundly as I can in this house. I'm up hours before the sun the next morning, determined to eat breakfast before anyone comes down to the dining room. I'm just passing through the kitchen when I see Mabel, hurrying around with a bushel of burning tree branches under her arm.

"What are you doing?" I call out in alarm. The whole downstairs is filling with smoke, choking with its sticky sweet scent, and I cough violently in its wake. Is she trying to set the house on fire?

I'm looking around for water and am reaching for a pitcher on the counter when she stops me, sneering. She looks me up and down, and I wonder if she's going to mention anything about yesterday, when she saw Charlie and me steal away.

"It's the *saining*," she says finally. "A New Year's tradition to cleanse the house. You fill the house with smoke from the juniper branches and then throw open the windows to let the fresh New Year air in." She frowns down at the branches. "I didn't do it last year, and look what happened. We need all the luck we can get."

She looks up, as if suddenly remembering to whom she's talking, and scowls before pushing past me.

I can't help but remember the time I watched her sink down into the darkness of the room below the tower, the room with the tree. Does she truly believe in this magic? That this ritual actually exerts power over this house?

What secrets does this strange woman hold?

CHAPTER 25

Next Friday, it's the day of the ball, and the whole house-hold is scurrying around like it's preparing for an invasion.

Poppy is supposed to be working on a paper for English class, due after the holiday break ends this coming Monday. The assignment is to write about her favorite book, so of course she chose *David Copperfield*. But she can barely get through a single sentence without looking up and asking me if I think the dress she picked out will be pretty enough, if there will be anyone her age at the ball, what is she supposed to do if a boy asks her to dance?

I finally leave the room, hoping that without me to distract her, she can get at least a little work done, but I don't have much confidence.

I can't blame her. I'm not even going to the ball, but I

can't focus on anything else either. I can't stop thinking about Charlie, how he'll be dancing with Blair all night. He'll hold her close and kiss her in front of everybody and be the loving, devoted husband-to-be that she wants him to be.

When guests start arriving, I shut myself up in my room with a stack of books from the library, hoping at least one of them will be able to distract me. But before I can choose one, there's a frantic knock on my door.

I open it to find Poppy, standing there in her pale blue dress, her blond hair expertly curled and pinned up by Blair's stylist.

"You have to come with me!" she insists before I can ask her what she's doing here.

"What?" I say with a laugh. She stares at me, her eyebrows raised, and my laughter fades. "Wait, you can't be serious?"

"I don't know anyone down there, and Charlie and Blair are going to be too busy to pay attention to me." She pauses. "Please?"

"Poppy, I don't know anyone down there either. And I'm an employee here—I'm not invited." No one ever told me not to come, of course, but Blair certainly didn't invite me either. Regardless, it's pretty clear that I'm not wanted down there.

By anyone except the very stubborn eleven-year-old girl

standing in front of me. "*I'm* inviting you," she declares, shrugging. "Please?"

She looks so nervous and worried that I know I won't be able to stand my ground on this one. I can just pop down with her and then disappear when she inevitably finds someone else to chat with. "Fine," I say. I run a hand through my hair to smooth it, and gesture her out the door.

"You can't go like that," she says, her expression a cross between concerned and bewildered.

I look down at my gray pants and forest green sweater. Right.

"You need a dress," she says, rolling her eyes dramatically, perfectly playing the role of a typical tween. She opens the door to my closet and starts rummaging through it until she finds what she's looking for.

"This'll do," she says triumphantly as she pulls out the dark plum cocktail dress I bought in town that day with her and Blair. "Put it on, quick!" she says, hurrying out the door and closing it behind her.

The thought of putting on this dress and walking down among all those people, as if I belong, makes a fluttering feeling rise in my stomach. Still, I pull the dress over my head and fumble with the zipper. I look at my face for a moment in the mirror, and before I can change my mind, I swipe on some blush and a bit of lip gloss. And then, because I'm getting into the spirit of things, I twist my hair back into a quick chignon, securing it with an army of bobby pins. It looks a little less messy that way, at least. I slip on the low black heels Poppy insisted I buy on that same shopping trip and try not to stumble as I fling the door open.

"Much better," Poppy says, and I almost roll my eyes at her to see how she likes it. Instead I just bite the inside of my lip and follow her down the stairs to the second floor, where we wind our way out of the medieval part of the castle and into the wing built in the seventeenth century, when the Moffats decided they needed a grand ballroom.

A grand ballroom that is currently packed with strangers. No wonder Poppy didn't feel like facing this crowd alone.

All the women are in long, formal dresses, some with poufy ball-gown skirts. I'm definitely underdressed in my knee-length skirt, but I there's nothing I can do about it now, so I straighten my shoulders and move forward into the room. *I'm just here for Poppy*, I tell myself over and over. I shouldn't care what anyone else thinks of me. But as soon as I enter the room, I start looking for Charlie. Will he see me? What will he think?

But instead of Charlie, I spot Blair. She's holding court near the center of the room, just before the dance floor. She's wearing a voluminous, billowing gray ball gown, the color of an approaching storm, which I only get peeks at through the crowd.

And then I see Charlie, standing right beside her.

I watch as his eyes go wide and his lips part just slightly as he notices me and takes me in. I exhale a shaky breath through my teeth and try to break my gaze from his, but find that I can't. And I can't disguise the pain—the aching need—that courses through me. He sees it all, as he always does.

The crowd closes in around us, and we're hidden from one another again. I turn to Poppy, who's now happily talking and laughing with a girl who looks to be around her age. "I'm just going to step outside for some air," I say, and Poppy smiles and nods, now apparently quite content to be left alone.

I push myself as politely as possible through the swell of people blocking the way until I've almost made it back to the entrance, but before I get there, I feel a hand on my arm. I know that it's him before I even turn around.

"Dance with me," Charlie says.

I want to refuse. I want to slip my arm from his and escape out that doorway and out of this castle into the cold winter air I need so desperately, but I can't think straight with his hand on me, when he's wearing a tuxedo that's tailored so perfectly. So I let him lead me out to the dance floor. The band is playing

Waltz no. 2 by Shostakovich, an epic and beautiful piece. The couples around us are a mix of old and young, some of them dancing the proper steps, some of them just swaying together to the rhythm. I try to focus on them as Charlie puts his hand on the small of my back, drawing me in until my body is pressed against his. My breath comes in shallow gasps. We're much too close, I know it. I look at the other couples, trying to tell if they're pressed as closely together as we are, while Charlie takes my arms and wraps them around his shoulders. Suddenly my focus is on him alone. We start moving together to the music, and I close my eyes. One of his hands stays pressed to the small of my back, and the other slides up into my hair, scattering a few of my bobby pins until my curls threaten to break free. My chest is pressed to his, so close that I can feel his heartbeat, racing just as fast as mine. I cling to his shoulders, pressing him even tighter to me.

Why doesn't he seem to care who sees us? Where is Blair? Shouldn't she be running over here to separate us? Why hasn't everyone else around us stopped to stare?

"Fiona," he says quietly. "Look at me."

I take a breath and lift my chin. I know my eyes are full of my desperation, and his gaze is only reflecting all of that right back at me.

There's no denying it now, not after his confession on New

Year's Eve, and now this. He wants me just as much as I want him. I should feel elated, but it's as if my body doesn't have the room right now for any more emotion.

We sway together for a few moments, our eyes locked. With every breath, I'm fighting the urge to press my lips to his. I can't kiss him. Not here in the middle of the ballroom.

Then his eyes drop to my lips, and I have to tighten my grasp on him to keep from stumbling on my shaky legs. We're torturing each other.

I bury my head in the crook of his neck, nuzzling there. At least now we can't see each other—or each other's lips. I breathe into his neck, now feeling as if I might cry. Because this is it. This is the one moment we'll have, I know it. It has to be. After this song, he will go back to Blair, and I will go back to being just a governess. And then all I'll be left with is the memory of how it feels to be pressed here against him, to feel his heartbeat, to know how perfectly my body fits into his.

I press my lips to his neck again, just above his collar. One kiss. One soft kiss. I feel his fingers tighten on my back, on my neck, and I know he felt it.

The music fades, and I stumble to a stop.

It's over. I have to let it be over.

I push my hands against his chest to break free of his embrace, and, before he can react, I am threading a path through the crowd until I'm finally out in the corridor again. I find an out-of-the-way spot where I can catch my breath before retreating back to my room.

Before I can, though, I look up to see a tall figure right in front of me. Gareth, standing in my way.

"Are you okay?" he asks.

"Yeah," I say quickly, wondering if he saw me dancing with Charlie. "Just not really my type of crowd."

"Fair enough," he says. He's dressed up, I realize. Not in a tux, but in a button-down shirt and slacks, a huge change from the rough flannel shirts and jeans that he usually wears.

He catches me looking curiously at his clothes and laughs. "Mabel asked all the staff to dress up for the night. The whole house has to look the part, apparently." He smiles at me again, more gently this time. "You look nice."

"I'm not really dressed up enough for *this*, though," I say, looking down at my dress and gesturing toward the ballroom. Mabel didn't tell me to dress up, probably assuming—or maybe hoping—that I would stay up in my room all night.

"Fee," he says, stepping closer. His easy, flirtatious tone is back, and he bends down to whisper in my ear, "You're the only girl worth looking at in this entire party."

I shiver. It feels wrong to hear someone else's whisper. I'm just about to step back, to end this stupid flirtation, when I see a figure approaching us out of the corner of my eye.

Gareth must hear the catch in my breath, because he turns around to see Charlie there.

"Gareth," Charlie says with a nod. His voice is polite enough, but then his eyes fasten on mine with a flash of intensity.

I watch Gareth look from Charlie to me and back again, and his entire body tenses up. "I should go check on the horses," he says, his voice low, almost angry-sounding. I can't even look at him before he walks away.

I can't look at anything but Charlie.

My lips are still buzzing, as if I can still feel the warm skin of his neck on them.

"Gareth was just joking around with me," I say, though I don't know why I'm explaining myself.

"Yeah, well, I don't like his kind of joking." He steps closer to me. "I don't like him near you." His words are harsh, but his tone is full of hurt.

I step closer to him, anger making me bold. There's no space between us now. "Why?" I ask, challenging him.

He clenches his jaw. "Let's go to the library," he says sternly. "You need to play me a song."

"What?" I ask, confused. "Why?"

He leans down so that his lips are right next to my ear as he whispers, "Because I want to tell you a secret."

"No," I say, drawing back, suddenly near tears. Angry tears— not the tears of pain that I've been crying these last few days. "No more games. You want to tell me something, then just tell me."

"Fiona." He says my name like it's a prayer.

I close my eyes. Because if I look at him for one more second, I'm either going to slap him or throw my arms around him and press my lips to his, and there are too many people in this corridor for me to do either of those things.

The feel of his hand on my cheek shocks my eyes back open. He says my name again, and this time it sounds like salvation on his lips. And then he's leaning toward me, his mouth nearing mine, and I'm pushing myself up on my tiptoes to meet him, and—

"What are you doing out here?" Blair's voice cuts between us like a blade.

I watch in horror as Charlie steps back from me, a mask of bored nonchalance falling over his face. "Nothing," he says, turning toward her.

She smiles at him. Smiles, as if she didn't see us mere inches from each other, about to collide. I fall back onto my heels, my shoes clacking on the stone floor.

"Well, come on, then," she says to him. "There are about a

million people waiting to meet you." She holds out her hand, and, after only a moment of hesitation, he takes it, linking his arm with hers and leading her back to the ballroom.

"Have a good night, Fee," she calls over her shoulder, her face flashing with a grotesque smile, a pointed, victorious grin, before she glides on with her fiancé securely in place.

He doesn't look back at me. Not even once.

I stare at the space where he just was, feeling like I've been drenched by a bucket of ice water.

I'm done. I'm so done. I'm not staying here anymore. I won't stand by and watch him choose her again and again. I won't let him get my hopes up anymore, only to dash them right back down again, even if he claims he doesn't mean to. Even if he's trying not to. I can't bear it anymore.

The guests in the corridor are watching me as angry tears finally start falling down my cheeks. I don't even care. Those people can't make me feel any more foolish than I already feel.

I turn away from them, toward the wall, and realize that I've been standing under the portrait of the Grey Lady. The goddamned Grey Lady.

I feel like I'm going to throw up. I spin back around and run for the staircase as best as I can in these stupid heels, the corridor now silent as everyone watches me run away like a madwoman.

I run through the maze of rooms to the servants' staircase, where I take the spinning steps two at a time, tripping and pitching forward with every footfall. I don't care. I just need to get up to my room, pack my things, and get the hell out of this place before my heart can break any more. Before my *mind* can break any more.

I've finally reached the top and am rounding the corner into the servants' hallway when I hear it.

Her laugh. My mother's laugh. She's here.

CHAPTER 26

I stand, frozen, in the empty hallway, her laughter right in my ear. That full-throated laugh, the one that poured out of her whenever she was overwhelmed with joy. I can almost see her, her head thrown back, her eyes wide with delight.

And then it stops, and everything is so silent.

"NO!" I wail, stepping forward, straining to hear her again. The best music in the world. But it's gone.

Keira pops her head around the corner, startling me. "Fee?" she says, looking around the hall, clearly surprised to find me alone. "Are you okay?"

"She was just here," I say, and the sound of my voice—so high-pitched and shaky—makes me cringe. There are new tears streaking down my cheeks, and I do my best to wipe them away. I can't imagine what a mess I must look like.

How unhinged.

"Do you want me to get somebody?" Keira asks. She's backed away from me the tiniest bit, and I don't blame her.

"No," I say, because there's no one to get. "No, I'm fine. I was just . . . startled, that's all."

She nods. "Okay," she says quietly before backing away completely, until she disappears into her room.

I wipe away the tears and focus on breathing deeply and slowly, in and out.

That laughter couldn't have been in my head; it was too real. I reach out and trail my fingers along the corridor walls, as if searching for some type of tape recorder that I know isn't there. Sure enough, there's nothing, just blank white walls and silence.

But I know the laughter was real and that Blair had something to do with it.

Because she's trying to make me think I'm going crazy.

Of course. It all makes sense now. She's the one behind those strange noises at night. She's kept me sleepless, exhausted, so that I feel like I'm just drifting through the day. She's trying to drive me insane so that she can drive me away. Maybe she even figured out what really happened to my mom and is using that—my family genes—against me.

I hide myself in my room. It doesn't matter what I've figured out. She's already won. I pull out my small duffel bag and start packing it with my old clothes, the ones I brought with me from Mulespur. I don't want to take anything that isn't truly mine, which includes everything I brought back from that shopping trip. I don't want anything from this house. An image of Charlie's face floats into my mind, but I shove it away.

I finish packing and peek out into the hall, stupidly hopeful and foolishly terrified that I'll find my mother out there, waiting for me. But the hallway is clear. I throw my bag over my shoulder and head downstairs.

There are a few guests lingering in the entrance hall, including one couple enthusiastically making out in a corner, only half-hidden by the suit of armor. I duck my head and scurry out to Albert's apartment above the garage unnoticed.

I bang loudly on the door, and I hear him mutter and trip over something before he answers it. "What is it?" he asks. "What's wrong?" His white hair is a mess, standing straight up on one end. He's wearing striped pajamas, and I'm so startled to see him out of his uniform that I stare at him for a few extended moments before remembering what I'm doing here.

"Can you take me to the train station?" I ask him, doing my best to sound measured and rational.

"It's ten o'clock at night!" he says, looking down at my duffel bag and then back up at me. "There aren't any more trains tonight. Fee, what's going on?"

"Nothing," I say. "Nothing important. Poppy's fine. I just have to go home."

"Have you told Charlie?" he asks, and his voice is so kind that I almost start crying again.

I have to bite the inside of my lip before I answer. "No."

He puts his hand on my shoulder. "Why don't you sleep on it? You can't go anywhere tonight anyway. If you wake up tomorrow and still want to leave, you can tell Mabel at breakfast, and we'll arrange to get you on the next train and flight home. Okay?"

I stare over my shoulder, out at the dark road winding away from us. I want so much to be free of this place.

He must see that want in my eyes, because he adds, "You don't want to leave without saying goodbye to Poppy, do you? That would make your absence even harder on the lass."

I think of Poppy, and the guilt crushes down on top of me. "Of course not," I whisper.

"Why don't you go to the kitchen and make some of that tea you like," he says softly. "Then you can get some sleep. Things will look better in the morning."

I nod, but in that instant, I feel a weight pressing down on me, making my entire body heavy. Something shackling me to this place. I cannot escape.

"Sorry for waking you," I mumble to Albert, turning to walk down his spiral staircase.

He says nothing, just watches me go as I hurry back to the house and to the kitchen for my tea.

I can make it one more night. That's all it is, I tell myself. One night. For Poppy.

CHAPTER 27

I feel the sunlight streaming into my room as I slowly struggle to pull myself out of a deep sleep. My limbs and eyelids feel heavy—too heavy. Judging by the intensity of the sun, I must have overslept by several hours. Why didn't anyone wake me? The whole staff must be busy recovering from the ball last night.

I groan, finally processing the pounding in my head. *What happened last night?*

I open my eyes a crack to let them adjust to the sunlight and stretch my legs under the sheets, trying to bring some life into them.

As I wake up bit by bit, I feel something cool in my hand. Cool and sticky. I lift my hand up, and then I'm screaming.

It's a knife. I'm holding a knife, and there's blood all over it. And there's blood on my sheets, too, everywhere. I drop the knife and draw my knees up, pulling myself into a crouch. I run my hands over my body, searching for the source of the blood. But there's nothing, not even a scratch. The blood staining my hand must have come from the knife.

Oh my God, what have I done?

My screams have dampened down to a whimper. All the servants must be up already, because no one has come to my door. No one can hear me.

I shove the knife underneath my mattress and rip the blood-stained sheets off the bed, stuffing them into my closet. That way, at least, the sight of them can't sicken me anymore. Then I grab a towel and hurry to the shower at the end of the hall. I need to get clean. Once I'm clean, I'll be able to think. I turn the hot water on full blast and watch as the red, red blood swirls down the drain. I scrub my hands and arms hard, erasing all traces of it. I'm sobbing now, my tears mixing with the hot water and the blood on the shower floor.

When my skin is finally scrubbed raw, I jump out of the shower and dry off, checking to make sure there's no trace of blood left on me. I have to figure out whose blood was on that knife. I have to find out what happened.

Oh, God, who did I hurt?

Back in my room, I throw on some clothes and run out again into the empty hallway and down the stairs. The kitchen and dining room are empty, and all the breakfast things have been cleared.

I throw open the front door and see Alice approaching.

"Where have you been all morning?" she asks, breaking the silence between us for the first time in weeks. I shouldn't have expected anything about this day would be normal.

"Where is everyone?" I ask her, my voice rushed and frantic as I blink at her in the late morning sunshine. Nothing fits today—it hasn't been sunny here for weeks.

"Out at the stables," Alice says, pulling me from my strange thoughts. "You better get out there."

"Why? What happened?" Even my tongue feels heavy, and the words come out slow and slurred.

She shakes her head, her lips curling in disgust. At what, I can't tell. "Just get out there. Poppy needs you."

Poppy. I start running.

My hair is still wet, and it freezes in the startlingly cold air as I run toward a crowd of household staff standing outside the barn. Two of the kitchen girls hold each other and sob. Mabel stands apart from the group, watching me approach, and says nothing as I fly past her into the barn.

Poppy sits outside of Copperfield's stall, bent over something massive I can't clearly see, practically lying on it. My heart stops as I watch her completely still form, but then she moves, running her hand down the thing in front of her, and I find that I'm gasping for air. *She's alive.* It wasn't her blood on that knife. She's okay, right here in front of me, healthy.

Before I can feel real relief, I sense someone approach and stand beside me. Gareth. His hand rests on my arm, warm and comforting. I look up at him. "I'm sorry," he murmurs. "I don't know what happened."

His words don't make sense until I turn again to Poppy and take in the whole scene.

Charlie sits beside Poppy, his arm around her shoulders, watching me as I slip from Gareth's hand and approach them. Poppy is keening, low moans and sobs pouring out of her, the sound of heartbreak, of unimaginable pain. I step forward again, and something squelches under my feet. The hay beneath me is soaked with blood. A wave of nausea hits me.

I swallow and look back up at the mound beneath Poppy's fingertips. The bristly, rust-colored hair. The long, silky mane. The elegant snout with those fiery brown eyes, now wide open and dull.

It's Copperfield. Copperfield has been killed.

Did I . . . did I *kill* Copperfield? How the hell . . . and if I *did*, why don't I remember any of it?

I sink down next to Poppy, my knees giving way underneath me.

Charlie is still watching me, and I raise my eyes slowly to his.

"She found him this morning," he says softly.

"What happened?" I ask, my voice scratchy as it comes out of my throat.

He nods down at the horse, as if it should be obvious. But I can't look back down at the red mess beneath me, the one open and staring eye. "It looks like he was stabbed," he whispers. "Gareth thinks it happened sometime last night, by the looks of him."

"There's a knife missing from the kitchen," Mabel says from behind me. "A butcher's knife."

I blink, dizzy.

"Who would have done something like this?" Blair asks, and it's only then that I realize she's there, sitting on the other side of Charlie. She's staring right at me. "What kind of monster would kill a child's horse?"

"Someone with a lot of determination," Albert says, making me jump. "Whoever did this stuck a knife right into his neck and wrenched it. Takes a lot of strength to do that."

I look back at him, my eyes wide. I think I'm going to be sick.

"Where have *you* been?" Blair turns to me and asks. "We haven't seen you all morning."

"I—I overslept," I say, trying to stop the bile rising up my throat.

Charlie's looking at me now, his brow furrowed. Concerned about me? Or suspicious?

I spin on my heel and run for the door, making it just outside the barn before I start dry heaving into the bushes.

Did I . . . did I actually get up in the middle of the night and . . . and kill Copperfield?

There's a hand on my back, and I look up to see Gareth standing over me. I straighten my shoulders, but his hand stays on the small of my back, anchoring me. "I'm sorry," I say. "I just . . ."

"I know," he says softly. "It's hard to take."

"Did you hear anything last night?"

He nods. "I heard Copperfield—he was whinnying like hell."

I close my eyes, shuddering.

"I hurried over here, saw someone running out of the barn."

"Who?" I ask, opening my eyes.

He shakes his head. "I don't know. Didn't get a good look. But I think it was a woman. She was running into the castle, and then I came straight here and found Copperfield thrashing on the ground. So I shot him in the head."

"You *what*?" I ask.

"Couldn't leave him in pain like that," he says, surprised. "It was the only thing I could do for him."

I rub my forehead, which only seems to inflame the headache I woke up with. "Right. Of course," I say.

"Fee," Gareth says, stepping even closer to me, his hand warm on my back. "Are you sure you're okay?"

I've no idea how to answer him, but before I can try to scramble for something to say, Charlie's voice hits me. "Fiona?"

He's standing in the barn's threshold, watching us, a stony look stamped on his face. Gareth pulls his hand away from my back, but not before I see Charlie notice it.

Charlie looks back up at me, his expression unreadable. "We need to get Poppy out of here," he says.

I nod, taking a deep breath before walking past him and back inside the barn. I crouch down beside Poppy, who is still making that horrible keening sound that I don't think I'll ever be able to forget.

I place my hands on her shoulders. "Come on, Poppy," I whisper. "We need to get you home and into a nice hot shower."

She doesn't seem to hear me, and she won't meet my eyes.

"Poppy?" Charlie says from behind me.

She doesn't move.

Charlie taps my shoulder, and I move out of his way. He leans down and wraps his arms around Poppy, lifting her up. She slings her arms around his neck as he puts his arm under her knees and carries her out of the barn. "Take care of him," he tells Gareth, his voice sharp, nodding back at the horse.

I trail after Charlie and Poppy and start the shower for her. She doesn't let go of Charlie until he places her on her feet gently, clothes and all, under the hot water.

For a few moments, she just stands there, letting the water pour over her. Just like I did this morning.

I shiver. We both had to wash Copperfield's blood off today.

She lifts up her left arm so she can watch the dark red blood stream off it. I grab her other hand and hold on, so that she knows someone is there with her.

She steps out from under the stream of water and looks at me.

"He was my horse," she says, her voice broken.

"I know."

"I loved him so much."

"I know."

"Why does everyone keep leaving me?" She begins sobbing: huge, choking sobs that shake her entire frame. She sinks to the floor and wraps her arms around her knees, the water stream-ing over her and mixing with her tears.

There's nothing to say, so I just sit there with her, outside the shower, holding her hand tight, and wait for her sobs to subside. Charlie sits beside me, his head in his hands.

Suddenly, he reaches over and gently takes my free hand in his. His fingers wrap securely over mine, the heat from them sparking a flame that shoots right up my arm, spreading through my entire body.

I told myself I was done. I should be gone by now, on a plane back to Texas. But right now I can't imagine being any-where else. I squeeze his hand for a moment, just once.

He squeezes back. And we sit there on the floor, the three of us, broken and shocked. But together. A family.

CHAPTER 28

An hour later, Poppy is in warm, dry clothes and back in bed for an early nap after an exhausting morning. I'll get her to eat something when she wakes up, but for now, I retreat to my spot on the windowsill in the library and pretend to read a book that I grab at random off the bookshelf.

There's no way I can leave now. Poppy's just been through a horrible trauma, and she needs safe, familiar faces around her. She doesn't need to deal with me leaving suddenly on top of everything else.

I leaf through the pages, but instead of the words in front of me, all I can see is the bloody knife in my hands, the pool of blood that I knelt in, the huge horse lying dead on the ground.

I woke up with every scrap of evidence in my hand, but . . . what if I wasn't the one who killed Copperfield? What if this was a trick, another move by Blair? Gareth said he saw a woman running out of the barn. What if it was Blair running back to the castle with the murder weapon so she could plant it on me?

My stomach turns. How could she be that twisted? To take that knife and plunge it into Copperfield's neck, just to scare me? What kind of demon would that make her?

I don't know what to think anymore. I'm glad I hid the knife under my mattress, though. Tonight, once it's dark, I'll sneak it out of the castle, maybe bury it in the woods somewhere.

And then, because he always finds me, Charlie is at the door.

"Is Poppy all right?" he asks.

"She's sound asleep."

He sighs, stepping farther into the room.

"I have to apologize for last night."

"Please," I whisper. "Don't." I know what he's going to say, and I know that I definitely don't want to hear it.

But he holds up his hand to stop me and says it anyway. "I'm sorry that I've been playing games with you. That I almost kissed you. I shouldn't have."

I close my eyes, pained. I should be a bit happy, I guess. At least I know I didn't imagine it. At least it actually happened.

But nothing about this moment is happy.

"I hate that I hurt you," he continues, and I can hear the

anguish in his voice. "I hate this entire situation. I hate trying to deny how I feel about you."

I hold my breath and wait for him to go on.

"I can't hurt Blair anymore. And I can't hurt *you* anymore. So I promise, from now on, I won't lead you on."

"You're choosing her," I say dully, finally opening my eyes. He's still so far away from me, but I can see his green eyes clearly, his strong jaw, his red-brown curls. All the features I love about the guy who will never be mine.

"I have to," he says.

Of course he does. He has to do the right thing, because he spent so many years of his life doing the wrong thing, and he wants more than anything to be a different guy.

I want to scream at him. I want to hit him and pull his hair and kick him and make him realize that this choice he's made is going to make us both miserable.

But deep down, I can't help but like him even more for making it.

"You're going to marry her."

Charlie clenches his jaw.

I hate that I asked him. I already know the answer, but I still don't want to hear it.

"Yes," he says softly.

I feel my heart fall right to the ground, and I wish that the floor would swallow me up. Because even though I've closed my eyes again, I can feel Charlie's gaze on me. And I know that he can sense every bit of pain and agony that this has caused.

It turns out that knowing the truth of something and hearing it out loud are two completely different things.

I know then, just as I've lost him completely, that I love him. I'm in love with him. And the world has never seemed so cruel.

I push myself off the window seat. "I should check on Poppy," I manage to whisper before walking out of the room as steadily as I can. I force myself to put one foot in front of the other until I reach the closest bathroom, where I sink to the floor and completely break down.

I tried so hard to ignore the fact that I had fallen for him. I wanted to believe that I could float above it all, that I'd be able to sit by and watch Blair and Charlie start a family together and my heart wouldn't break into a million little shards, puncturing my body like shattered glass from the inside out.

But I can't ignore it anymore. I love him. I love the way he looks at me like he can see every little secret inside me. I love the way he smiles, always with a bit of surprise, like he wasn't expecting to. I love the way he brightens the moment his sister enters the room.

It's why I couldn't leave, why I played the secret-for-a-song game, why, as much as I wanted to let him go, I couldn't.

I love him, every part of him. His past, who he is now, who he wants to be.

And he loves her. Or, at least, he's choosing her. And all that love that I have for him will shatter inside me, ruining me.

CHAPTER 29

When I've cried myself out, I run the bathroom sink and splash some cold water on my face. I wait until my eyes are a little less red and puffy before heading to the kitchen to search for some lunch—or dinner, rather, seeing as it's almost evening. The kitchen is much more crowded than I expected, filled with footmen and housemaids gathering in a huddle with the cook and her helpers. They turn to look at me when I enter, all of them pressing their lips tightly shut.

"What is it?" I ask. "What happened?"

After a brief silence, Alice speaks up. "They found the butcher knife. The one used to kill Copperfield."

The blood rushes from my head, leaving me dizzy and swaying. The knife. I forgot about the knife, bloody and incriminating underneath my mattress.

"Mabel wants to talk to you," Alice says as I grasp the countertop for support. "She's in her office."

I look around the room, taking a deep breath. No one has on a friendly face, and one of the maids regards me with an expression of open disgust.

I make my way through the kitchen and into the hallway that leads to Mabel's office. I know what will happen now. I'll be fired and sent away, maybe even to jail. I'll never see Poppy or Charlie again.

Tears form in my eyes, but I blink them away. I won't cry. I will not let myself cry, not in front of Mabel.

She's sitting behind her desk, going through a stack of receipts, when I enter. "Sit down," she says sharply when she sees me.

I sink into the hard, uncomfortable chair across from her.

"I'm sure you know by now that we conducted a search of all the rooms in the castle once we learned the knife was missing," she says. "I'm sure you also know that we found it in your room." She pauses, staring into my eyes. "Do you want to explain yourself?"

"I don't know what happened," I say in a rush. "I went to bed after the ball and I . . . I just woke up with it like that—with the knife in my hand, and it was so bloody, and I was horrified. I had no idea where it came from or whose blood was on it."

"You don't remember stealing the knife, going out to the stables, and stabbing the horse?" she asks. Her voice is cool, but there's a gleam in her eyes as she watches me. How excited she must be to have a reason to fire me. She blinks, and that gleam is gone.

I shake my head furiously. "I didn't. I couldn't have. I mean, I would never—I would never hurt Poppy like that. I would never hurt *Copperfield* like that!"

Her features become even more strained as she continues to stare at me. "It's troubling to me that you could commit such a heinous act and not even remember it."

"But I didn't! You have to believe me. I think . . ." I stop myself, trying to gather my thoughts before I dare come out in public with the crazy suspicion I've been harboring for hours now. "Mabel, I think Blair did it. I think she killed Copperfield and then made it look like *I* did it."

"*Blair?*" Mabel says, her eyebrows raised in shock. "You're trying to accuse *Blair* of killing the horse?"

"I know it sounds crazy—"

"Yes," she interrupts, and I flinch. "Yes, it *does* sound crazy. You're accusing a poor girl, who is still recovering from a horrible miscarriage, of murdering a child's beloved horse and then planting the knife in your room to frame you? Who on earth do you think you are, lass?"

Of course she doesn't believe me. No one would ever believe a story like that. I don't know how to make any of this make sense, so I keep my lips pressed together.

I take one twisted moment to appreciate how well Blair has played this game. She has spent every moment in this castle making herself so sympathetic and beloved that everything I could say to contradict that impression makes me sound insane.

She's won.

"I think I've heard enough. We need to send you someplace where they can take care of you. Give you the help you need," Mabel says.

"What?" I say. It takes me a few moments to interpret her words. "You want to send me to—what, a hospital? Why not just fire me, send me home?"

She stands and clasps her hands in front of her. "I think you need help. I do care about my staff, after all. There's a very good facility in Twicken, in the Borders. It's the best in the country for people like you."

She's talking about a mental hospital. She wants me to go to some *asylum*, where they'll diagnose me with schizophrenia and lock me up forever.

"You can just fire me," I say. "I'll go, no arguments, no fuss. But I won't let you put me in some asylum."

She twists her lips into a grimace and nods, as if she was

expecting me to respond this way. "Very well. If you refuse to go, then we'll have to press charges. You just murdered a giant *horse*, for heaven's sake. You're too dangerous to be let free. And if you're not . . . in need of some psychiatric help, then you have nothing to fear from a doctor's evaluation. It's your only option."

I stand and back up into the doorway. "I won't go. You can't make me."

She stands up, too, glowering at me. "Fine. Refuse to come quietly. We have plenty of evidence to make a very convincing court case." Her words are full of warning, just daring me to defy her.

I shake my head. "I won't go." I inch further into the hallway, ready to run, but instead I back up right into someone's arms.

I spin around, terrified that whoever's holding me has orders to drag me to the asylum whether I agree to it or not. But instead I see Charlie. I sag into him with relief, but then he lets go of my shoulders, focusing a powerful glare at Mabel.

"What's going on? Someone told me you've accused Fiona of killing Copperfield."

Mabel straightens her spine. "We found the missing knife in her room, under her mattress. Covered in the horse's blood."

Charlie looks at me, wary.

"I didn't do it," I assure him. I tell him how I woke up with the knife in my hand, how I'm not even strong enough to injure a horse so big, how there's no way I could have committed such a horrible crime and then not remembered it.

"She says Blair did it," Mabel interjects before I can finish convincing him that I'm not crazy.

"You think Blair stabbed Copperfield?" he asks, confusion in his eyes and voice.

"I don't—I don't know who did it," I say, stumbling over my words. I realize then how dangerous it was for me to confess my suspicions to Mabel.

"She went on and on about how Blair is trying to frame her," Mabel says.

"Is that true?" Charlie asks, looking down at me.

"Gareth said he saw a woman running out of the stables last night," I say, fumbling for words. "I don't—I mean, it's possible that Blair—"

"Why would she hurt Copperfield?" Charlie asks. I can hardly hear him. I can barely concentrate on anything except the way he's looking at me, with confusion and . . . pity. Like I really am crazy and he's only realizing it now.

I can't bear for him to look at me like that, so I hide my head in my hands. "I don't know. I don't—I'm sorry. I just know that I didn't do it."

Mabel whispers something to Charlie. All I hear is the word

"hospital," and I just keep my face hidden, my eyes closed, as if it'll make all this disappear.

Maybe they're right. Maybe I really am crazy. I woke up this morning with a headache and no memory. Was that some kind of aftereffect of a psychotic episode?

It doesn't make any sense, but nothing about going crazy ever does.

My only hope—the only light that I can hold on to—is that Blair really is the one to blame. Now it's not just me she's trying to convince—she's got the whole castle thinking I'm crazy, so they'll push me out of the house and away from Charlie.

I sit back down on Mabel's uncomfortable guest chair, and Charlie kneels in front of me. "Fee?" he says softly.

So I'm Fee now to him. No longer Fiona. I feel the sting of my nickname as if it were a knife stabbed into my neck.

He tugs at my arm, wants me to uncover my face and look at him, but I can't. "Fee, I'm worried about you," he murmurs. "I think maybe it would be a good idea for you to talk to a doctor. Just talk. Nothing permanent. What do you think?"

There's no going back. He thinks I'm crazy now. No matter what the doctors say, he won't ever see me as anything else.

I'm numb as I finally uncover my face and meet his concerned gaze. I nod.

"Okay. Okay, then," he says, resting back on his heels. "Can I get you anything? Tea or . . . anything?"

"Can I see Poppy?"

He opens his mouth to speak, and then he must think better of it, because he just breathes out heavily instead. "I don't think that would be a good idea," he says finally.

I can't do anything but nod.

He waits with me in silence until Mabel comes back. "I've called the hospital," she says. "Dr. Furnham agreed to meet with Fiona tonight. Albert is getting the car ready, and he'll take her there now."

"Great. Well, let's get this all sorted, then," Charlie says, falsely cheerful. He stretches a hand out to me, and I take it. But he lets go of my hand as soon as I'm up, and I'm left with no lingering warmth.

I follow him out of Mabel's office and into the grand part of the house. I look around, trying to memorize every little detail I can of these beautiful rooms. It's the last time I'll ever be here, in the castle, I know it.

We cross in front of the main staircase, and I look up. Blair is at the top, looking down at us. Charlie doesn't seem to notice her as he opens the front door. I watch her as I step through after him, and as he starts to close the door behind me, I swear I see her start to smile. A dangerous, wicked curve of a smile.

I slide into the backseat of the car and take a deep breath. I have to be strong, for Poppy's sake. I have to prove that I am sane, not a danger to anyone. Maybe after proving this to the doctors, I can go back to the house and everything can go back to normal.

"How are you feeling, Fee?" Albert asks as Charlie and I buckle our seat belts. I catch his eyes in the rearview mirror, and I see the wary assessment in them.

"I didn't kill Copperfield, Albert," I say as calmly as possible. He doesn't respond.

CHAPTER 30

The drive there is painful. I'm sitting next to the guy who nearly kissed me last night in a room full of strangers, and now he's turned away from me, staring out the window as if I'm not even here, mere inches from him. Because he thinks I killed his little sister's horse.

If I weren't so hurt and terrified, I would laugh. Because this whole situation is just so insane.

We pull up in front of a small official building, and I realize it's the same hospital in Beasley where Blair supposedly miscarried.

"I thought we were going to the . . . facility in Twicken?" I say to Charlie.

His eyes are filled with caution as he looks at me, as if I'm an unexploded bomb. "It's too far away, and Mabel says they stopped accepting new patients for the night. So Dr. Furnham has agreed to do your consultation here. Depending on what he says, we'll take you to Twicken tomorrow."

"Fine," I say, trying to sound reasonable and compliant.

I get out of the car and follow Charlie inside. Albert says he'll meet us at the front desk.

We walk into the waiting room, and I see the same doctor from last time, Blair's doctor, standing there. Waiting for us, I realize, as Charlie approaches him.

"Miss Smith," he says, shaking my hand with a firm grip. "I'm Dr. Furnham. Nice to meet you." He looks beyond me, and I follow his gaze to see Albert, who's just walked in. Albert is looking at him with a blank expression on his face, and he doesn't introduce himself.

Dr. Furnham looks back at me. "I understand you've had a rough day. If you'll follow me into my office, we can talk there."

"I'll wait out here," Charlie says, and I look up at him, horrified.

"You're not going to come with me?" I ask. I hate how desperate my voice sounds in the cold stillness of the room.

Charlie glances at the doctor, then back at me. "I think it's better if you two talk alone. Albert and I will be right out here."

I have to be strong, I remind myself. *Strong and sane. I can handle this.*

I pull my shoulders back, nod, and follow the doctor into his office. It's small, with only a desk and one bookshelf stacked with thick medical books and a few framed photographs of him and a woman—his wife, I assume.

He gestures to the chair across from his desk, and I settle into it. It's more comfortable than the chair in Mabel's office, at least.

"So you're a psychiatrist as well as an OB/GYN?" I ask before he can say anything.

He shifts in his seat. "I'm a general physician, Miss Smith. I have training in many areas of medicine. There aren't many specialists in this part of the country, I'm afraid."

His temple is beaded with sweat. He's nervous. Is it me? Is he worried about what I might do or say in here?

"So, tell me, Fiona. What exactly happened last night?"

I try to answer as succinctly as I can. "I came back from the ball, and I had a mug of tea and read a bit. I was asleep by midnight."

"What were you reading?"

"A book about Bonnie Prince Charlie."

The doctor raises his eyebrows at the name, and I hope I'm not blushing. "Is he a favorite subject of yours?" he asks.

"No," I say quickly. "Poppy's studying him in school, so I wanted to do some research so I could be more helpful to her."

He nods slowly. "Okay. So you went to bed," he prompts.

"And then I woke up in the morning with a headache and a bloody knife in my hand."

"That must have been disorienting," he says, his tone mild.

"It was *terrifying*," I correct him. "I felt as if I'd been drugged. As if someone drugged me and put a knife in my hands in the middle of the night."

"Who would have done something like that?"

"I don't know," I say as calmly as I can.

"I spoke to the head housekeeper, Ms. Faraday, on the phone." He must mean Mabel. "She said you believed Ms. Rifely, Blair, did this? That she was trying to frame you?"

I twist my hands together but try to keep my voice steady. "Yes, I mentioned something like that to Mabel, but she seems to have exaggerated my words. I only know what Gareth said— that he saw a woman running out of the stables, and when he went to check on the horses, he found Copperfield, stabbed. I don't know if Blair was involved—all I told Mabel was that, based on what Gareth saw, we can't rule her out."

"There are several women who work and live at the castle, are there not?" he says. He's clicking his pen, out and in, over and over. I want to reach over and stop him, grab the pen, but I focus all my energy on staying still.

I grit my teeth. "Yes, there are. Blair was just the first one who came to mind, that's all. But I suppose it could have been any of them."

"Why this fixation on Blair? Why do you think she'd want to frame you?"

I lift my chin. "There's no reason that I know of. I don't know why I said her name. Really. All I know is that I did not hurt that horse."

"Have you experienced anything like this before? Episodes where you've lost time or memories?"

"No," I say emphatically.

He asks me several more questions, trying to get me to say anything that proves I'm crazy and unstable, like: Have I ever had violent fantasies? Do I often think people are trying to target me? Do I ever hear voices?

I lie when I answer that last question, telling him I've never heard voices before.

"How would you have been drugged?" he asks finally.

I've been asking myself that same question ever since this morning. I think back to last night. I ate dinner with the staff in the kitchen before the ball. After that, I had nothing to eat or drink. Until . . . "The tea," I say finally. "Someone must have slipped something in my tea. I drink chamomile tea every night to help me sleep. Everybody at the castle knows that."

"You've been having trouble sleeping?"

"No. Not *trouble* trouble. I'm a light sleeper, so I sometimes wake up in the middle of the night and have trouble falling back asleep. But the tea helps."

He nods, disinterested. "Tell me a bit about your family history."

"My family history?" I repeat.

"Yes," he says, peering at me closely. "Do you have any family members who suffer from any illnesses? Specifically mental illness?"

I eye the stack of files on his desk. Is one of them mine? Does he have access to my family's medical history?

I meet his eyes. "There's nothing that I know of on my dad's side. My aunt never mentioned anything."

"And your mother's side?"

If I lie, and he knows the truth, I'm guilty. Insane. But if I tell the truth, how on earth would I be able to convince him that I haven't inherited my mother's schizophrenia?

"I don't know of anything on her side either," I whisper.

He glances down at the sheet of paper in front of him, and I hold my breath.

"Ms. Faraday informed me that, prior to her death, Lady Moffat told her that your mother was a paranoid schizophrenic who committed suicide."

I close my eyes and feel my entire world crumbling around me. *Mabel knew? This whole time she knew about my mother?*

"I didn't—I mean, what I meant by that was that I'm *nothing* like my mother. I won't turn out like her."

Of course Mabel knew. Lily would have wanted her to know, so she could watch out for any signs that might affect Poppy. And now she thinks I'm the same.

The doctor asks me a few more questions about my mother, but I'm barely paying attention anymore. It's all over.

Finally, Dr. Furnham stops asking questions and stands up. "Why don't we rejoin Lord Moffat outside?" I stand up and follow him listlessly to the waiting room.

Albert's not there, but Charlie sits in a dingy plastic chair, his hair looking more tousled than usual. He's worried. Is he worried about what will happen to me? Or about what a danger I'd posed to Poppy?

"I think Miss Smith would benefit from an extended stay at the Twicken facility," Dr. Furnham says, "especially considering her family history. We'll keep her here overnight and take her there in the morning."

"Sorry, what family history?" Charlie asks.

Both of them look at me. "My mother," I say quietly. "My mother was schizophrenic."

Charlie doesn't recoil. His eyes don't fill with horror. He doesn't look at me with a grimace of betrayal or disgust. Instead, he hugs me close to his side. "I'm so sorry, Fee. I didn't know."

I sink into his hug, allow it to comfort me. But he's still calling me Fee.

I step out of his arms. "Watch over Poppy, okay?" I say, meeting his eyes finally to show him how serious I am. "Keep her safe?"

"Of course," he says. "She'll be fine, Fee, I promise. And so will you."

I nod. "Then let's see the padded room," I say, trying to part on a somewhat lighthearted note.

I turn around and let Dr. Furnham lead me. I don't want to watch Charlie leave. I can't. But I feel his presence leave just the same, and then, once again, I'm all alone in this life.

CHAPTER 31

The doctor leads me to what appears to be a standard hospital room, no padded walls to be seen.

"I'll need you to give us your permission to strap you to your bed with soft cuffs tonight. They won't hurt, I promise. It's just to keep you safe."

"Do I look like I'm having a psychotic episode?" I ask, my voice a defiant snap. "I absolutely *don't* give my permission."

The thought of being chained to the bed, like a rabid animal, makes me queasy.

He looks like he wants to say something more, but he stops himself. "A nurse will be in soon to check your vitals," he says.

I nod, sitting down on the bed and looking away from him.

He leaves the room, and through the small window on top of my door, I see him standing at the nurses' station across the hall, filling out paperwork. I walk to the window and flip the blinds closed.

For a moment, I stand in the middle of the room and let all my doubts wash over me. What if all this is really happening? What if I'm spiraling into schizophrenia, the way I've always feared I would? I'm the right age; I'm experiencing my first period of great stress. It all makes sense.

You're not crazy, says my mother's voice in my head. But it just makes me feel worse. I hear voices. I feel my mother's presence everywhere. And this morning, I woke up with a bloody knife in my hands.

I sink to my knees and finally, *finally,* I don't push aside the thought I've been trying to avoid like hell for the past three months.

What if I'm going crazy?

It's the simplest answer to so many things that haven't made sense. Hearing whispers at night, my mom's laughter, the voices in my head. The overwhelming, irrational fear I felt in the rain that day in the woods. Potentially killing Copperfield in some kind of fit of psychotic rage so intense that my body won't let me remember it now. I'm breaking. It's all me. There's no evil girl with an intricate plot to get me. My fear of Blair is nothing but the product of a paranoid delusion. The idea that I'm the only one who can see through her? A delusion of grandeur. I really do need help.

Time in a psychiatric institution can't be that bad. These days, those kinds of places can be really nice. It will be clean and calm and filled with other people who understand what I'm going through. People who won't judge me for suffering from a disease I can't control. They'll give me the medicine I need and teach me how to manage the symptoms. A place like that could have helped my mother—maybe it'll help me, too.

Maybe I should just stop fighting and accept this fate.

But then I think of Blair, remembering all those times her careful control over her expression would slip, revealing a triumphant smile or a hateful glare.

I stand up and wipe away the tears that have fallen down my cheeks.

Maybe I am crazy. But with everything I've seen, all I know about Blair, I need to bet on myself now. I have to.

Of course I can't stay here. I can't just offer myself up for the slaughter like this. Blair has that doctor in her pocket, I know it, and the two of them are going to lock me away somewhere I'll never be able to leave. I won't let her win that easily.

But how do I get out of here? I forgot my cell phone at the castle, and I don't have anyone to call anyway. The nurses' station outside is continuously staffed. Everyone on duty knows exactly why I'm here, thinks I'm dangerous, and will be keeping a close eye on me.

I go to the window on the other side of the room. I unlock the clasp and slide the pane up only to find a set of metal bars blocking my way.

Past the nurses' station it is.

I have to act fast; someone will be in soon to take my vitals and force me into a hospital gown, at which point I'll be even more trapped than I am now.

I open the blinds and glance out into the hallway. I see two nurses sitting in front of computers, but the doctor is nowhere in sight. I suck a breath in and open the door as quietly as possible.

The nurses don't look up. The hospital rooms are arranged around the station, and I'll have to go halfway across the circle to get to the hallway that hopefully leads to an elevator and the exit.

There are a few patients and family members walking around the floor. I try to blend in with them, walking as casually as possible out of my room and around the station. The nurses never even glance at me, and I start breathing again.

I reach the hall. There's an elevator at the end of it. I'm heading toward it when I notice a nurse look up from a chart and spot me. She smiles politely, and I do my best to smile back through my almost paralyzing fear.

Suddenly, though, the smile falls off her face and is replaced by a look of dawning recognition.

"Wait," she says as I slip past her and into the elevator. I push the button for the first floor. "Wait!" she shouts, and I press down frantically on the door-close button. She's running for the elevator when the door slides shut in her face with a satisfying *snick*.

I bounce on the balls of my feet as the elevator sails down to the first floor, and when it opens, I abandon all attempts to act normal and start running. I sprint past a few bewildered nurses and families in the waiting room, and then I'm out the door and free.

I just have no idea what to do now.

I stand for a second in the dim lights of the hospital parking lot and try to figure out a plan.

I didn't pay enough attention during the drive here to know which direction to go. The village of Beasley is slightly larger than Almsley, but still nothing is open at this hour, and I don't have any money.

I have to set off into the wilderness if I want to have any hope of escaping.

I bypass the main road and follow a side street until I'm out of the village. The one-lane road before me stretches out into the darkness. Am I really going to do this?

I should keep to the road, I decide. I know that if I venture into the countryside, I'll most likely become irrevocably lost.

I hop over the low stone wall that runs alongside the pavement and head toward the tree line, about ten feet away from it. I'm close enough to the wall to follow it, but far enough that I won't be seen.

It's a cold night, and while I'm grateful for the thick coat I'm wearing, I'm shivering before long. The rush of adrenaline I felt while escaping has faded away, and I'm more tired than I've been all day. And more frightened. I have no plan, no place to go. What am I going to do?

The night is filled with all kinds of squeaking and scurrying animal sounds, and the wind has grown vicious and wild. The cold air sears my lungs. Each breath becomes a struggle, until it's all I can focus on.

Just as I'm wondering if I'm going to be able to survive the night, a yellow light flashes behind me.

Headlights, approaching fast. Without thinking, I dart into some rough bushes beside me, crouch down, and hide, waiting for the car to pass.

It's warmer here, among the leaves and close to the ground.

I must have been walking for only a couple of hours, but I'm so cold, so utterly exhausted, that I doubt I can get much farther. This will have to do. I curl up on the ground, hugging my coat around me. The ground is soft with bracken, and I thank whatever lucky stars I have that the snow has melted over the last few days. The ground is still damp, but I do my best to ignore it, and soon enough, I'm drifting off to sleep.

CHAPTER 32

I must wake every fifteen minutes or so during the night, curling closer and closer into myself to escape the cold. Finally, I decide I've slept enough, and I open my eyes to a foggy, freezing-cold morning. It feels as if my fingers and toes have frozen together, and I stretch them carefully as I stand. There's no one in sight, no cars on the road, so I walk along it.

Cars start to appear as the sun rises higher in the sky, around midmorning. I retreat into the edge of the woods and keep walking parallel to the lane. I imagine those cars are full of families heading to church or to Sunday lunch. That thought makes me feel even more alone.

Right on cue, I hear my mother's voice in my head. *You'll be fine, hen,* she coos. *You'll find your way home soon.*

It does nothing to comfort me, and I do my best to ignore it.

The road meanders through the hills. I pass fields of shaggy Highland cows, farmhouses and ruins of old churches and abandoned cabins, lakes so still that they reflect the cloudy sky and the mountains that rise above them as clearly as a mirror. It's beautiful here.

The sun disappears behind a blanket of clouds in late morning, taking the relatively mild temperature with it, and does not come out again. The wind grows wilder, more vengeful, and finally, the clouds give way and snow begins to flutter down. It falls harder and harder, until it begins sticking to the ground, and I'm crunching it underneath my boots. It pelts me, making me blink every few seconds as water drips from my eyelashes down my cheek. Soon I feel as if I'm trapped inside a frozen cocoon, as if the snow has captured me, is keeping me from the world outside.

I try to keep my disoriented eyes on the road, as if it can reassure me. But I don't know where I'm going. I barely know where I am. I need to get someplace warm soon, or I don't even want to think about what could happen to me in these conditions.

It must be late afternoon when I come upon a cluster of houses and stores. I see it a few hundred yards in the distance, and I speed up until my half-numb feet are nearly at a jog.

I've figured out what to do: I'll call Hex and ask her to get me a plane ticket home. I know she doesn't have that kind of money on hand, but she's Hex—she'll figure out a way.

As I draw closer to the village, I realize I recognize these shops. I'm in Perthton. The village near Dunraven Manor.

Suddenly, an idea—a crazy idea—begins to form in my mind.

My lips are on the verge of a smile when a voice calls out, making me stop in my tracks.

"Fee!"

I turn around to see Gareth walking toward me. I stare at him, hardly believing he's really there. But it's certainly him, in his heavy black coat and work boots, a concerned frown on his face.

"What are you doing here?" I ask as he gets closer.

He doesn't answer. Instead, as soon as he reaches me, he wraps his arms around me and pulls me into a hug.

I'm so surprised that, for a short moment, I don't hug him back. But finally I reach my arms around his waist and let myself lean into him. I don't realize how much I needed this until now.

He steps back but keeps his hands on my shoulders. "Where have you been?" he asks, reaching up and plucking a leaf from the tangles of my hair.

"I couldn't—I had to run." I don't even know where to begin, and he must see the frantic confusion rising within me, because he squeezes my shoulders before I can continue on.

"Here," he says, looking around. "Let's get inside." He takes my hand and gently pulls me into the pub on the corner. He points me to a booth in the back, away from the crowd near the bar, and goes up to order us something.

There's a roaring fire a few feet away, and I can't help but sigh as I start to thaw out a bit.

I think of the fireplace in the pub I waited in the first day I arrived in the Highlands. Where I met the boy with firelit red-brown curls and pale green eyes for the first time.

I shove that memory aside and look around to discover that most of the people in this tiny place are watching me. I don't blame them. I must look frightful, with my red hair even messier than normal and my face streaked with dirt.

Gareth walks over to me with two tumblers of whisky and a bowl of almonds, and I watch as the women in the pub shift their attention from me to him. Evidently, they like the way his muddy-brown hair glints in the firelight. Or maybe it's his broad shoulders that catch their eyes.

I remember what happened in front of the fire in his cottage and blush down at my drink.

"Drink up," Gareth says, nodding at my whisky. "It'll warm you up a bit. And then why don't you tell me everything that's happened, from the beginning?"

So I do. I tell him everything, from my suspicions about

Blair to our strange argument that she denied ever having and on through the horrible events of the past few days.

Gareth listens to it all without interrupting. I try to read his expression, but all I can see is attentiveness.

When I'm finally done, I tell him, "Now it's your turn. Why are you here? Were you out looking for me?"

He takes a long sip of his drink before answering. "The whole house is out looking for you, in all the nearby villages," he says. "Albert lent me a car, said you might be here. He said he took you here once? Anyway, I'm supposed to call as soon as I find you."

"You can't tell him," I say quickly, but he holds his hands up.

"Don't worry. I'm not going to."

"Do you believe me? That Blair is orchestrating all this?"

He opens his mouth, then closes it. He takes a deep breath before finally saying, "I don't think you're crazy, Fee."

I close my eyes, breathing a sigh of relief. Because every-one—Mabel, Albert, Charlie, the doctor—*everyone* has spent the last few days doubting me. I can't stop thinking about that look in Charlie's eyes, the pity as I told him about my mom's schizo-phrenia, the sorrow as he ascribed that disease to me as well.

But Gareth believes me.

I reach across the table, and he takes my hand in his and squeezes it. "We'll figure it out, Fee. We'll figure something out."

I nod, too overwhelmed with emotion to speak. Finally, when I get myself under control, I have to ask him, "Why do you believe me?"

He brushes his thumb back and forth across the back of my hand. "Because I know you. And the woman I saw running away that night from the stables—I don't know if she was you. I mean, I don't think she was you," he says in a rush.

"Who do you think she was?"

"I don't know, but I'm certain I would have recognized you."

"Do you think it could have been Blair?"

"I don't think so," he says with a small frown, trying to remember.

I pull my hand from his and bury my head in my arms. "She set it all up so perfectly," I groan.

"Why do you think she hates you so much?" he asks. There's a careful tone to his voice that makes me look up, and when I do, I see that he can't meet my eyes.

"Because of Charlie," I whisper, though I can tell he already knows.

"You like him," he says.

I can't lie. Not to Gareth. Not when he's the one person in the world who's stood by my side. "I love him," I admit.

He meets my eyes and nods once, quickly. "I'll get us another round. Be right back, okay? And then we can make a plan."

I nod, my eyes brimming with grateful tears, and settle back into the booth as he heads for the bar. I eat the rest of the almonds and finish my drink and let the burning warmth from the whisky and the fire spread through me. I'm safe.

When I look back toward the bar, though, Gareth isn't there. I search the crowd, and he's definitely not among them.

I stand up, a feeling of dread growing in the pit of my stomach. I walk past all the patrons, through the door, and back out into the cold. And find Gareth on his cell phone.

CHAPTER 33

"Just hurry," he says before hanging up and turning around to come back inside.

As soon as he spots me, I start running. "Fee!" he calls out, but I'm into the woods before he can catch me.

He'll go for the car now and try to track me down. I keep running, deeper into the woods but still following the road as closely as I dare toward Dunraven Manor. It's a couple of miles away, and I know Gareth will overtake me soon. But if I stay far enough from the road, hidden in the dense trees, maybe he won't see me.

Evening is falling, and there are plenty of cars zipping by. I don't stop to look for Gareth's. I just stumble along as best as I can, pushing my way through the scratching, searching trees. The whisky and the fire have brought some feeling back into my feet, and I feel the blood pumping through me, warming me, as I run faster.

I'm out of breath with a painful stitch in my side by the time I finally reach a tall stone wall. The edge of the Dunraven Manor property. I climb over the wall as quickly and quietly as possible, then sprint for the manor house. I know every camera in the trees is pointed at me, but I don't care. I want them to know that I'm here.

Once I'm inside that house, I'll be safe. I hope.

Sure enough, before I'm less than halfway to the house, someone behind me yells, "Stop!"

I whirl around to face the same guard who found me the first time I came here. He recognizes me just as I recognize him. "What are you doing here?" he asks gruffly. "You need to leave." He grabs my arm and starts dragging me off.

"Wait," I say, pulling my arm from his grasp. "You have to let me inside. I have to see the Cavendishes."

He frowns at me, the wrinkles deepening in his weathered face. "Then you can call and make an appointment. But you're not getting anywhere near them tonight."

He starts dragging me off again, but I stand my ground.

"My name is Fiona," I say. "I'm Moira's daughter."

He stares at me, his brow furrowed. "I don't understand," he says after a stretch of silence.

"Mr. and Mrs. Cavendish are my grandparents. And I need to see them. Now."

He drops my arm and takes a step back. "Is this a joke? I've never heard anything about Moira having a child."

Maybe my grandparents really never knew about me. Either that or they were too ashamed to tell anyone. "I was born in Texas. My mother raised me until she committed suicide. My mother was their daughter, and I'm their granddaughter."

The guard blinks, then looks from me to the manor house and back again. "Well . . . I suppose we'll see what Mrs. Drummond has to say about this," he says, stumbling over his words.

"Thank you," I say with as much dignity as I can muster.

We walk in silence, glancing at each other out of the corners of our eyes every so often.

The housekeeper is standing outside the front door, watching us walk up.

"You're the girl who was here last month. The trespasser," she says once we're close enough to hear. "I thought it was you on the security camera. What's this about?" she asks the guard.

"She says she's their granddaughter."

"Granddaughter?" Mrs. Drummond says with a laugh. It fades when she sees the serious look on my face.

I tell her who my mother is, but she still looks confused.

"I'm sorry," I say, taking one step closer to her. "But could you please just talk to them? Ask them if they'll see me?"

She wrings her hands in worry but finally nods. "Wait here," she says.

The guard stays with me, and we wait in silence until Mrs. Drummond comes back. Her expression is so grave that for a moment I'm sure they've refused to meet with me.

But instead, she gives me a small nod of assent. "They'll see you," she says somewhat uncertainly. "But you have to understand, they're very old, and not well. If this is some kind of joke, or a trick—"

"It's not," I say, looking her right in the eye. "I promise."

She studies me for a moment, then gestures toward the door. "Come with me."

We climb up a grand staircase, the railing matching the gold filigree details on the walls. There is nothing medieval about this manor house—it's only a couple of centuries old, and well planned. No twisty staircases or uneven floors to be found.

As we climb, I try to wrap my head around that the fact that this is where my mother grew up. She knew every inch of these elaborate rooms, was familiar with every piece of antique furniture, knew the story behind every portrait lining the walls. This was her home, where she had her family. The one she left behind without a second glance.

I think with a quiver: *Maybe I shouldn't be here.* I don't know anything about these people, except for that it's quite possible they don't know about me. Or maybe it's that they don't want to know me. My mother ran away from them as quickly as she could, as soon as she got the chance. Why would they help me?

Even if they don't help me, I still want answers. And this is the only way I'm going to get them. That determination propels me up the last few steps.

Mrs. Drummond knocks quietly on the door in front of us. "Come in," a very strong, clear voice calls out. My grandmother?

We walk into another ornate room, with a large fireplace, one of the grandest grand pianos I've ever seen, and so many portraits of kilted men along the walls that it's as if they're covered in plaid wallpaper.

And then I see them, my mother's parents, sitting on a curved Victorian sofa in the middle of the room. Mr. Cavendish reads a newspaper—Charlie's newspaper—and Mrs. Cavendish is writing something on a small lap desk. A letter. Mr. Cavendish looks up when I walk in, but she keeps writing.

They are both small, smaller than I thought they would be given my mother's willowy height. Mrs. Cavendish's hair is coiled into an elegant bun, and Mr. Cavendish wears a well-tailored three-piece suit, as if they've decided they must dress to match the opulence of their home. Tentatively, I step closer, examining their faces for familiar traits, anything that might remind me of my mother. Or myself.

Mr. Cavendish's mouth has dropped open at the sight of me. "Your hair—" he chokes out. He turns to Mrs. Cavendish, and she finally looks at me. "She has Moira's hair."

They both stare at me, as if marveling at my long red curls, and I awkwardly shift from one foot to the other.

"That will be all, Mrs. Drummond," Mrs. Cavendish says. Mrs. Drummond nods and slips back out the door, leaving me alone with them.

"Well, girl," my grandmother says finally, her voice dry. "What do you have to say for yourself?" She sets aside her lap desk and crosses her hands together, studying me. Everything about her breathes elegance and refinement, even though she wears only a simple gold wedding band and no makeup. It's the way she moves, her posture. My mother had that same gracefulness.

"Let's start at the beginning," Mrs. Cavendish says, surely noticing that I'm too overwhelmed to speak. "You claim to be our granddaughter."

"Y-yes," I stutter out.

"Moira never had a child."

So they never heard about me. Which means I need to start with the hardest part. "My name is Fiona. My mother, Moira

Cavendish, gave birth to me in Austin, Texas, about seven years after she left yo—after she left Scotland. She raised me there until she . . . she died when I was twelve."

I pause, watching them, waiting for their reaction.

They look at each other, solemn and sad. They knew she was dead. "Did Lily tell you?" I ask.

"Lily told us, yes. About her suicide," my grandfather says slowly, and I can hear the grief in his voice, still so fresh after all these years. "But she never mentioned anything about a daughter."

Why? Why would Lily try to hide me from them?

"Lily was always keeping us in the loop on Moira's life in the States. Why wouldn't she tell us about you?" my grandmother asks, echoing my thoughts, her left eyebrow arching.

Was that lie, that omission, part of an old promise to my mother? Did Lily think she was somehow protecting me from the Cavendishes? Or was she keeping me from them for some other reason? What secrets had she been hiding?

"Suppose what you say is true," my grandmother continues. "What mother would commit suicide when she had a young daughter to raise? Who could be that irresponsible?"

"She was sick," I say. "With schizophrenia. Didn't Lily tell you that?" I ask.

My grandparents glance at each other again. "We know of

the family illness," my grandfather says finally, his voice much softer than his wife's. "My aunt suffered from it as well."

"We raised Moira to be stronger than any illness," my grandmother says, her voice cutting in over her husband's.

I straighten my shoulders, staring at this hard woman in shock. "Schizophrenics can't help their actions," I say slowly, trying to make her hear me. "Not without medication."

"And was she on medication?" my grandmother asks, delicately arching an eyebrow again.

"No," I admit.

She nods, receiving the answer she expected. "This is all ridiculous. A ridiculous fairy tale spun by a poor American who thinks she can strike it rich by preying on our sympathies. We won't fall for it."

I stand up, furious. "I don't want your money."

I see now how stupid I was to come here. These people— or at least this woman—would never lift a finger to help me, especially not if I told them I was currently being accused of having the same "family illness" as my mother. I'm wasting my time.

My grandmother stands at the same time I do, straightening out imaginary wrinkles in her pale pink skirt suit. She is short, only coming up to my shoulder, but she stares me down with plenty of authority. "Any money that you might have been after wouldn't have gone to you anyhow. All of our fortune will go to the poor Moffat children, the ones who truly deserve it."

"The Moffats?" I say, thinking I must have heard her wrong.

She quirks that eyebrow up again. "Yes. Lily was like a daughter to us, much more loyal and obedient than Moira ever was. She stayed near, always visited," she adds, and her voice breaks slightly, revealing the hurt underneath. "Lily was our family, and her children are our family, too. You are nothing but a fraud. A mistake."

Her words sting, but I brush them aside. Their money—their considerable fortune, this house, everything—is going to the Moffats.

Because they didn't know that they had a granddaughter.

Of course. That's why Lily never told my grandparents about me. She probably passed it off to my mother like she was just keeping her promise to her, but really she wanted my inheritance. The newspaper was failing, and if she wanted to keep the castle and her fancy lifestyle, she needed money however she could get it.

So why bring me here, mere miles away from my grandparents' home? It doesn't make sense.

I don't say another word to the Cavendishes. I can't. Instead, I flee the room, running down the staircase and out into the entry hall. I need to shift my focus back to Blair.

CHAPTER 34

Mrs. Drummond is waiting for me at the front door. "Is everything all right?" she asks, her voice full of concern.

"Yes, fine," I lie. "I just need to go."

"Should I call Albert to come get you?" she asks softly.

I shake my head, the horror of Albert coming here and taking me right back to the hospital eclipsing the threat of tears. And Gareth is still out there somewhere, in the Fintair car. Will he come looking for me? Did Albert tell him I might come here? "No," I croak out. "I—I don't want to bother him. Is there someone here who could drive me back to Fintair Castle?"

"I can," Mrs. Drummond says, pulling a set of keys out of a drawer by the door.

"I don't want to mess up your day—" I begin, but she waves her hand at me.

"It's the least I can do," she says, and in her expression, I see that she believes me. I know that she knows I'm truly Moira's daughter. "Wait here."

She rushes out the door and pulls around a few moments later in a big black car with tinted windows. "Get in," she calls.

I climb into the passenger seat, and we start driving away from Dunraven Manor. I look in the side mirror at it for a few moments as the estate fades away into the distance, a heavy sense of disappointment settling over me. I certainly didn't expect an unquestioningly warm welcome from my grandparents, but I would never have imagined them to be so cruel. To dismiss schizophrenia as some kind of weakness of character . . . my hands are still shaking with anger.

I have to focus on what I can do at the castle to prove that Blair isn't who she says she is. I have to do that for Charlie. And for Poppy, too.

He didn't believe you, the nasty voice in my head says. *He left you in that hospital. Why should you do anything for him?*

Of course he didn't believe me. There was overwhelming evidence that I was not trustworthy, that I was a danger. Evidence that Blair planted incredibly convincingly.

And then there is the fact that I love him.

I love him, no matter what he does or doesn't feel about me. I can't let him be with a girl evil and twisted enough to cook up this plot against me. He deserves to be happy, not to give his life over to a psychopath.

And if she is the one who killed Copperfield, she's even more dangerous than I originally thought. Just thinking about it makes me feel sick to my stomach. I have to save Poppy and Charlie from her. I have to at least try.

That sickening feeling intensifies as we get closer and closer to the castle. I pick at the cuticle of my left index finger until it bleeds, trying to come up with some sort of plan. All I can think to do is sneak in and head straight for Lily's desk. I remember that tempting locked drawer, and I know that if Lily was hiding any secrets, that's where they would be. And I remember the time Blair came into the study, claiming to be looking for Charlie when Alice and I were in there cleaning. Was she really going for that drawer?

There have to be some answers in there. About why Lily never told my grandparents about me. About why Blair has been trying to drive me crazy. About *something*.

It's not much of a plan, but it's all I've got.

We reach the familiar landmarks leading up to the turnoff for the castle, and I can't keep still.

"Could you drop me off here?" I ask before we get to the turnoff.

Mrs. Drummond pulls the car over and stops. "Are you sure?" she asks. Her concern is growing.

"Yes, I—I just want to walk," I say, trying to sound assuring. "I need to clear my head."

"Okay."

She's silent as I get out of the car, then she waves goodbye and drives off. I can only hope that she won't call Albert or Mabel and tell them that I'm on the property.

I take a deep breath, square my shoulders, then head for the low stone wall that surrounds the grounds. I hop over it quickly, dusting off my hands as I crash onward. There are no security cameras here like there are at Dunraven Manor, but I can't shake the nervous feeling that I'm being watched.

Dusk is falling, and the fog is rolling in. Soon it will be so thick that it'll swallow me whole. I hurry onward. I know the estate well enough to navigate it now, but the fog of the witching hour has a way of turning me around and tricking me. I have to get through a patch of woods before I reach the open lawn around the castle.

I start running, the bushes and tree trunks grasping for me, trying to trip me and scratch me up. Now I'll look even more like a wild animal than I already do.

I'm not quick enough. The fog enshrouds me before I'm halfway to the castle.

I slow to a walk, trying to catch my breath, which sounds much too loud in this small space that my world has become. I can barely see a foot in front of me, but I do my best not to panic, holding my hands out to feel my way through. The branches scratch at my skin, and I stumble over rocks every few steps.

Just when I'm sure I'm completely lost, I hear a noise to my left, something that sounds so much like a human sigh. All the breath evaporates from my body. Then another sound: the swish of a long skirt. Blair?

The Grey Lady?

Mom?

I force myself to keep moving, to keep putting one foot in front of the other in a straight line. I can do this. I have to do this.

Something nudges my left elbow, hard, and I scream. My wail is lost in the fog.

I finally stop screaming, and now there is nothing but silence. The nudge has pushed me slightly off course, to the right. Is someone trying to push me off the path? Or trying to guide me?

"Who are you?" I whisper into the silence.

No answer. I try to tell myself that I'm just imagining things, but there's no way I can actually believe that. Not right now, not in this fog. There is someone—something—out here with me, I'm sure of it.

Strangely, though, I'm not frightened. I don't understand it, but there's something about the air around me that feels . . . comforting somehow. So do I return to the path I was on before, or do I follow the one the nudge suggested?

"I'm trusting you," I whisper, setting off in the new direction.

I creep forward, slowly now, picking my way across the rocky soil and bracing myself at every moment for another nudge.

It never comes, though, and soon enough I'm out of the woods and onto the lawn. And a few minutes later, I find a gnarled tree in front of me. I recognize it—it's the old tree that stands only about thirty feet from the main entrance.

I praise the fog now as I skirt around the castle and head for the back door. I overshoot it by a few feet, but I find it easily enough. And there's no one around.

I open the door, quickly and soundlessly, and peek into the empty back hallway. I scurry down it toward the main staircase, but before I can reach it, two of Alice's fellow maids clatter out of a nearby room.

I dive for the nearest doorway, catapulting into one of the sitting rooms. I close the door behind me and hold my breath. The door is thick, and I can barely hear the brightly chirping voices of the girls as they pass by my hiding place. When I'm sure they're gone, I try to even out my shaky breath and head back into the hallway.

I make it up the main staircase, and I'm pretty sure no one sees me. The servants will all be following Mabel's rules and sticking to the servants' area of the house.

Poppy's bedroom door is open. I try not to breathe as I creep toward it. I can't hear anything inside, and after a few quiet moments, I lean forward and peek in. I want to feel relieved when I see that it's empty, but I can't help but feel a pang of sadness as I take in the frilly pink room that's become so familiar and comfortable to me these past few months. I might never see this room again.

I shake my head and return my focus to my task, scurrying for the door to the master suite.

It's locked. Of course.

I realize I've only ever been here with Alice before. Alice, who has the key.

For one brief, awful moment, I consider seeking her out and asking for her help. But of course that's stupid and would only result in her turning me over to Blair or Mabel or the hospital. Even if she didn't already hate me, she thinks I killed Copperfield, just like everyone else. And begging her to help me break into the master suite will only make me seem crazier.

I dash back to Poppy's room, wishing I had paid more

attention to Hex's occasional lessons on breaking and entering. She considered picking locks a survival skill, though she swore up and down that it was one she hadn't used in years.

I scramble through Poppy's hair-accessory drawer, brushing aside headbands and sparkly hair clips until I find a few bobby pins. I grab them and rush back to the door, kneeling down in front of the lock and bending the pins into what I hope are the right shapes. I try to remember how to angle one pin and twist the other, like Hex taught me, but my hands are shaking. I close my eyes, take a deep breath, and try to feel my way.

Finally, the lock clicks, I open the door, and I'm in.

I hurry through the opulent room into the small office and repeat the process on the desk drawer lock.

As I fumble with the lock, I think about exactly how much trouble I'll be in if they catch me. I won't just be packed off to an asylum, I'll be charged with breaking and entering. Even Charlie won't have any sympathy for me if I'm found rummaging through his mother's private things.

But I have no choice. I have to know. I have to understand why this woman hid me from my grandparents. Why she brought me here.

I nearly crow when the lock clicks open, but I press my lips together and open the drawer.

I stare at the treasure inside. The drawer is filled with papers and photos and all kinds of miscellaneous objects, including an old tape recorder. I reach for a glass perfume bottle in the back corner. Highland Heather. My mom's scent. The one that filled my room here that one night, as if my mother were passing through it. I set the bottle down and take out a few of the papers. They're emails, from my mom to Lily, printed out and marked up. Some of them are brief, only a few lines assuring Lily that she's fine. Some of them are longer, and I skim them through with tears in my eyes. She writes about my first words, my first day of kindergarten, the stories she tells me as I fall asleep each night. There's a sentence about the bluebird princess story, which Lily highlighted. Several passages have been highlighted, I realize, including the recipe for the "shortbread with a kick" that she used to make for me.

I click play on the tape recorder, and my mother's laugh rings out from the small speakers. Just like I knew it would. "Lily, what are you doing?" my mother says, and her voice sounds so young. So carefree. "What am I supposed to say?"

"Say your name, and what piece you're going to play," a high-pitched voice answers.

"My name is Moira Cavendish, and I'll be playing Beethoven's *Moonlight Sonata*."

Mom. This drawer is full of her.

"You found her," someone says, and I click off the tape recorder, slipping it into my coat pocket as I whirl around to see through my tears that Mabel is standing in the doorway of the office, and Blair is peeking over her right shoulder.

Mabel is holding a gun.

And she's pointing it right at me.

CHAPTER 35

Mabel?

I stare at her, trying to blink away my tears to focus on the gun. I recognize it: It's one of a pair of antique dueling pistols that I saw in a spare bedroom once when I was following Alice around. "What are you doing?" I ask, more confused than frightened.

"What she wanted me to do," Mabel says. There's something different about her voice. It almost reminds me of the dark times, when Mom was in the midst of one of her episodes, and her words would come out too fast. Unsettled. Unhinged.

"What Blair wants you to do?" I ask. I want to keep her talking. I spare a glance at Blair, who is standing silently behind Mabel, her face pale, her eyes piercing into me.

Mabel shakes her head, drawing my attention back to her. "Not Blair. My lady."

"Lily?" I ask.

"Don't you dare speak her name," Mabel spits out.

"She wanted you to kill me?"

"She wanted me to shut you up, put you somewhere no one could ever find you."

Of course. "Somewhere my grandparents could never find me, you mean. Why?"

Mabel doesn't answer. I look back at Blair, but her face doesn't offer me anything either.

"Money?" I say finally. "She wanted my grandparents' money, is that it?"

"And her children will get it," Mabel says firmly. The strange darkness in her voice is gone now, and I finally feel a frisson of terror. She sounds determined.

I glance again at Blair, but she says nothing. She makes no move to help me, just stands there.

"Why does it matter so much to you? Why get so involved with her personal affairs?" I ask Mabel.

She blinks, as if she thinks the questions I've asked are absurd. "This is my *family*. Lillian—I knew her from when she was just a wee bairn. I raised her, better than her own mother ever could have. I wanted the world for her. She deserved so much more than the life she was born into. She deserved this castle, and the old magic that keeps it safe." Her voice falters for a moment, and for just that moment, she lowers the gun a fraction. But then it's right back up, level with the space between my eyes. "I should have paid more attention to the rituals. If I had, they would have protected her."

I think of her disappearing into the darkness of the tree room, carrying the burning bundle of juniper branches through the house on New Year's Day. All because she thinks those strange rituals would keep this family—*her* family—safe.

I've been so blind. I've been so focused on Blair that I didn't recognize the larger enemy.

"I'm sorry," I say softly. "I'm so sorry for your loss."

She wraps her free arm around herself, as if she's trying to hold all that loss inside her. The gun is still shakily pointed at me. "I will not let her children lose any more than they already have."

I spread my hands in front of me, trying to look as unthreatening as possible. "The inheritance is theirs. Even if the Cavendishes did offer it to me, I wouldn't take it. I'd refuse it. I want what's best for Poppy, too. And for Charlie."

My voice catches on his name, and Blair finally reacts, her

eyes narrowing and snapping to mine. They are filled with venom.

"Charles is *mine*," she hisses. "I won't let you take him from me."

"Of course. I would *never* try to take him from you," I vow, trying to ignore the sadness that curls through me as I say it. "I just want to go back to Texas, back home. I won't say anything to anyone. Please, just let me go home."

"Blair, go make sure everyone is where they're supposed to be," Mabel says. And, like a good little servant, Blair nods her head and hurries away.

Mabel's been in charge all along.

The two of us are now alone. Mabel raises the gun a little higher, pointing it right at my forehead. Her hand is steady, no longer shaking, and I can see the determination in her eyes. She knows I'm lying. She knows I'd never leave Poppy and Charlie here in the same house with a madwoman. With two madwomen. She's not going to let me go.

So, before she can say anything else, before she can pull the trigger and do what she thinks must be done, I act.

I run straight at her, pushing her to the floor, my terror making me strong. And there's a horrible explosion from the gun.

I suck in a breath, but I don't feel any pain. I must have

knocked the gun off course. I sprint down the hall, screaming for help.

But no one is answering me. Can't anyone hear me? Time seems to slow, and my legs feel impossibly heavy. I can't push them any faster. I wait to hear Mabel's footsteps right behind me, for the sound of the next gunshot.

Finally, I make it to the main staircase, leaping down the steps three at a time. I'm almost to the next landing when my feet slip from under me, and I'm rolling to the bottom.

I can't breathe. I can't even tell if I'm injured. For a moment, all I can do is lie there in a heap, stunned, the world spinning.

I have to move. I have to get up.

I hear footsteps above me, and, in a haze, I see Mabel hurrying down to me. There's no one to help me. I have to help myself.

I shove myself up, finally getting some good breath in my lungs but also feeling a sharp, searing pain shooting from my left ankle.

I keep running down the stairs, trying to ignore the pain that feels like lightning cracking up my leg.

I keep screaming. *Where is everyone?*

There is another explosion, and something whizzes past my ear.

I push myself faster, my ankle now screaming in protest.

I turn and hurry to the back door, limping, my teeth gritted in sheer determination. She can't kill me. I won't die this way, right now.

I push open the back door and hurry out into the snow. I'm running toward Gareth's cabin, desperate to find someone, any-one, who might not want to kill me, but when I get there I see that there are no lights on inside. He's not home. *Where* is *everyone?*

Another bullet rushes past my left ear, burying itself in the wood side of Gareth's cabin, and I instinctively veer right, my eyes landing on the large hedge maze. The fog envelops me as I find the entrance and run in.

It's only when I've made a few random turns and gone deeper inside that I realize what a mistake I've made. I've trapped myself in a disorienting, confining structure with just one entrance. This maze doesn't lead to an exit but to a foun-tain in the center, which means the way I came in is the only way out. I'm cornered.

Desperate, I try to scramble up the hedges, hoping I can climb over them and run out into the woods. But the shrubs aren't sturdy enough, and they collapse beneath my weight. They're too dense for me to push my way through, no matter how much I scrabble at the branches.

I clap a hand over my mouth to muffle a scream of terror and frustration.

I can hear faint footsteps now. Mabel. Stalking me. I creep away from them, making more random turns until I come to a dead end.

Her footsteps are closer now.

I'm going to die.

CHAPTER 36

I press myself back against the hedges, trying to think of what to do.

"I knew your mother, did you know that?" Mabel calls out from somewhere in the maze. "She was always ordering my lady around, ever since they were children. She grew up in that big manor, and my lady's parents could hardly afford their little house in town, so Moira thought she was better than her. But then your awful mother ran off with your winking, devilish father, and my lady finally got everything that she deserved."

I can hardly focus on her menacing words; I'm too distracted by how much better I can hear them. She's getting closer.

The venom in her voice grows sharper. "I hated her. I hated

your mother. My lady and I celebrated when we found out that all along she was crazy. We knew there was something wrong with her."

I need something to fight with. I slip my hand into my coat pocket, wishing I still had my cell phone. But it's gone, left behind when I went to the hospital to be evaluated. In its place, there's the tape recorder that I found in Lily's drawer.

The tape recorder. For a moment, I consider pressing play. Then at least I can hear my mother's voice one last time before I die.

But then I get another idea.

I do press play, but I hurl it over the hedge across from me. The notes of *Moonlight Sonata* float through the air, the melody moving farther and farther away from me. And I hear Mabel's footsteps hurry after it.

I'm off like a shot, sprinting out of my dead end and back onto the path I came from. My twisted ankle is white-hot with searing pain, but still I run blindly, fueled by a desperate hope. Then, somehow, I find my way out of the maze again.

I'm nearly sobbing in relief, checking over my shoulder to make sure Mabel's not behind me, when I run right into something. No, someone.

I choke on the sob in my throat, sure that Mabel or Blair has caught me.

Instead, I look up to see Alice.

"Fee," she says, clearly shocked, her hands on my shoulders, bracing me. "What—"

"She has a gun," I whisper frantically. "Mabel—she has a gun, and she's after me." I'm tugging on her hand, my eyes on the entrance to the maze. "Hurry!"

Alice lets me pull her along a few steps, then plants her feet, stopping the both of us. "Fee, what's happened? You sound—"

"Crazy?" I finish for her. "I sound crazy, yes, but we have to go. Please!"

She looks back at the maze, and that's when we see Mabel running out of it. Her hand still clutches the antique dueling pistol.

Alice sucks in a startled breath as Mabel raises the gun and fires. She's still running as she shoots, though, and her aim is unsteady. The bullet flies wide, and finally Alice starts running.

I don't know where to go. I have no idea where we'll be safe. Suddenly my ankle gives way, and I slip on the fresh snow, but Alice grabs my arms and pulls me back up before I can fall.

She keeps pulling me onward. We hurry around the castle and out to the garage, and finally I see why no one answered my calls inside the castle. This is where everyone's been. I choke out a sob of relief.

The whole staff is crowded around the staircase to Albert's

apartment, some of them moving in our direction. They must have heard the shot. I see Poppy standing at the edge of the group, weeping into the cook's arms.

"Mabel," Alice says as I kneel over, trying to catch my breath. "She's out of her mind. And she's got a gun."

Then, as if I'm in a dream, I see Charlie striding down the stairs from Albert's door, his expression almost comically frozen in shock as he spots me. And then I watch his expression shift to pure horror as he sees Mabel careening around the side of the house, gun in hand.

"What the . . . ?" he starts to ask, but then Mabel raises her arm once again, still intent on killing me. And he runs.

Right in front of me.

And for once, Mabel's bullet finds a mark.

CHAPTER 37

Charlie stumbles back, and I cry out.

I hook my arms under his shoulders as he falls backward, trying to soften his fall. There's a shock of red on the snow beside him—his blood.

Everyone around me is screaming, including Mabel, who has sunk to her knees in the snow, her face twisted in sorrow and regret, her gun dropped and forgotten beside her.

I bend over Charlie. The bullet must be in his left leg, in his thigh. "Charlie?" I ask, frantic, my fingers searching him. There's so much blood; I need to stop it.

His eyelids flicker, then close, and I scream his name. His eyes startle open again, and he looks up at me.

"I'm okay," he says, the weakness of his voice completely contradicting him.

I look down at his leg. The pool of blood around his left thigh has grown even larger. It's too much blood.

Without thinking, I rise to my knees, unbuckle the thin belt around my waist, yank it off, and wrap it around his upper thigh, as a tourniquet. I pull it tight, then tighter still, and press my hands against the wound until he groans and the blood seems to stop pouring out of him quite so quickly.

"You stupid idiot. You stupid, stupid idiot," I murmur, over and over.

Charlie looks up and smiles faintly at me. "Nice thanks I get for saving your life."

"Shut up," I growl, but the tears start pouring down my cheeks. And before I can think better of it, I bend down and brush my lips against his, a flutter of a kiss. A small spark.

But the moment ends when I hear a sudden commotion coming from Albert's door. I look up to find Albert himself standing there, staring down at us, and at first I almost don't recognize him. He's flanked on either side by a footman and a maid, each holding on to an arm, and I realize it's because he's trying to launch himself at us. At *me*. There is fury in his eyes, a crazed anger that shocks me.

He looks at me as if he hates me.

It doesn't make sense. Ever since he picked me up from the

train station that first day, he's been a friend, an ally, someone who's helped and advised me. He's had me completely fooled.

Several more pieces of the puzzle start to fit together in my mind, but the revelation is interrupted as an ambulance comes blaring onto the scene.

"You've ruined everything!" Albert snarls.

The ambulance has come much too quickly to have been meant for Charlie. As it comes to a halt in front of us, I understand why everyone has been rounded up and gathered around the garage. Albert knew I was here. Maybe he told everyone I was crazy and back for more blood, then told them to call an ambulance and wait here until I was taken away. Somehow, he removed everyone from the castle so that Mabel could hunt me down.

He hates me as much as she does.

I can't believe that this kind man, one of my only friends here, has been plotting against me this entire time. I don't want to believe it. I registered Mabel's animosity toward me immediately and chose to ignore it, but I didn't see one inch past Albert's false kindness. And I didn't understand how deeply devoted they were to this family. How intensely they hated me, how much of a threat to this family's continued fortune they thought I was.

As he glares at me now, like he wants to kill me with his bare hands, I finally see the real Albert.

The footman pushes him down, trapping his hands behind his back. Another footman kicks the gun even farther from Mabel's side and stands guard over her.

The paramedics descend upon Charlie, and I focus back on him. "His left leg's been shot," I tell them as they begin moving him onto a stretcher. "I made a tourniquet, but I don't know if it's helping."

One of the paramedics checks the belt I've knotted tightly around Charlie's thigh and takes over pressing down on the wound, pushing my hands out of the way. "We need to get him in now," he says.

I hear a small, choked sob behind me and know instantly that it's Poppy. I had forgotten about her. I whirl around to see her tearstained face, her eyes wide with horror. "He's going to be okay," I tell her softly. "They'll take good care of him."

I want to reach forward, to hug her, but my hands are covered in his blood. I wipe them off as much as I can on my jeans.

Quickly, I turn to Alice. "Blair was with Mabel. She was after me, too, when they first found me in the house. I don't know where she is now."

Alice nods. "We'll find her. Just worry about Charlie now."

"Are you coming?" the paramedic asks. They've loaded him into the ambulance.

I crawl in beside him, taking Poppy with me. "Only one person allowed back here," the paramedic says.

"Not tonight," I tell him with an icy stare, and he finally nods. I'm not letting Poppy out of my sight. Albert and Mabel are handled, but I don't know where Blair disappeared to. Or where Gareth is, whether he's on their side, if he's still hanging around Perthton, looking for me. All I know is that Poppy is with me, and we're both getting the hell out of here.

The ambulance doors close, and we are speeding away from the castle.

CHAPTER 38

The next few hours are a blur of bright white lights and shouts and the cold stillness of the waiting room as they do emergency surgery on Charlie.

We're back in the hospital at Beasley, the place I escaped just the night before, but Dr. Furnham is nowhere to be found, and none of the nurses seem to recognize me.

A doctor insists on looking at my ankle. It's just a twist, and she puts a light splint on it and gives me a couple of over-the-counter pain pills.

We're alone in the waiting room. I can't sit still, so I hobble around the room, unable to think of anything but the bright red stain on the snow, the feel of Charlie's lips on mine, the sight of Poppy's terrified face. I still have some of his blood on my jeans, and it makes my stomach turn.

Poppy is too frightened and freaked out to even speak. She can't lose him. *I* can't lose him.

He stepped in front of me. To save me. He didn't even think about it, he just acted. He doesn't know about Blair yet, that she's been planning my demise with Mabel, but it doesn't matter. I saw it in his eyes as he bled out there in the snow: He loves me, too.

And now he might die.

I've nearly worn a rut in the floor by the time the automatic hospital doors slide open and Alice enters the waiting room.

"How is he?" she asks, though her face falls when she sees mine.

I shake my head. "I don't know. He's been in there for hours. They haven't told me anything."

She slips a hand in mine and pulls me to a chair out of Poppy's earshot. "Here, sit," she tells me. "You'll drive yourself crazy if you keep pacing like that."

I choke out a laugh, and her lips twist in a wry smile.

"What was going on at Albert's?" I ask her. "Why was everyone out there?"

The smile falls off her face. "He collapsed. He said he was having a heart attack. That ambulance was coming for him. Lucky it was, too, or else . . ."

"He faked a heart attack to distract everyone?"

She nods. "He and Mabel have both been arrested, thank God. I still don't understand, though. Why would he and Mabel want to *kill* you?"

I tell her the story—all of it. Who I really am, my grandparents, my mother, why Lily hired me, the inheritance, everything. She takes everything in with ever-widening eyes and doesn't ask any questions until I'm done.

"Unbelievable. So Blair was a part of it, too?"

I nod. "Where is she? Did you find her?"

"No. I looked everywhere around the castle, and the police are searching the grounds. No one's seen her."

I shiver, knowing she's still out there. I look out the dark hospital windows, but all I can see is a reflection of my own pale, drawn face.

"And Gareth?" I ask. "Do you think Gareth had anything to do with what Mabel did?"

"Gareth?" she asks, looking at me hard.

"They sent him out to look for me. He found me at Perthton, and he called someone to tell them I was there."

She shakes her head slowly. "*Everyone* was looking for you. We thought you had some kind of psychotic break." She takes a deep breath. "You have to know, even *I* would have called Mabel if I had been the one to find you. She said you were a danger to us and to yourself."

I grit my teeth.

She sighs, her eyes full of regret. "You can't blame us, Fee. We thought you killed that horse. We were worried about you. We wanted to get you someplace safe, where you could get help."

"I know," I say. "I'm sorry."

"Gareth probably thought he was doing what was best for you."

"He said he believed me. I just—I really thought he did."

She doesn't say anything, and I know we're both thinking about the event that led to our fight. The reason we haven't spoken in weeks. She's tried to downplay her feelings for Gareth since they split, but it can't be easy seeing him every day. And it definitely couldn't have been easy to receive a photo of her new friend making out with her ex. I feel awful about it all, but so grateful she's talking to me again.

Maybe Alice is right. Gareth was only doing what he thought he should. I don't blame Charlie for believing Mabel's claims about my mental state, so I can hardly blame Gareth.

Still, he had seemed so sincere when he promised me I was safe with him. I had clung to that, had needed to hear it so badly. And it had turned out to be a lie.

A woman in scrubs walks through the door, and I jump to my feet. Poppy does the same and rushes to my side.

"How is he?" I ask before the doctor can say anything.

"He's fine," she says with a reassuring smile. "He lost a lot of blood; the bullet nicked the femoral artery. But we got him into surgery just in time. No complications."

I breathe out a sigh of relief, tears springing to my eyes. "Okay," I say, my voice choked with unshed tears. "Okay."

"You're the girl who made the tourniquet?" she asks, resting a hand on my shoulder.

I nod, unable to look at anything but the floor.

"You saved his life," she says, and then I'm sobbing, and Alice and Poppy are hugging me. *He's okay. He's going to be okay.*

The doctor tells us that they're transferring him to a room, and we can see him in a few minutes. I call the house to update Mrs. Mackenzie and the other servants, and then wait impatiently.

When they finally let us see him, he's sedated. His face is pale, and there are dark purple circles underneath his eyes, but he's breathing. He's still alive.

Poppy bursts into tears again when she sees him, and I wrap my arms around her. She holds on to me for a moment before pulling a chair to his bedside. I draw another chair up to his other side and clasp his hand in mine.

I don't let go. Not for hours.

Poppy and I don't talk. There's nothing to say. There's nothing to do but wait.

It's almost three hours, deep into the middle of the night, before his eyes finally flicker open. He fades in and out of consciousness for a while, still groggy from the pain medication and anesthesia. But every time his gaze lands on Poppy or me, he smiles that familiar, comforting smile.

A couple of hours later, when the first streaks of dawn are lighting up the sky outside, he finally wakes up enough to talk.

"Hi," he says to Poppy, his voice creaky. He squeezes her hand in his, and I back up to the wall, giving them some space. I can't bring myself to leave the room, though. I can't stop looking at him.

He reassures her that he's all right, and when she starts yawning, he tells her to go home and sleep.

"No," I say, startling him. "Go find Alice in the waiting room," I tell Poppy. "She'll help you find a place to rest. You two should stay here for now, okay? It's the safest place."

She nods. By now Poppy knows enough about Blair to know she should be avoided at all costs. Alice keeps checking in with Mrs. Mackenzie and updating us, and we still don't know where Blair is. Until someone finds her and she's locked away in a cell somewhere, I don't want Poppy too far from me.

Charlie looks at both of us with a confused expression, but Poppy says nothing as she kisses his forehead before leaving the room. Leaving him alone with me.

He looks at me, his gaze so intense that it takes my breath away. "Come here," he says, his voice rough.

I push myself off the wall, back into my chair beside him. "No," he says, softly now. He scoots over in bed, making room. "Come here."

"I don't want to hurt you," I whisper.

"You won't," he says. His eyes burn into mine as I slip into the bed beside him. He stretches out his arm for me to rest my head in the crook of his shoulder, and I press my cheek against his chest.

I start to cry again, softly, as he kisses the top of my head, his hand stroking my hair. "It's okay," he murmurs. "I'm okay."

"It's all my fault," I choke out.

He laughs. "Somehow I doubt that."

I raise my head so I can look him in the eye. "It is," I whisper. And then I tell him everything.

By the time I finish, he's furious. But not at me.

"She just stood there?" he asks. "Blair just stood there as Mabel pointed a gun at you?"

I nod, trying to pull back a little, but his hand presses gently against my back, keeping me close.

"She lied to me. All this time, she lied to me. How couldn't I have seen it?" I watch a dark range of emotions war across his face: anger, fear, sadness. In the end, the sadness wins out.

"The baby," he says finally. "Do you think the baby was ever real?"

"I don't know," I say, but I know he hears the doubt in my voice.

"I really didn't know her at all," he murmurs. He looks up at me. "I'm so sorry, Fiona. For everything. For not believing you."

He props himself up on his elbow and lets out a short hiss of pain. I startle, ready to jump off the bed, but he shakes his head. He tangles his hand in my hair, bringing me closer to him. I'm lost in his eyes, the warm green that darkens as he watches me.

"Fiona," he says, and then he's kissing me. This is no flutter of a kiss. His lips are strong against mine, and he pulls me closer, my body pushing against his. I open my lips, deepening the kiss. And we are lost in each other.

I thought about this moment so many times, but I never imagined it would feel like this. Like the whole world has disappeared around us, like nothing else exists.

We break apart, both of us gasping for air, staring at each other in wonder. He smiles and moves his lips to my cheeks, to the line of my jaw, to my neck. It feels heavenly, but I bring my lips back to his, greedy for more.

I'm nearly lying on top of him now, and when I shift my leg, he gives another small gasp of pain. I yelp, pulling myself off him.

He smiles at me. "It's okay, I'm fine."

"I hurt you."

"It's worth it."

I shake my head at him, but I can't help smiling as I rest my head back in the crook of his arm. He's mine. After all this time, he's finally mine.

We fall asleep together for the rest of the morning, the nurses clucking disapprovingly at us every time they come to check on him. But we don't care.

CHAPTER 39

Charlie's still asleep in the early afternoon, so I go out to the waiting room to see if anyone from the household is outside with news.

I stop short, horrified, when I see Gareth pacing in front of the information desk. He looks up and rushes over before I can hide.

"Get away from me," I say loudly, putting my hands up and backing away.

He stops. "Fee, I didn't know. I swear. I—I had no idea what Blair and Mabel were up to, I . . ." He stops, his eyes full of regret as he watches me. "You have to believe me, I would never have called Albert if I knew."

I take a deep breath, remembering what Alice told me. I believe him, I do. He's so sincere, his emotions so raw, I can't help but believe his frazzled, frantic apology is honest. But I'm also exhausted, still so terrified, and I don't know if I can trust my own instincts right now. So I tell him, "I just need some time."

He nods solemnly. "How is he?"

"He's going to be fine."

He watches me closely, seemingly intent on reading all the emotion in my face. "You really love him, don't you?" he asks.

"Yes," I say, looking him right in the eye. "I do."

He slips his hands into his pockets and clears his throat. "I should get back. The police have been around, and we're all looking for Blair."

"Good," I say. "Thank you, Gareth."

He looks at me again, then lowers his gaze and walks away.

I take a deep breath and try to forgive myself for hurting him as I head toward the waiting room.

Alice is asleep, spread out over four of the uncomfortable plastic chairs. I gently shake her awake, and she stretches and blinks before looking up at me.

"Is Charlie okay?" she asks, standing up slowly.

"He's going to be. Gareth was just here. He says they're still looking for Blair."

She sighs. "What's taking so long? She can't have gone far."

"Where's Poppy?" I ask, looking around the room, empty except for us. "Is someone watching her?"

Alice blinks. "What do you mean? I thought she was in Charlie's room with you."

We stare at each other, a strong sense of alarm growing between us.

"Blair," I whisper. "Blair has her."

"We don't know that," Alice says quickly, but she stands up, grabbing car keys from her purse.

I run to the nurses' station. "Did you see a little girl, Poppy, last night around midnight? Eleven years old, blond hair?"

"Oh, yes, and I met her au pair," the nurse says, unconcerned. "She said she was taking her home."

"Home?" I ask, pressing my hand to my stomach as a wave of horror crashes through me.

"Yes," says the nurse. "The poor girl was still half-asleep when she carried her out. I did hear her say something to the little girl—something about going to see a special tree?"

Alice looks at me, her confusion reflecting mine, and then it clicks. The tree underneath the house. Blair snatched Poppy from the hospital and has her down in that dark cavern with that creepy tree.

I'm going to kill her.

CHAPTER 40

"Do you have your phone?" I ask Alice as I run for the exit, ignoring the dull but persistent ache in my ankle.

She pulls her cell out of her purse as she runs after me.

"Call the police. Tell them to get to Fintair immediately. Tell them someone is holding a little girl hostage in an underground room."

She does, talking to the operator while unlocking her car and starting it up.

She hangs up, and we tear out of the parking lot, tires squealing. "Why would she take her down to the holly tree?" she asks.

I try to put myself in the shoes of a woman whose master plan has crashed and burned around her, who is crazed and angry enough to kidnap a child. "It's an easy location, I guess. One entrance, no other exit. She can control the situation."

"Should we have someone tell Charlie?"

He should know about this, but when the image of him lying in that hospital bed, weak and lucky to be alive, flashes through my mind, I just shake my head. "He's just been through a huge trauma. If we tell him, he'll try to break out of the hospital to look for her."

Alice glances at me. "But maybe he could reason with her. He could tell Blair what she wants to hear, calm her down."

"I'm the one she wants," I say. "She knew the nurse would hear what she said about the tree and tell me. She's too smart to just let something like that slip by accident."

It's not much of an argument, but Alice seems to accept it. I don't want to tell her the real reason I don't want Charlie there: If he came and told her that he didn't love her anymore, that he loved me, there's a very real chance we could all die. She could snap, and we'd be putting Poppy in an even more dangerous situation.

No, I don't want him near her. I don't want to see him try to comfort her or touch her or feel sorry for her, even if he's pretending. I don't think I could bear it.

So Blair gets me instead. She gets to spew her venom at me, while I work to find a way to get her to give Poppy back.

For the remainder of the drive, I keep curling my hands in and out of fists on top of my knees, doing my best not to pick at my fingernails. I can tell Alice is just as tense as I am, and she's speeding fast to get us home.

The sun is hidden behind a thick blanket of clouds when we reach the castle. No one greets us at the front door, and Alice and I run through the halls alone. When we reach that narrow spiral staircase to the basement, I launch myself down it, hardly feeling the pain in my ankle, but Alice's voice stops me.

"Wait!" she hisses, staring at me in horror. "Let's just stop and think for a minute before you go down there. She's dangerous. She could have a weapon. We need to get the police, someone who knows what they're doing."

"Poppy's down there," I say, my voice pleading.

She looks at me for a quick moment of hesitation, then nods. "Should I go with you?"

"No," I whisper. "Stay here. Wait for the cops." I look down at the staircase descending into darkness, steeling myself. "I'm the one that she wants anyway."

I creep down the stairs, running my right hand along the rough rope rail and my left along the cold stone wall to keep my balance. As the darkness envelops me completely, I reach the door at the bottom. It's closed, sealing Blair and Poppy off from the rest of the world.

I press my ear to the door, but I can't hear anything from inside the room. I take a deep breath and knock. A long, silent moment passes, but then suddenly the door creaks open a bit. "Blair," I say softly, trying not to sound angry or menacing. "It's me. I'm alone."

She pushes the door open wider, and the electric lantern in her hand, casting shadows all around us, lights the bottom of the stairwell.

She peeks around the edge, and even in the strange lantern light, I see how different she looks. There's no facade on her face, no carefully pleasant structure overlying her features. Her long black hair is limp and tangled, her face bare without any hint of the perfectly applied makeup she usually wears. She's no longer trying to deceive anyone.

She glares at me with such undisguised hatred that I almost don't notice what she's holding in her hand. A gun. One of the pair of the antique dueling pistols. It can't be Mabel's—they would have taken that one away. It must be the other one. And then I see Poppy.

And I don't know whether I want to scream or faint or hit something very, very hard.

Because she's tied to the tree in the middle of the room, roughly bound there by Blair as if she were an ancient sacrifice.

Her hands are wrapped and tied with some kind of cord behind her, low around the tree. "Fee?" she asks, her voice slurred. She's shaking her head, as if trying to clear it. As if

she's been drugged. Of course. That's how Blair got her out of
the hospital.

I look to Blair, breathing steadily and trying to remain calm.
I keep my hands high above my head and move slowly so that I
don't startle her. "Okay, Blair. You've got me here. Alone. What
do you want?"

"What do I *want*?" she asks, as if the question is ludicrous.
"I *want* you to have never been born. I *want* you to have never
come to this house." She stops talking and approaches me,
bringing her face so close to mine that I can see the swirling
storm in her blue eyes, that row of perfect little white teeth bit-
ing her lower lip. She doesn't look crazy, like Mabel did. She
looks sad, in despair. Like she doesn't know what to do now.

"I want you to have never met him," she says finally, her
voice breaking. "You've ruined everything. *I'm* the love of
Charles's life. I'm the one he's supposed to want. But day after
day, I had to watch him want *you*. And I couldn't do a bloody
thing about it."

She steps back, and I can breathe again.

I need to keep her talking. It's what I used to do with Mom,
keep her talking until she calmed down. "There wasn't anything
you could do about it until Mabel told you about Lily's plan,"
I say.

Blair lets out a sad laugh, and it's a chilling thing. I see

Poppy's eyes widen even further, and I have to close my eyes for a second to stop myself from running over there and ripping her from that cursed tree.

"She really thought she was a part of this family," Blair says. "She would come down to this stupid tree and worship it like it was a deity. She thought it protected the family and that her role was to serve it. Seriously mental."

Blair's entire voice has changed. Her words are rushing out without her usual careful control. Her Scottish brogue is much more pronounced, too—not as crisp and polished as usual. I remember my first impression of her, thinking that her accent sounded labored, as if she were affecting an upper-class voice. I guess I was right.

"So you tried to make me think *I* was going crazy."

For a moment, she brightens. She smiles, that pointed, victorious smile that I've only caught glimpses of before now. "We did a rather good job, don't you think? I was out in the woods the night Charles came back, when you saw me. Did you think you were hallucinating?" She laughs again, and I try not to let my mouth drop open in horror. "We made the short-bread your mother used to make. We planted a recording of her voice in the air vent of the hallway to make you think you were hearing things. We drugged your tea leaves the night of the ball, after Albert told us you were going to leave. Did we really make you think you might have done it? Did you think you were going crazy?"

I nod tightly, remembering that moment when I was left alone, trapped in the hospital room. That one small moment when my perception shifted, and I thought my headache and lethargy might be symptoms of some psychotic break. In that moment, I truly thought I was crazy. And I hate her for that.

I remember that morning, the fierce headache I woke up with. Of course it was the tea. Albert was the one who told me to make it. And like a fool, I did exactly what he told me to.

"You should have seen yourself when you saw Copperfield!" she crows.

"Did you do it, Blair?" Poppy asks, her voice twisted with tears and fear. "Did you kill Copperfield?" I shoot a look at her, telling her to be quiet. I don't want Blair to think about Poppy right now. I just need to distract her until the police can get here.

Blair glances at her, her mouth contorted in a grimace. "Mabel took care of that, thank goodness. So disgusting. She really is the crazy one, you know?" She looks up at me, and I see the pure conviction in her wild eyes. She truly thinks that Mabel was the deranged one, the only one who spun out of control.

What's her plan now? She's kidnapped Charlie's sister, but she's never going to get away with it, even if she kills us. She's never going to get him back—she has to know that. She's desperate and out of her head, and I can't make one false move.

I nod, trying to appease her. "And you made those strange sounds next to me in the middle of the night, right?" I ask, trying to draw her attention away from Poppy.

"Did you never figure it out?" she asks, laughing in that chilling way again. "Mabel showed me. There's a secret passageway that runs right by your room. There's a hidden entrance in the hall, and it leads down to one of the spare bedrooms. Mabel said it was used when a guest wanted . . . *particular* overnight company from among the servants. So that's where we went, to hide right beside your bed and drive you crazy all night long. Or just turn on the recording. You freaked out perfectly, by the way. Played right into our hand."

I bite down on my bottom lip, hard, and don't say anything.

Blair steps closer, her head cocked, considering me. She starts to speak, but her voice is lower, softer. Full of pain again. "Why does he want you? You're nothing. I've been in love with him since our first year at university, and it took me *two years* to get him to fall for me. He's all I ever wanted." The words are pouring out now, and I wonder if she even remembers that I'm here. "Even when he cheated on me, even when he didn't call or forgot my birthday or stood me up for a date, he just . . . he had this way of making me feel like I was the luckiest girl. All he had to do was look at me, and I felt like I was the only girl in the world."

"Did you fake the pregnancy, too?" I ask softly.

She is crying now, angry tears spilling down her cheeks as she stares at me. "He wouldn't have taken me back any other way. He told me, when he broke up with me after his parents died, that he needed a fresh start. That he couldn't be the person he wanted to be if he stayed with me. It was the only thing I could think of. I *need* him. Albert helped me when he found out I was lying about the baby. He knew Dr. Furnham was having an affair with a nurse and threatened to tell his wife unless he helped me."

"He got him to recommend committing me, too?"

She nods, dropping down to the floor. She keeps the gun up, pointed right at me, but her body shakes with sobs.

I start to speak, even though every voice in my head is screaming at me not to. "You tried to make me think I had imagined the fight we had, about Poppy's horse show. You used my memories of my mother against me. You used every fear I had against me." I stop, trying to rein in my anger.

There's a creak on a step above me, but I don't react. I try not to show that I heard anything unusual.

But Blair heard it. She whirls up and grabs Poppy by her

ponytail, pulling her face closer to her. Poppy yelps as Blair lifts the gun and rests it on her temple.

"Don't," I say quickly. "Don't hurt her. She's just a kid, Blair. And hurting her won't help you with anything."

She stares at me, venom in her eyes. Then, all of a sudden, that venom disappears, and all that's left is misery. "He's never going to love me, is he?" she whispers, her voice raw and broken.

"Just let her go, Blair. And everything will be okay," I lie.

Poppy stares at me, her eyes filled with fear.

We all stay there, frozen, for a few moments. And then finally, Blair shoves Poppy's head down and lets go of her hair.

And turns the gun on herself.

CHAPTER 41

I don't think.

I dart around Poppy and run for Blair, tackling her before she can pull the trigger. The pistol falls to the floor just as I do.

The wind is knocked out of me, and distantly, I hear Poppy scream. There are footsteps on the stones, so many footsteps. Someone—a stranger—is kneeling over me, telling me that it's okay, that I'll be able to breathe soon. There are stars at the edge of my vision, and I open my mouth, desperate for air that won't enter my lungs.

I remember the last time I saw stars, when I forgot to breathe around Charlie. That was much more pleasant.

Finally, with a rush, I get a breath in, and my vision clears. The room is filled with cops, and they're pulling Blair up the staircase, her wrists in handcuffs. I let one cop help me onto my feet, and Poppy, free from the tree, launches herself into my arms. I wrap them around her tightly. "It's okay now," I murmur to her, over and over. "It's okay."

Alice is waiting for us when we finally climb the staircase back into the real world. "Thank God you two are all right! What happened?" she asks.

"She tried—" I start to say, but then suddenly it all crashes over me. I just watched a woman pull a gun on herself. And I stopped it.

The way I always wished I had been able to stop my mother.

I sink to my knees, unable to stand any longer. Alice kneels beside me, her arm around my shoulder. Poppy kneels on my other side, and together they let me cry. I'm crying for all those years of grief and pain, and for these last few months of aching love and fear.

"I'm sorry," I say when I can finally speak.

"It's okay," Poppy says, repeating my own useless words back to me. But somehow they're comforting. "You just needed someone to sit with you." She smiles at me, and I squeeze her hand.

Poppy and I give the cops our statements, and when we're finally free to go, Alice takes us straight to Charlie's hospital room.

He gasps, a mixture of a sob and a laugh, when he sees Poppy in the doorway. She runs to his side, and he bends his head down toward hers. "I'm sorry," he says, his deep voice overflowing with sorrow and relief. "I'm so sorry."

He looks up at me, his expression unreadable.

I can guess what he's thinking, though. He must be furious at me for leaving the hospital without an explanation. For not telling him how much danger his sister was in.

I'm planning out what I'll say to him, when he asks Poppy if he can talk to me alone for a second. I watch her go, her hand securely in Alice's, and then I'm left to face Charlie alone.

I wait for him to ask me how I could do this to him. For him to yell at me. For him to tell me that he can't trust me anymore, that whatever fragile relationship we started building last night is now over.

But he doesn't. Instead, he reaches for me, pulling me to him, and kisses me fiercely. I hardly have time to kiss him back before he leans back on his pillow and looks at me. "I'm so sorry," he says. "I'm sorry I let her into our lives."

He kisses me again, and this time, I'm prepared for it. I kiss him back just as fiercely, nuzzling close to him and wrapping my arms around his shoulders.

We break apart again, and I'm about to tell him that it's not his fault, that he couldn't have known, but he speaks first.

"I love you," he says. "I love you."

My lips part as I stare at him in awe. He loves me. I can see in his eyes that it's the truth, but I still can hardly believe it.

He looks at me with a broad smile full of joy. "I think I've loved you since the night I first met you in the pub, when I couldn't stop staring at you."

I laugh at the memory.

He tucks one of my wild curls behind my ear. "I looked up from the fire, and all of a sudden you were there, like I'd conjured you up. I think I couldn't stop staring because I recognized something in you. Something I needed. I think even then, I knew you were going to save me." He brushes his palm down my cheek. "And then I got to know you, and I started up that stupid secret-for-a-song game because I wanted an excuse to open myself up to you. I'd never wanted to let anyone in until I met you. I couldn't stop seeking you out, inventing any excuse to see you."

"I wasn't all that hard to find," I point out. "I think I spent all that time in the library because I was hoping you would come and demand a song." I kiss him again, my lips lingering on his for a moment before I pull back. "I love you, too," I whisper.

CHAPTER 42

Charlie is finally discharged a few days later, and we take a cab from the hospital. Neither of us says anything as we slide into the backseat of the taxi, but I know we're both thinking about Albert. He, Mabel, and Blair are locked up, awaiting psychiatric evaluations and trials. Dr. Furnham has been arrested as well, on numerous counts of fraud and malpractice.

Thankfully, the police have interviewed the rest of the staff and have determined that no one else was part of their mad plot.

"Dunraven Manor," I tell the driver.

Charlie looks at me, a question in his eyes.

"Do you mind?" I ask. "There's something I have to do."

He sits beside me in the back of the cab, taking my hand in his. "Of course not."

We arrive at Dunraven, and my stomach feels as if it has

twisted itself into a permanent knot. I don't know if I can face these people, who've already rejected me, again. But I have to. I have to tell them one last thing.

Charlie gets out with me as Mrs. Drummond opens the front door. She beams at him, though her bright smile falters a bit when she sees me. "Lord Moffat," she says. "I'm so happy to see you up and about."

He smiles at her as we approach the front door. "Thank you, Mrs. Drummond."

She turns her attention to me. "Shall I tell your grandparents that you're here?" she asks softly.

I nod, my throat too dry to attempt to speak.

She has us wait in a grand sitting room while she hurries up to tell her employers that their unwanted granddaughter is waiting for an audience. I sigh, craning my neck up to look at the intricate plasterwork ceiling, the leaves and musical instruments and cherubs that adorn it. Much less interesting than the ceiling fresco of the dragon above the entryway.

Charlie takes my hand in his.

"I didn't know about the money," I say softly. "I just wanted . . . I just wanted a family."

"We can't choose what we inherit. Or who we're related to," he says with a touch of bitterness, and I know he's thinking about his mother.

I squeeze his hand. "Your mother did what she did because she loved you and Poppy so much. She wanted to take care of you."

"By hurting you," he says, pulling his hand from my grasp and standing up. He runs that hand through his hair and looks down at me. "She loved me so much that she planned to have an innocent girl committed, just so her grandparents would never find out about her. For money."

I stand, staring him down. "But she loved you," I say again. "At least you had a family."

He stares at me for a moment, then reaches for me, his hand settling on my waist and pulling me closer. "You do have a family," he says softly, his other hand cupping my chin, lifting my eyes up to his. "You have Poppy. And you have me."

Despite how nervous I am, I can't help but smile at him. And when he leans down to kiss me, all I want to do is melt into him. I press myself as close as possible to him, but it still doesn't feel close enough. By the time we break apart, I'm dizzy with wanting.

He looks down at me, his smile holding something like wonder in it. As if he can't believe how lucky he is. I want to tell him that he's got it the wrong way around, that I'm the lucky one, but I press my lips to his again instead. Maybe we're both lucky.

The sound of someone clearing her throat breaks us apart, and I blush when I turn to find Mrs. Drummond back in the doorway. "Your grandparents will see you now," she says with a kind smile.

"Do you want me to come with you?" Charlie asks when I look back at him.

It would be comforting to have him there, standing firmly beside me, but I shake my head. "I should do this on my own."

I follow Mrs. Drummond up the ornate staircase to that beautiful receiving room once again and find my grandparents seated on that plush couch, absorbed in their newspaper and letter writing, as if they haven't moved since I left them.

Mrs. Cavendish looks up from her lap desk as I enter the room. "We heard there was quite a bit of noise at Fintair Castle the other night," she says drily.

Quite a bit of noise. An unusual way to describe the house-keeper's attempt to murder me, but shooting Charlie instead, and then his fiancée's kidnapping of his sister.

I look over at the grand piano, the one that must have inspired my mom's love of music. I draw strength from it now, from her memory.

I grit my teeth and say what I came here to say. "I want you to know that I don't want anything from you. Because you already gave me the best mother I could ever have had. Despite everything, despite having grown up in this cold house, she was warm. She always made sure my world was filled with love. So I won't bother you anymore."

I spin on my heels and walk out of the room before Mrs. Cavendish can say another venom-tipped word. I make my way down the stairs back to Charlie. Back to my real family.

He springs up from the silk armchair he was sitting on. "Ready to go already?" he asks.

"Yes, please," I say with a small smile. It's all the cheer I can manage.

Before I can rush out the door, though, Charlie rests a hand on my arm, stopping me. He's looking toward the other doorway. Where Mr. Cavendish is standing.

I blink a couple of times, as if I'm unsure he's really there.

"I wanted to catch you before you go," he says, walking to me. He's searching my eyes, and I know what he's looking for. My mother. I wonder if he can see her in my freckles, in the way my nose tapers just so, in my long eyelashes.

He must, because he holds his hands out to me, and before I know it, I'm wrapped up in his arms. "Your mother was a remarkable young woman. And so are you."

I press my face into his shoulder, trying to memorize the

feel of this first hug from my grandfather, a man I'd wondered about for so long. He's small and frail, but his grip is strong.

"Greer will come around. She always does. She's lost her child, you see—she's hurt. Moira ran away from us, and we tried to keep up with her through Lily, but our daughter didn't want anything to do with us. Not after we'd tried so hard to keep her from that boy. So Greer just needs time." He steps back, looking down at me. "Don't give up on her yet."

I nod slowly. "Okay."

"You're family," he says, his voice full of conviction. "I'm setting up a trust for you, so that you can live your own life. You'll have everything you need, all that we can give you. But I hope— I hope you stay near us. Give us a chance to be your family."

I blink at him. "I don't—"

"We've plenty of money, lass," he says firmly. "I don't want to hear another word about it," he finishes with a smile.

I think about what Charlie said, that we don't choose what we inherit from our family. But we can choose what to do with it. "I—I don't know what to say," I say finally. "Thank you."

He pulls me in for another hug before letting me go. "Come back as often as you like, hen. I want to get to know you."

He calls me "hen," just like my mother used to. "Okay," I say again, not knowing if I'm about to laugh or cry.

Charlie wraps his arm around me, keeping me close as we walk back to the cab.

Both of us are quiet as we drive up the long avenue of trees. I feel as if the castle will have changed appearance since I've been gone. As if it will be darker, a mark of the evil and madness that it held within it.

But then it comes into view, and it is the same castle it always was, with the massive medieval tower and sprawled-out wings.

Charlie pays the driver as I get out and take a good, long look at this place that hid its secrets from me for so long. I can't help the shiver that courses through me as I remember the shadows in the underground tree room. How certain I felt that I would die in the maze, the crazed anger in Mabel's eyes, the loathing in Albert's. The snow has melted, but I still have the memory of Charlie's blood pooled there.

Charlie takes my hand, and when I look at him, those visions shift away. This place isn't dark. It isn't hateful. It's where my family is. It's where I'm meant to be.

"So what now?" Charlie asks.

I turn to him, my mind made up. "I want to stay here. With you and Poppy."

He smiles. "Good. We both need you."

"And if the Cavendishes agree, I want to be an angel investor for the paper," I say. "I want to help fund the new website."

"Fee, you don't have to—" he starts, but I interrupt him with a wave of my hand.

"You'll have to make me a good deal," I say with a smile. "But I believe in you."

He watches me for a moment, as if he can't believe what I'm offering. Finally, his lips curve in a smile. "I can't think of anything I'd like better than to partner with you," he says, sweeping me up for a kiss.

I hold tight to him, to this moment of perfect happiness and hope.

"Ready to go inside?" he asks softly when I finally let him go.

I kiss him again quickly. "Yes."

We walk into the castle together.

ACKNOWLEDGMENTS

There are so many people who helped bring *Fiona* into the world, and I'm going to do my best to thank them all here.

First, I have to thank Alexandra Machinist, agent extraordinaire. There's no one I'd rather have in my corner.

Thank you so much to Liz Tingue, my editor, for all your hard work and insight. Fiona and I are so lucky to have you.

Thank you to Tara Shanahan, my publicist, for shining a spotlight on Fiona, and to the Razorbill Team: Vivian Kirklin, Deborah Kaplan, Laura Cheung, Christian Fuenfhausen (for the GORGEOUS cover!), Jessica Harriton, and Marissa Grossman. And to Ben Schrank, for leading it all.

To the Fearless Fifteeners and all my wonderful writing and blogging friends on Twitter, Instagram, and Facebook. Everyone always says writing is a solitary profession, but it's never felt that way to me, and I owe that to all of you.

Thank you to my brilliant critique group: Angélique Jamail, Shirley Redwine, Brenda Liebling-Goldberg, Lucie Scott Smith, Gabrielle Hale, Adam Holt, and Jenny Waldo. You read the earliest, worst drafts of my books and somehow help me make sense of them, and I can't thank you enough for that.

To Allison Maffitt, Christina Scharar, Rosalee Maffitt, Chelsea Grate, Aly Sider, Valerie Grainger Henderson, Alex

Begley, Charlotte Mitchell Loreman, Ali Bodin Ho, and Nellen Hawkins for being the best friends (and "fan club") a girl could ask for. And to all my friends and family members who've cheered me on ever since I started this whole crazy writing thing. Special thanks to Nic Buckley for all of the writing retreats and *Friends* marathons. And to Denise Delaney and Ross Netherway, for giving me a home base in London before I went exploring in the Scottish Highlands.

To Liz Ghrist, Grandma, for taking me on fabulous vacations. And for leading by example.

To Greg, Jenn, Olga, Lucy, Jimmy, and Louis, for all the pizza, board games, and bad reality TV. And for being my favorite people in the world.

And, as always, to Dad, for being my support system and my partner in crime. I love you.